DESCENT

SON OF A MERMAID ~ BOOK ONE

KATIE O'SULLIVAN

Wicked W
Publishing

First Edition: July 2015

(First published as Son of a Mermaid by Crescent Moon Press, May 2013)

Cover Design: Cape Cod Scribe, K.R. Conway

Library of Congress Cataloging-in-Publication Data

O'Sullivan, Katie

Descent/ by Katie O'Sullivan – First Edition.

  Pages: 338

  Summary: When fifteen-year-old Shea MacNamara is uprooted from his life in Oklahoma and brought to seaside Cape Cod, he discovers his bloodline runs deeper than the ocean itself and quickly finds himself caught in an undersea war, determined to help the unlikely girl who has stolen his heart.

Wicked Whale Publishing

Bourne MA 02532

www.WickedWhalePublishing.com

ISBN: 978-0-9962789-0-4

Published in the United States of America

DEDICATION

For Brian and Teagan, who loved this story from the start.

You encourage and inspire me every day.

DESCENT

CHAPTER ONE
PLAINVILLE, OKLAHOMA

What started as an ordinary Thursday quickly spiraled out of Shea's control…and it wasn't even third period.

Tingling sensations coursed through his legs, zinging from his toes to his stomach. It was as if some switch in his body flipped into high gear at the same moment the school's emergency system started its loud electronic beeping. Each beep over the monitors sent another vibration racing through his bloodstream.

Could it be just the stupid tornado drill putting him on edge?

He sat with his back against the cinderblock wall, at the very top of the gym bleachers, desperately hoping no one would notice the sweat dripping from his forehead. He closed his eyes, as if that would make him invisible.

1

Logically, he knew tornadoes and tornado drills were brutal facts of life in central Oklahoma. Plainville High's cavernous gym had more than enough room to hold the entire student body. It wasn't claustrophobia or nerves that had him on edge. It was something else. Something more. Almost as if there was a charge in the air and Shea's body was the magnet attracting it.

Finally, the all-clear bell rang. He heaved a sigh of relief as the tingling slowly subsided.

"Okay, people." Mr. Kelley raised his voice to get the attention of the students milling next to the bleachers. "The drill's over. Line up and head to class."

Shea stood, testing his legs to make sure they would make it down the stairs without an embarrassing fall. When he reached the gym floor, John Hansen spotted him and made his way to Shea's side. Taller than most of the other freshmen, John was built like a brick wall. The other students – and teachers – cleared out of his way. "There you are, MacNamara! Where were you hiding?"

Shea shrugged. He didn't want to admit anything was wrong. Especially when he didn't understand why his body freaked out during the drill.

A wide grin lit John's face. "I was so saved by the bell this morning. No way was I ready for my history presentation. Western Civ has got to be my least favorite class ever."

Just shy of six feet, Shea was considered big for a freshman, but even he felt dwarfed next to John. The pair had been friends forever, and Shea knew even though John towered over their classmates, he was all heart. "Yeah, Mr. Kelley can be harsh," he agreed. "I never get all those dates right."

"What are you talking about?" John laughed, a low rumble that caused the girls in front of them to turn and giggle. "You ace every quiz."

He scowled. "No I don't."

John kept laughing and shook his head. "Whatever. So...did you ask yet about Saturday? Mom said you could spend the night Friday so we can get an early start."

He didn't answer, distracted by another little zing crackling along his spine. He'd never experienced anything like it before, but it almost felt like his body *remembered* the strange sensations.

"Hello, Shea?"

It took a minute before John's question registered. "What? Oh, yeah, the Redhawks game. I forgot to ask."

"Oh come on. It's gonna be your birthday."

"It depends on whether we get the rest of the fields planted before then. Otherwise, I'll have to stay and help."

"Your dad never lets you do anything fun."

3

With the overhead lights still off, the slatted blinds painted bold stripes of light along the desks closest to the windows, leaving the rest of the room in shadow. Darkness made no difference to Shea. His eyes always adjusted to whatever light was available, which came in handy when it came to early morning chores like feeding chickens or milking the cow.

John dropped his backpack next to his desk. "If I didn't know better, MacNamara, I'd think your dad was trying to keep you locked away from the world."

"Don't be an idiot." Shea's mouth quirked into a half grin. "Why would he do that?"

John shrugged. "Beats me. Hey, what if there was a tornado, and it sucked away that John Deere of yours?"

"Yeah, right. I'd never be so lucky." Shea gestured toward the partially opened window next to his desk. Brilliant blue skies peeked through the blinds. "Not a storm cloud to be seen. Besides, that would mean I'd miss the game for sure, since we'd have to buy a new tractor."

The last few students entered the room and flipped on the lights. Two girls leaned against the front row desk of Bobby Joe Peters. *Jeannie Sanderson and Maria Garcia*, Shea noted. *Of course the prettiest girls flirt with the richest boy in school.* Shea scowled as Jeannie tossed her long red ponytail and smiled at some silly thing B.J. said.

Jeannie glanced up, catching Shea's stare. She leaned over to whisper in Maria's ear. The pair both glanced his way and smiled. Shea felt his cheeks start to burn as John elbowed him in the ribs. "Dude, we're not in middle school anymore. They're cheerleaders now. Way out of our league."

"Speak for yourself, dude." Shea smiled at the girls.

"Oh, yeah." John snorted. "At least I play a sport. You're not even on their radar."

"So what? B.J. doesn't play a sport either."

"He's rich. You're not. And besides, it's not like your dad would let you out on a *date* when he won't even let you come to Oklahoma City with me for a baseball game."

Up in the front, B.J. noticed Jeannie's attention had wandered. He spotted Shea and his eyes narrowed. Suddenly, B.J. pointed his nose toward the ceiling and sniffed loudly. "Do you smell something?"

The girls giggled as B.J. flared his nostrils and swiveled his head toward the back of the room. "Oh right, the *farmboys* are in this class! You should bathe more, Hansen. You too, MacNamara. The stench of manure isn't as cool as you might think." Laughter filled the classroom. Shea clenched his teeth, his right hand curling into a fist. B.J.'s next words cut through him like an old fashioned scythe. "No wonder your mommy ran out on you, MacNamara. She couldn't stand the smell."

5

Shea's throat constricted so fast he could barely breathe. He shot to his feet, his chair slamming over sideways with a loud bang.

"Ignore him." John's fingers dug deep into Shea's flesh, holding him in place. "He's an idiot."

"Someone needs to teach him a lesson." Shea yanked his arm from John's grasp.

"Totally true. But still not worth another detention."

Before Shea could decide what to do, Mr. Kelley entered the classroom. "All right, all right, settle down." The tapping of his foot on the tiled floor got progressively louder while students shuffled to their seats. Shea took a deep breath and bent to pick up his fallen chair, banging it into place and dropping himself into it. He jammed his elbows onto the hard surface of his desk, and pressed the heels of both hands against his eyes until it felt like they were digging into his skull. *Just breathe*, he told himself. *Make it through the next ten minutes of class and then catch a ride home. To hell with school.*

Up front, the teacher barked at the class. "Settle down and I'll hand out last Friday's quizzes. We can go over them before I take them back to keep in your files for the fourth term." When he reached Shea's desk, he stopped. "Mr. MacNamara." Shea dropped his hands from his face. "Can you guess how many questions you answered correctly?"

"Umm, I don't know?" Shea heard Jeannie muffle a giggle. His cheeks flamed in response.

"You got one wrong." Mr. Kelley's eyes glittered like they usually did when he was annoyed. The rest of the class turned to watch the exchange. Shea felt the burn from his cheeks creep down the back of his neck while the teacher placed the test paper in the exact center of Shea's desk. His index finger skewered the page to the surface. "It bothered me, because it's a question I was sure you answered the week before." The teacher paused, his eyes never leaving Shea. "So I checked."

Shea dropped his gaze, wishing a hole would open in the floor to swallow him. He thought he'd been careful, but apparently not careful enough.

"I went back through *all* your test papers. It seems you get one or two questions wrong every week. Regardless of whether it's something you've gotten correct before. If I didn't know better, I'd think you were answering wrong on purpose. Now, why would that be?"

"Um, Mr. Kelley... I..."

A knock on the classroom door interrupted, giving him a few extra minutes to scramble for an excuse that wouldn't sound completely lame. How could he explain he was trying not to stand out? Or that...

"Is there a Shea MacNamara here?"

His head jerked at the sound of his name. A state trooper stood in the doorway, mirrored sunglasses hiding his eyes. At his side was the assistant principal, wringing his hands and looking like he'd rather be anywhere else on the planet. A cold ball formed in the pit of Shea's stomach. His arm felt like lead when he raised his hand.

"Come with me, son," commanded the trooper. Shea stood, grabbing his backpack from the floor next to his chair. Moments ago he'd been busy planning his escape from school, but suddenly he knew he'd rather stay.

Twenty pairs of eyes followed his long walk to the front of the room. "We'll finish this discussion tomorrow," Mr. Kelley called after him.

Shea kept walking.

CHAPTER TWO

The nightmares started the day after the tornado but it wasn't the swirling storm clouds haunting Shea's dreams. It was the ocean, leaving him drenched in sweat and tearing at the bed sheets as he tried to escape the watery depths in his mind.

There really had been a tornado in the area when the warning bells sounded. A small but powerful microburst twister appeared out of the clear blue sky and disappeared almost as fast. But not before wreaking havoc.

Tornadoes were the real threat in Oklahoma. Unpredictable and deadly, he knew he should be having nightmares about the killer storm that had the weathermen puzzled and everyone talking. People from Plainville didn't generally drown at sea, since the closest ocean was more than six hundred miles south, down in the Gulf of Mexico. The

Atlantic coastline was even further. And yet... Shea knew it was the Atlantic that haunted him. Called to him.

Or, at least, his grandmother called. Martha MacNamara wanted Shea to come "home" to Cape Cod. A place he'd never even visited. He looked it up on the computer and saw a thin stretch of land curling out into the ocean like a body builder flexing his bicep, surrounded by water on all sides. A far cry from land-locked Oklahoma.

He lay in the extra bed in John's room listening to his friend's rhythmic snoring. Shea struggled to keep his eyelids open, fighting the tired aches of his body, not wanting to fall asleep.

The school counselor stopped by the Hansen's home for a visit, a few days after the tornado. He tried to be reassuring, in that school-counselor-Psych-101 kind of way. He said people often dream of drowning when they feel helpless or out of control. That it was a normal reaction.

Shea didn't think that explained the dreams.

Not all the way.

The door to the bedroom creaked opened, a yellow shaft of light piercing the blackness of the room. Louise Hansen poked her head partway through the opening. "Are you boys still awake?"

"Just me," Shea answered. "Sorry."

She opened the door the rest of the way. The light from the hallway spilled into the bedroom, widening into a triangle along the floor. "No need to apologize," she said with a sigh. "It's been a tough week. Losing your daddy is never easy."

He blinked back the hot tears filling his eyes. One escaped and rolled down his cheek to wet the pillow. He was glad for the darkness, knowing she couldn't see him cry. "I wish he'd turn up. Somewhere. So we'd know for sure."

"Shea…" she started, but her voice trailed off. She gripped the doorframe with one hand to steady herself and cleared her throat. "Your grandmother should arrive here in Plainville tomorrow. She called from Logan Airport to give us the flight information."

"Logan?" He tried to think where he'd heard that name before, as a few more salty tears seared a silent path down his cheek. "Is that Cape Cod?"

"Boston. A few hours from the Cape." She sighed. "That's where you're going to live with your grandparents."

His eyes closed, his stomach clenched into a hard knot. Massachusetts was almost two thousand miles away from Oklahoma. Away from his friends. Away from anything familiar. "It's just her. My grandfather and my uncle died two months ago."

Silence stretched through the darkness. "I remember now," Mrs. Hansen finally said. "You stayed here with us that week your father flew home for their funerals."

His next words gushed like a fast-moving river. "Can't I stay here with you guys? John said he'd be happy to share his room full-time, I mean, since Tanner's off to university. And I'm handy around the farm –"

Mrs. Hansen cut him off. "No, honey. You have to go." There was a long pause before she added, "She's your family." Slowly, she closed the bedroom door, the shaft of light receding, along with any hope Shea had of staying in Plainville.

"But I've never even met her," he whispered into the blackness.

The blue-green coolness swirled around him as his body tumbled through the water, arms and legs flailing. He struggled to hold his breath. Millions of tiny bubbles of precious air traced the path of his descent, escaping from his clothing and through his nose.

Eyes wide, he watched a huge school of shimmering minnows part down the middle as they swam around him, surrounding him like a silvery box. Turning his face upward to the surface, he could see the blue sky receding further and further while he sank deeper into the water's depths.

His throat and lungs burned from the effort of holding his breath. Darkness pressed hard against his eyes, and swirls of strange colors danced in front of him. His whole body strained against the lack of oxygen.

I need to breathe, he thought wildly, his whole body feeling like it was on fire. *I can't hold out much longer.* His feet hit the mucky bottom with a thud, coming to a stop. The mud swirled around his legs.

There, hovering before him in the water, swam a beautiful woman with flowing golden hair...and a green fish tail, golden flecks sparkling among the scales.

A mermaid.

Her big green eyes looked familiar, just like the ones he saw in the mirror every morning. She smiled at him, reaching for his hand. His head pounded while searing pain ripped through his throat, as if his entire body would tear apart any second from the effort of holding his breath.

The mermaid squeezed his hand and the pain receded. Shea stared into her eyes, lost in their green depths. He opened his mouth to exhale the stale air that pounded like a jackhammer in his lungs. Large bubbles rushed to the surface. He struggled to breathe, but there was no air, only salty ocean water rushing in to fill his mouth, his lungs, his body...

Shea woke with a start, clawing at the sheets and disoriented for a full minute before remembering where he was. At the Hansen's house. Because his own home – the farm where he'd lived and worked all his life – was gone, swept away and crushed by the freak tornado.

And his dad was nowhere to be found.

Chapter Three

Guilty thoughts plagued Shea as he surveyed the damage to his former home. *Why am I still alive?* The flattened fields looked like an army of soldiers trampled them, leaving nothing in their wake. Broken hunks of wood and window dotted the yard, all that remained of the two-story farmhouse. Beyond the edges of the farm, everything was normal. The rogue twister only targeted the acres belonging to Tom MacNamara.

I should've been home. Maybe I could've saved him. He turned from the flattened fields and saw a thin plume of dust rising along the road. A yellow cab. A shiver ran through him, remembering the last taxicab to come out this far from the city, bringing his dad home from the airport. Shea stayed in Oklahoma to mind the farm while his dad went to Cape Cod to bury his father and brother. A murderous wave rolled their

15

fishing boat, killing them both in one fell swoop. It had been a hard few months for the men of the MacNamara family.

The taxi stopped halfway up the drive, where the John Deere tractor lay on its back blocking the road like some passing giant's discarded toy. The rear passenger door opened and a wisp of a figure emerged, dressed all in black. Shea watched the woman lean in to say something to the driver before turning toward him. Tilting her head to one side, she cupped a hand to her mouth and called out, "Are you Shea Thomas MacNamara?"

He nodded, not trusting his voice. He watched her pick her way around the John Deere, walking the rest of the way up the graveled driveway to where he stood rooted. Spreading her arms wide, she gave him a sad smile. "Come give me a hug. I'm your Gramma." When he didn't move, she lowered her arms and sighed. "I guess boys these days don't hug. More's the pity." She closed the distance between them and extended her right hand. "I'm Martha MacNamara. But you can call me Gramma."

So this was the grandmother he'd never met.

"You're sure to be having lots of questions," she continued, as if sensing his curiosity, "but there'll be plenty of time for catching up. First things first, let's have a look at you." She put both hands on his shoulders and squinted her eyes behind her half-moon glasses, nodding to herself. He could see that behind the lenses her eyes were blue, just like his dad's were. Had been. "And how old are you now, lad? Fourteen, is it?"

"Fifteen," he corrected, squirming under her scrutiny. "My birthday was Saturday." He'd planned to spend the day in Oklahoma City, watching baseball and celebrating with his best friend. Instead, he'd spent the day sitting by the Hansen's phone, waiting in vain for word about his father.

She cocked her head to one side, her eyes glittering brightly. "Is that so? Fifteen already? My, oh, my, how the time does fly." She shook her head and took a step back when John and his father approached. Mr. Hansen and his sons had been checking to see if any farm equipment could be salvaged from the collapsed barn.

"Hello there!" Mr. Hansen reached a meaty fist toward Martha, enveloping her entire hand with a hearty shake. Even in the midst of the devastated farmland, it was hard for the big man to tone down his boisterous nature. "You must be Tom's mother. My wife called to say you stopped at our house first. I'm so sorry for your loss."

John sidled over to Shea. "She looks like she might be okay," he whispered. Shea didn't acknowledge John's words or even spare him a glance. His eyes were riveted on the woman who claimed to be kin, sizing her up as she chatted with John's dad. Mr. Hansen's blond bulk towered over the thin, grey-haired woman with the sharp blue eyes, and yet Shea had the feeling the little old lady would be the victor of any argument. There was something odd about her, but he couldn't quite put a finger on it.

She looked nothing like his father, for starters. Except for the eyes. And while her long braided hair was steely grey and her clothes screamed "old lady alert," there were very few wrinkles on her face. Behind those half-moon glasses, her eyes looked clear. As he made his assessment, she turned those sharp eyes toward him, catching him with her gaze.

"Let's not dawdle then," she said, cutting off whatever it was John's dad had been babbling about. "We need to get your things, dearie, and get a move on." She kept her eyes locked with Shea's.

Mr. Hansen was startled. "But surely you're not leaving right away. Aren't you going to stay for the funeral service?"

Martha narrowed her eyes. "Have you found my son, then?"

The big man shuffled awkwardly under her piercing gaze. "Well, as a matter of plain fact, no. But folks here thought it would be the decent thing to have a ceremony. Put some closure on this tragedy."

"Tragedy it is," she agreed, taking her glasses off. She pulled a lace handkerchief from somewhere up her left sleeve and polished the lenses while they stood watching her. She took her time, rubbing first one lens and then the other, sliding the handkerchief along the brass while everyone else stood silent. She finally slipped the half-moons back on, her eyes sparkling more brightly. "But I'm afraid there will be no closure for now. Nothing is *over*," she added cryptically. "It's only just begun."

CHAPTER FOUR

ONE WEEK LATER
SOUTHERN ATLANTIC OCEAN
OFF THE COAST OF BRAZIL

The decision to follow Prince Demyan's demands for the past decade had been one that Zan never questioned. His loyalties were born out of necessity, for Prince Demyan knew the truth. Zan had killed two children when he was only four years old.

Their deaths were an accident, Zan told himself, but he knew the High Court in Atlantis would see it as murder.

And so Zan followed Demyan's every whim, no matter how terrible, as an act of self-preservation. It wasn't until he was older that Zan began to wonder if Demyan had his own reasons for helping him so long ago.

But now, at seventeen, Zan knew Demyan had secrets too. Brutal secrets, destined to overthrow kingdoms, which started with Demyan quietly murdering the Queen, leaving her six-year-old son to inherit the crown.

Zan understood that he and Prince Demyan were both murderers, but the carnage that stretched out over the battlefield left little doubt to one fact: Zan had become a pawn in a tyrant's game of thrones. The prince was more of a monster than any leviathan lurking in the ocean's depths. Two years of bloody warfare proved the point beyond any doubt.

The broken bodies from the latest skirmish lay strewn across the fields before him, evidence of the ruthless efficiency of the prince's soldiers. Although the Adluo clan reigned in the Southern Ocean, they made significant inroads into the Southern Atlantic over the last few years. Demyan's unrelenting army swam northward day by day, destroying any resistance in their path. Before today's slaughter, this land belonged to Lord Telfonns, a cousin to the King of the Atlantic Ocean. Now the lord lay somewhere on the ocean floor, slain by Prince Demyan.

The battle leaders assembled at the edge of the field, straightening the blue sashes marking them as Adluo warriors. The sashes dripped with fresh blood, but none more than the one across Prince Demyan's chest.

"You'd think even farmers would put up more of a fight." Demyan's lips twisted in a cruel smile as he scrubbed a hand through his short, muck-colored hair. The prince always seemed happiest on the battlefield. Especially when covered in blood. "The bounty of Lord Telfonns now belongs to the Adluo clan."

"A great victory," Zan agreed, trying not to grimace. Before them lay miles of trampled kelp beds, the green of the food stained red with thick merman blood, crushed under the limp bodies of the fallen. Most of the Adluos already left the site to tend their own wounded, leaving their enemies where they lay, the water heavily scented with iron.

The scavengers would arrive soon.

Prince Demyan looked around the gathered circle. "Where are the Aequorean farmers I told you to round up?" Blank stares met his gaze.

One of the young pages finally spoke up, pride in his voice as if answering an easy riddle. "Dead, my Lord."

Zan cringed, knowing what would surely happen next but unable to look away. The prince propelled himself toward the boy in a flash of speed. His hand shot forward, fingers extended. He cut through the water and struck the boy hard and square in the chest. A resounding crack echoed off nearby boulders as young bones broke. Drawing his sword, Demyan looked upon the quaking merman with obvious disdain, his fingers still hard against the newly cracked breastbone. "Who is your master, boy?"

"You are, my Lord," the boy wheezed between labored breaths, his lungs obviously feeling the press of broken ribs as thin streams of bubbles rose from his gills.

Demyan smiled and withdrew his fingers from the boy's chest. "I expected you to point out your supervisor. You are wise beyond your years, with such a politic answer. To which of these mermen do you submit your wise reports?"

The boy raised his arm slowly and pointed. With a quick flash of his tail, Demyan closed the distance between himself and the one singled out by the boy. The prince thrust his sword deep into the advisor's belly, the golden blade disappearing all the way to the ruby encrusted hilt, and the merman gasped, stricken.

"My orders were clear, were they not?" demanded Demyan, leaning in close to the dying merman. "We needed the farmers to tend the field, and yet now they lie dead. You will join them for your stupidity." With his victim slowly sinking to the ground, Demyan whispered in his face, "Are my orders clear now?"

A gurgle of blood was all that trickled from the advisor's lips, as his black eyes rolled upward, leaving only the whites staring blindly. Lifeless.

Demyan released his hold on the blade dangling from the now limp body. Turning to face the rest of the war council, he bellowed, "DOES ANYONE ELSE DARE DEFY MY ORDERS?"

Demyan's eyes, the color of pure octopus ink, scrutinized the mermen one by one, none of them able to meet his gaze. Finally, he squared off in front of Zan and flipped one hand toward the boy now cowering near the fallen body. "Take this one away to be trained. We seem to have a shortage of mermen who can follow directions properly."

Yes, because you keep killing anyone who questions your authority, Zan thought, but he dared not voice his sentiment out loud. Instead, he nodded and lowered his eyes. "Yes, my Lord." He grabbed the boy and dragged him away from the circle in the direction of the army wagons. Once out of sight, Zan placed one hand on the boy's shoulder, the other on his chest, letting the magick flow through the trembling merman to repair the cracked ribs and punctured lung. "Go now, rejoin your company. And never again speak in the presence of the prince."

"But, my training? Prince Demyan said…"

Zan closed his eyes. "Trust me, boy. The further you stay from the prince, the longer you will live." With one last puzzled look, the young merman zoomed off to rejoin his comrades. A long stream of bubbles exhaled from Zan's gills as he watched him swim away. "Not even a thank you for fixing his ribs."

When he returned to the circle, the other members of the war council were busy nodding in agreement with Prince Demyan's plans for the next day's battle, all too afraid to voice a true opinion, afraid to be the next victim of Demyan's wrath. Zan looked at the maps scratched in the sand and envisioned more bloody fields and ruined crops. There had to be a better way. "Perhaps you should send an emissary to King Koios? To negotiate peace with the Aequoreans?"

Demyan was still bent over, drawing attack lines across his maps with the tip of his golden sword. He straightened slowly to his full height, the bulging muscles of his torso tensed as if ready for another battle. "Negotiate peace?"

The rest of the advisors backed away, widening the circle. Zan held his ground, the rapid fluttering of his tailfin creating a sandstorm on the ocean floor. He'd been with Demyan long enough to know he swam a fine line, and yet he also knew he was right. "Yes, my Lord."

His next words thundered with anger. "By Poseidon's beard, you want me to SURRENDER?"

He held the prince's eyes without flinching. "No, my Lord. The Atlantic King should surrender. To you."

Demyan paused, his eyebrows raised in surprise. "I like the way you think, Zan. Why continue to battle our way northward if there's a faster solution? And here I thought I was about to lose my favorite sorcerer because of an impertinent tongue." He sheathed his sword and dismissed the rest of the advisors, who swam from the circle with the utmost haste.

Before Zan could leave, Demyan grabbed his arm in an iron grip. "I want you to travel north immediately. Negotiate with the Atlantic King on my behalf. I want his daughter's hand in marriage."

Small green crabs scuttled forward, claws clicking in excitement at the bloody feast before them, fighting for the more tender bits. A stream of bubbles shot from Zan's gills as he exhaled, forcing his gaze away as a crab tore off the dead merman's ear. He swallowed the lump in his throat, knowing his next question might be the one to send Demyan over the edge. "Surely you mean for your cousin, King Theosisto, to marry the Atlantic princess? She is heir to her father's throne, after all. A marriage between the rulers of our oceans would bind our clans more permanently."

Demyan's lip curled to show a row of perfect white teeth. "Of course that's what I meant. Arrange for the marriage as part of the peace treaty. My young cousin will be thrilled to have a new mother figure in his life, if only for a brief time."

Understanding dawned. "You plan to kill King Theo?"

The prince's laughter mocked him. "Did you have any doubt as to my end game? I merely needed the young king in power during wartime to give me – what is it they call it? *Plausible deniability.* I don't intend to remain his regent forever." As the only other living member of the Adluo royal family, the High Court appointed Prince Demyan as regent for his young cousin, to advise the boy until he came of age and could rule on his own.

Zan knew the boy was a mere puppet in Demyan's schemes, but had no idea another murder had already been planned. His eyes widened at the news, but bit his tongue as Demyan continued. "The princess can hardly refuse such a treaty, my magick-wielding friend. Especially if it means an end to the bloodshed."

Questions zoomed through Zan's mind at this unexpected turn of events. Arranged marriages were common enough among royals, but to demand a bride in return for peace was unheard of. And this particular princess had been marked by the gods with the trident-shaped birthmark proving she would be heir to her father's throne. Realization hit him

27

like a physical blow. "It's because she bears the Mark of Poseidon."

Demyan's bared his teeth in a cruel smile. "As will our child. My son will never have to fight to prove his worth, or fight to be accepted by the High Chancellor at royal gatherings. He will rule both the Southern and Atlantic Oceans, just like his father."

Zan's eyebrows came together as he frowned. "My prince, you don't rule the Atlantic. You don't even rule the Southern Ocean."

"But I will. It will all belong to me in due time. And you, my loyal sorcerer, will continue to aid me in my quest." He turned and swam through the bloodied field to where his carriage and the rest of his soldiers awaited their next orders.

Zan stared after him, wondering how different things would have been if the accident hadn't happened all those years ago. Guilt knotted his stomach and twisted his gut, the pain suddenly sharp at the memories. It didn't matter if the deaths were accidental, or if the killer was only a scared four-year-old. Killing a member of the royal family carried a death penalty. Even thirteen years later, Zan's life would still be forfeit if the truth came out.

His fingers curled into tight fists. He had no alternative but to do as Demyan commanded. Closing his eyes, he wondered for a moment how different his world would be if he had choices.

Chapter Five

Two weeks later
Cape Cod, Massachusetts

The beach probably looked this same way for decades, Shea decided. He stared out across the vast stretch of undulating blue. Centuries, even. Since before anyone started measuring time.

It sure looked exactly the same for the last few weeks.

Moving to Cape Cod was a huge mistake, he thought for the millionth time. He might be with his so-called family, but he'd never felt so alone in his life. *I should have stayed in Plainville and kept searching for Dad.*

He watched a wave catch the sunlight, the edge shimmering in the brightness, part of the endless and intricate dance of foam and spray. The saltwater rippled and curled, crashing to a grand finale on the empty shore as the sparkles melted into the sand. The sound and the power of the waves felt calming, although he couldn't understand why.

Turning his back on the dancing waves, he tramped through the soft sand. He'd watched the sun rise over this stretch of neighborhood beach each morning since his arrival on Cape Cod. Shea couldn't believe it had only been a few weeks. It already felt like Oklahoma belonged in a different lifetime.

At first, John called almost every day to share the news from Plainville High, like the fact that B.J. and Jeannie were now a couple and the high school baseball team qualified for the playoff tournament. John hadn't called yet this week, probably because of the tournament, but Shea already felt like he was losing his friend. The only good part was Martha hadn't made him sign up at the local school. Good and bad. At least if she'd made him go to school, he would have met other kids his age. For now, it was just Martha and him.

He tossed the bag of garbage into the blue barrel before turning toward the ocean. He went through the bizarre list of trash in his head, a habit he'd fallen into.

3 aluminum cans, 5 Styrofoam coffee cups, 2 plastic coffee cup lids, 3 popped blue balloons on yellow string tangled with seaweed, 1 water bottle, 1 Matchbox racecar, and a red shovel.

He started picking up the trash littered along the shore after his very first walk. Appalled by the number of empty cans and washed-up debris lying tangled with the seaweed, he stuffed plastic supermarket bags into his pockets and collected the garbage. It felt like the right thing to do. And it was something he could control. The rest of his life definitely felt out of his control. And the nightmares were getting worse, too. He dreaded falling asleep.

Most of the dreams took place underwater, far below the surface of the ocean, with hideous creatures chasing after him as he swam for his life. In some he was caught in bloody undersea battles, where the fish all had faces and arms and fought each other with steel swords. In others, he found himself locked inside a cold room made of stone, an underwater prison with no hope of escape. Sea monsters and mermaids and other mythical creatures floated in and out of his nightmares, jarring him awake with their sharp teeth. Night after night he lay tangled in sweat-soaked sheets, counting the hours until daylight.

He had no one to talk with about the strange dreams. He considered confiding in Martha, but dismissed the idea. After her cryptic remark in Oklahoma about the tragedy only beginning, she hadn't wanted to discuss anything with him – not about his father, or the tornado, or anything. Not even his mom. He knew his mom lived around here and figured Martha might know something, but she shut him down every time. She said she was giving him time to settle in. That they needed to wait.

Wait? For what?

He shook his head and returned to the present, adding today's list of garbage to the catalog already in his head. He needed something to focus on, and it seemed as good a hobby as any. If he kept obsessing over his mother or thinking about his father, he'd turn into one of those weepy emo types, wearing guy-liner and smoking behind the school auditorium. He imagined his father getting a call like that from the assistant principal and smirked, before it punched him in the gut again that his dad was gone.

Back to the garbage. If anyone asked, he could recite every bit of garbage he'd collected in the last two weeks. Not that anyone would ask. He never saw anyone else on the beach this early in the morning. But he didn't have a choice in the matter. Things just stuck in his head.

His dad called it a "perfect photographic memory." It was another of those odd things he couldn't explain, like his remarkable eyesight and his acute hearing. Which is why he'd started getting test answers wrong on purpose. He hadn't messed around on the standardized tests the year before. He knew he was smart, and wanted to see how he measured up. According to the guidance counselor, his scores were off their charts. Way off. His dad had been so proud.

And then his dad asked him to start getting answers wrong. On purpose.

How did that make sense?

He concentrated on the waves rolling onto the shore, crashing on the sand, and tried to steady his ragged breathing. He shouldn't think about his dad. It hurt too much.

Gramma's dog was still chasing seagulls. Shea whistled and waited, watching the dog turn away from the squawking birds and bound toward him. To his right, the beach stretched about a mile, ending at the river jetty where the Herring River spilled out into the ocean. Grass-covered sand dunes lined the edge of the beach. Private wooden walkways led through the dune grasses to stately mansions, now shuttered and quiet, waiting patiently for their summer people to return. Each house was large enough to hold at least two or three of Martha's smaller sized home, and Shea wondered why anyone needed so much space. The very last house before the river even had its own old-fashioned windmill attached to it, something Shea had only seen in storybooks. Windmills in Oklahoma tended to be of the more modern variety, sleek and efficient for electricity production.

Where Shea stood bordered on the public beach, complete with lifeguard stands and a brick building with public restrooms. A large paved parking lot edged against the top of the boardwalk. Over by the entrance stood a little white hut, now boarded up and empty. He figured that must be where someone stood to collect parking fees from summer tourists. At the far side of this beach stood a long rock jetty, jutting out into the crashing waves. A dozen seagulls huddled in a group on the rocks, keeping their distance from the loud black dog.

Lucky finally returned. He bent to clip the leash onto the dog's collar for the walk back to Martha's house. While he felt comfortable letting the dog run loose on the beach, he worried about the cars on the road. Suddenly the dog barked, bolting toward the water and pulling the leash from Shea's hand.

"No, Lucky!" He ran down the beach after him. "We're supposed to get off the beach before anyone shows up!" The sign posted next to the garbage barrel warned of stiff penalties for walking pets on the beach and he didn't have the money to pay the hundred dollar fine.

He caught Lucky at the ocean's edge, stomping on the water-soaked leash before he could get too far. A familiar shiver ran up his spine as a cold wave grabbed at his ankles. He remembered that feeling. From the day of the tornado.

When the wave pulled back from the shore, an odd stone sat upon the bare sand, glinting in the morning sunlight. He grabbed it along with the wet leash. Round and smooth, the stone felt almost polished. A strange hexagon-shaped hole cut right through its heart. The skin on his palm tingled beneath the weight of the rock.

Lucky barked again, jerking Shea's attention to the water's surface. Something splashed nearby. "What was it, boy? One of those seals Gramma talks about?" He raised his empty hand to shade his eyes. He waited for the creature to surface again. After several long minutes, he looked at the dog. "We've got to go. Maybe next time we'll get to see the seal."

Slipping the stone into the front pocket of his jeans, he tugged on the leash. The pair walked in silence through the dunes, back to the road leading to his grandmother's house.

****

Ten yards from shore, a blonde head surfaced among the waves. Her wide-set green eyes followed the boy and his dog until they were through the dunes and gone from view. She sighed and furrowed her brow, annoyed with herself for being afraid.

"Why didn't I talk to him?" She slapped her hand flat against the water's surface as she berated herself. "I'm such a jellyfish! I mean, he seems nice enough…"

She meant to pause her morning swim only for a moment, but it was unusual to see someone – anyone – picking up the garbage that lay on the beach. Hiding amidst the waves, she watched him walk the length of the beach and back again, gathering the debris all too common along the shoreline. Something about him fascinated her.

She wasn't supposed to talk to strangers at the beach. That was a hard and fast rule she'd only broken once before. But those had been girls, and they'd been much younger. This was a boy…and a cute one.

Her father would have a fit if he knew. If she even said hello. She pictured her father turning red as a snapping fish, yelling at her for breaking the rules. Tossing her long, wet hair away from her face, she froze, her hand flying to her neckline.

Her medallion was gone.

"The cord must've broken!" Her dad might resemble a red snapper after all. "But it has to be right here!" She dove under the water, forgetting the human boy for the moment as she searched the sandy bottom for her shiny black stone with the hole cut through the center.

CHAPTER SIX

Shea led Lucky through the gate in the stockade fence by the side of the house. Martha's backyard was small but functional, much like everything else about the house. A plain wooden shed sat on the back property line, with a clothesline strung from one corner over to the yard's sole pine tree in the other corner. A row of faded towels fluttered in the breeze.

The neatly trimmed patch of green was mostly grass, with generous sections of clover and chickweed sprinkled about for good measure. Rows of tall perennials lined the garden bed running the length of the house, with many strange shoots and leaves he didn't recognize. The only flowers he could name for certain were the daisies, which had barely started to open their sunny faces. The garden hose coiled neatly on one of those metal reel contraptions, like a giant spool of fishing line.

"C'mon boy, you know the drill." He grabbed the end of the hose and turned on the faucet while the dog whined his disapproval. "We need to get the salt water off your fur and off my feet. 'No ocean in the house,' Gramma says. And you don't want to mess with her."

With a distinct air of resignation, the dog submitted to the hose. Shea focused the spray onto the sleek black fur. A brilliant rainbow formed over the animal, the sunlight illuminating the gushing water.

Martha told him the black lab arrived at her door one day with no collar or tags of any sort. An hour later, her telephone rang with the news of the tornado on the MacNamara farm. She'd called the police station and rescue league, but no one had yet claimed ownership, so Martha allowed Shea to keep the dog. Shea named him "Lucky," and felt lucky to have one friend he could count on in his strange new surroundings.

"Shea? Are you back from the beach?" Martha peered out through the screen door. "I haven't finished making your pancakes."

"That's okay." He kicked off his sandals and hosed the sand from between his toes. "I'm not hungry." He grabbed one of the towels hanging from the clothesline and dried the dog's fur.

"What did you say?" She opened the door, her dull blue housedress looking even more faded in the bright sunshine. "You know my hearing is not what it used to be."

He narrowed his eyes, not believing for a minute her hearing was anything less than perfect. Shea didn't think she was as frail as she pretended. Ducking under her arm, he entered the kitchen. Lucky followed, padding across the linoleum to hide in the shadows underneath the kitchen table. The screen door swung shut behind them with a resounding bang. "Can I skip breakfast this morning?" He inched his way toward the opposite doorway, hoping to escape the thick scent of bacon grease lingering in the air. His stomach growled, betraying his hunger.

"Absolutely not." Martha bustled to the stove, where a cast iron griddle sat over flames of blue gas. "Your grandfather always said a good breakfast is the key to a good day. Sit your body down."

He dropped into one of the chairs next to the Formica table, the plastic seat cushion letting out a sigh. "Could I have a bowl of cereal instead, Gramma? I'm not used to eating such a big breakfast."

This was a lie. Shea found himself telling more and more of them since moving to Cape Cod. It felt easier than remembering the truth. The truth tended to hurt.

Breakfast had been an important part of life on the MacNamara farm. In the summertime, his dad employed a full-time cook to feed the hired farmhands and the interns from the university's agricultural program. "Aggies," his dad called the students. Pancakes were an everyday staple. Just the smell of the maple syrup on Gramma's table made his chest tight. His stomach muscles clenched into a knot as he pictured the Aggies around the breakfast table, fighting over the syrup pitcher.

Martha turned from the stove to squint at him. "Is something wrong?"

"What do you mean?"

"You seem – I don't know – unhappy." She shrugged and turned her attention to the griddle.

He didn't reply for a whole minute. *Of course I'm unhappy. I miss Dad and I miss the farm. I don't know anyone here. I miss John even if he won't call me back. I even miss those stuck-up cheerleaders. My legs ache and I'm afraid to fall asleep at night.*

Everything is different here and it all sucks.

He shrugged. "I'm fine."

Martha put the plate of food on the table in front of him and sat in the opposite chair. He grabbed the plastic bottle of maple syrup and squirted a thin stream over everything on his plate. He poked at the pancakes with his fork and tried to think of something to say.

"You look like your father."

His grandmother's blunt statement confused him. "Dad wasn't blond," he mumbled, the corners of his mouth dipping sharply. He held his fork above the plate, watching the syrup drip onto the golden cakes.

Martha nodded slowly. "Oh yes, the sun bleached his hair each spring, setting off those blue eyes of his. The girls… Well, the girls were all crazy for him. Especially your Mum."

He raised his eyes. His father never talked about his mother. Ever. The subject had been taboo in the farmhouse as far back as he could remember. And up until this moment, Martha hadn't wanted to talk about her either.

Maybe he could finally get some answers.

"If she was crazy for Dad, why'd she leave him?" He wanted to add, *"Why did she leave me?"* but that question hurt too much to think, let alone say out loud.

Martha looked away, unable to meet his eyes. "Her father didn't approve." After a long pause, she added, "I can't believe your father didn't tell you any of this. I certainly would have thought he'd tell you about your mum. Especially now that you are older. There are things you need to know."

So many questions popped into his head he couldn't decide which one to ask first. His mind raced while his lips remained firmly glued.

41

"You have her eyes, you know." She rose from her seat at the table. "The same shade of green."

His eyebrows shot up, shocked by this small revelation. He had no idea what his mother looked like. His dad didn't keep a single photo of her.

Martha turned on the hot water and donned the bright yellow rubber gloves from under the sink. For a minute he thought she'd forgotten about the conversation as she washed the mixing bowl she'd used to stir the pancake batter. He waited for her to continue. When she didn't, he prodded. "Could you, maybe, tell me…you know, about my mother?"

Long seconds of silence stretched between them. He held his breath, waiting. Finally, Martha sighed. "You're old enough to know."

"Know what?"

"Everything," she said with a curt nod, her hands still busy washing dishes. "But I should start at the beginning."

Shea leaned back in his chair, waiting for some big revelation.

"Your mum was what we call 'summer people'," his grandmother began, still facing the sink. "Folks who live somewhere else for most of the year, but spend their summers on Cape Cod." She paused. "Some of them even decide to stay. We call those 'wash-ashores,' since they 'wash up' on Cape Cod from other places."

42

He rolled his eyes before realizing Martha was watching him. His cheeks burned, as if he'd been caught doing something worse. "Umm, you were saying?"

She gave him a stern look before returning her attention to the dishes. "There are all kinds of summer people. A lot of those big houses right along the water belong to the rich ones. Which seems like such a waste for the other ten months of the year, but it keeps our economy alive."

"Whatever." He trailed his fork through the syrup pooled on the edge of his plate. He'd already heard her rant about the summer people more than once in the few short weeks he'd lived with her. He started to lose hope Martha had anything important to tell him. *What do summer people have to do with anything? Who cares about rich people or their big houses?*

"Some summer people aren't wealthy, but instead they come to work here, as lifeguards or waitresses or landscapers. And of course there are always the tourists, the lifeblood of Cape Cod. They come for the day or a weekend, or even for a week at a time to vacation in the sun. Many of them are fine people, but you always get the ones who, for one reason or another, feel superior to those of us who live here year round."

Shea remembered Bobby Joe Peters and the way he always acted superior. He thought about his dad growing up that way, with summer people putting him down. Dad

43

probably enjoyed that as much as Shea enjoyed Bobby Joe's teasing. "What about my mother?"

"Your mum was from a wealthy family, and her father definitely felt superior." His grandmother placed the last dish in the drying rack and pulled a fresh dishtowel out of the pocket of her apron. She dried her hands before peeling off the rubber gloves. "Your daddy was so in love with her. He took a second job running fishing charters so he could buy that fancy ring."

"What ring?"

"The engagement ring, of course."

"You mean like a diamond?"

Martha shook her head. "Your mum thought diamonds were cold things." She held out her hand. "See the ring your grandfather gave me? It's called a moonstone. The same kind of ring your dad gave your mum."

Surprise shot through him. He'd never seen anything like the milky stone with the swirling streaks of blue running through it. "Did they, you know, ever go through with it? Ever get married?"

Martha nodded. "You didn't know even that?" He shook his head, and she frowned. "Of course they were married, but without her father's blessing as it were. A judge performed the ceremony in Hyannis. Your Uncle Richard, Tom's twin, was the best man, and one of your

44

mum's…friends came to be her maid of honor. Your grandfather and I were the only audience. Didn't you notice the photograph in the living room?"

Shea shook his head again, and Martha walked out of the kitchen. When she didn't return, he followed her to the next room and found her on the sofa, her blue dress blending with the blue and white checked slipcover.

"This is the one I was thinking of." A silver frame lay in her lap. Shea crossed the threadbare oriental carpet and maneuvered around the coffee table. He eased onto the couch next to her, holding his breath.

He'd never paid attention to the photos in this room, the ones covering the mantle. Wrapped in his cocoon of depression, he hadn't noticed much of anything. Now he looked – really looked – at the photo.

The lady in the white dress was beautiful, with huge green eyes and a cascade of blonde curls surrounding her perfect oval face. Strong, defiant, and totally in love.

And exactly like the mermaid in his nightmares.

He blinked and shifted his gaze to the groom. Although he recognized the man in the tuxedo as his father, he'd never seen a smile like that on his dad's face. Or that look of pure happiness in his eyes.

The room was quiet as they sat staring at the photograph. Shea tried to make sense of this new bit of information. He didn't know there'd even been a wedding. He'd decided long ago that his birth must have been unplanned and unwelcome. He knew things like that happened all the time. But apparently that wasn't true.

His parents had been married.

And in love.

And somehow he'd been dreaming about his mother rescuing him from drowning?

"So…what happened?"

Martha sighed. "They sat here, in this very room, planning their life together. Deciding where they could go that her family wouldn't find them. Oklahoma should have been far enough away, smack dab in the middle of the country as it were." The old woman stared again at the photo, lost in thought.

"Why did she leave?"

Martha sighed again and shook her head. "She wanted you to be born near the ocean. So they came for a short stretch. But then your mum went into labor early, one afternoon when they were out on the fishing boat. Your dad got her to the medical center on Nantucket just in time."

Shea felt a lump form in his throat. "Did she die?"

Martha shook her head. There was a long pause before she finally smiled, putting a gentle hand on his knee. "Did you know your Daddy planned to bring you here to

Cape Cod to meet her, later this very summer? Now that you've turned fifteen?"

A whole minute passed before Shea realized his jaw hung open. He snapped it shut, his teeth clicking together. "He never said anything about it. I didn't know that they, you know, kept in touch."

"I don't think Thomas has seen her since you were born. He hadn't even visited the coast to see me until…until the funerals. But he and your mum exchanged letters over the years. She's heard all about you, and what a great help you are on the farm. She loves you, you know."

Shea snorted, feeling a familiar rush of anger bubbling inside of him. "No, Gramma, I don't know. She left when I was a little baby. She. Left. Me."

Martha narrowed her eyes. "No need for that tone of voice, young man. Maybe this is enough information for now. We'll talk more after you've sorted this through." Abruptly, she rose and left the room, leaving the silver frame on the couch.

Other photographs lined the mantel over the fireplace. There were old black and whites of a much younger Martha in her own wedding gown, and many of his dad and twin brother when they were young. In one of the frames was a photo of Tom holding a baby. The expression on his father's face looked happy and sad at the same time.

47

He reached for the silver frame lying on the cushion next to him. He stared at the photograph. His empty hand clenched into a ball, until he felt his stubby fingernails biting into his palms.

Why hadn't his father told him any of this? What had he been waiting for?

Chapter Seven

6 aluminum cans, 3 plastic coffee cup lids, a kid's sand bucket with a crack down the side, 4 whole silver candy wrappers and 4 more pieces of wrappers, broken red plastic from some kind of reflector, 3 water bottles and a long piece of smelly rope.

Shea catalogued the contents of the flimsy plastic bag, now bulging with the addition of that last soda can. Unable to sleep, he rose before the sun and slipped out of his grandmother's house, Lucky padding silently behind him through the pre-dawn darkness.

The sun was only now peeking out to greet the day, painting the horizon in pale shades of pink and dusky purple. He finished the daily two-mile trek along the shoreline, his head still spinning with the revelations of the prior morning. "If Dad really kept in touch with my mother, why didn't he tell me? Why wait until I'm fifteen?" His brain hurt, trying to wrap itself around this new twist. Having a mom would've been a lot more useful in, say, preschool than in high school.

After being so chatty at breakfast, his grandmother wouldn't say anything more on the subject for the rest of the day. He tried to coax it out of her at lunch, but she'd refused to talk about it. Dinner had been something of a silent affair.

He whistled for Lucky and turned toward the dunes, impatient to dump today's collection of garbage. The waterlogged rope smelled bad, even stuffed at the bottom of the bag. The dog's sharp bark stopped him in his tracks. He whipped his head toward the ocean.

Lucky stood at the far end of the beach barking frantically at a little girl with blonde ringlets of hair and huge eyes. She perched on top of the rock jetty with her knees pulled tight to her chest. He dropped the bag of trash and broke into a sprint. "Leave her alone, Lucky!" He slowed when he got closer. With one last bark, the dog walked to Shea's side, and lay on the sand.

"Don't be afraid. He's usually very friendly." The girl turned her eyes toward him, and he thought he saw a flash of recognition flit across her face before she relaxed the grip on her knees. As she uncurled her long body, he realized the girl wasn't so little after all. Actually, she might even be about his own age. Despite the early hour and the chill in the air, she wore a bikini, her curly hair dripping wet like she'd already been swimming.

"You're the Garbage Boy, aren't you?" Her voice sounded like a cross between a whisper and a summer breeze. "I saw you here yesterday."

He squinted at her. Long damp hair curled down her back and clung to the tops of her arms, her large green eyes too big for her face. He decided that even though she wasn't as pretty as Jeannie, or even Maria, this girl was…interesting. When she smiled at him his stomach muscles clenched into a tight ball of nervousness. "The name's Shea MacNamara, not Garbage Boy."

"Shea MacNamara." When the girl said his name, it tingled in his ears like music touching him all the way to his toes. Goosebumps prickled up his arms.

He cleared his throat. "So what's your name?"

"My name's Kae." She smiled, her lips parting to show perfect pearly white teeth. "Kaa – ee," she enunciated again. She stood and stretched her arms toward the sky. She was easily the same height as he was. "You must pronounce all the sounds."

"Kaa – ee," he repeated in the same exaggerated fashion and shook his head. "I haven't seen you on the beach before."

"You're the new one." Kae tucked her wet hair behind her ears. "My family is here every summer."

Rich summer people? He remembered his conversation with Martha and tried to imagine what a rich guy like Bobby Joe would do if he met someone like Kae on the beach. *Probably not stare at her like a complete fool,* he told himself with a mental kick. But he still couldn't tear his eyes from her face.

"Why do you do it?"

His eyebrows shot up at her question. "Do what?"

"Collect the garbage, for Neptune's sake. Your efforts amount to less than a drop in the ocean." She jumped from the rocks and stood next to him on the beach. "And the trash belongs to the land, not the sea."

He stared at her, trying to figure out if she was making fun of him. She stared back, unblinking, cocking her head to one side and running her fingers through her hair. He noticed those shining blonde curls were almost completely dry already. *Does some hair dry faster than others?*

"Well?"

He shook his head. "It offends me when people treat the ocean like their private garbage dump. And I'm not throwing it in the ocean. I put it in the barrel so it leaves the beach." She smiled at him again and he felt his heart beat faster, uncomfortable under her watchful eyes. "Why aren't you in school?" He wanted to change the subject, away from

52

him, away from the trash on the beach. "I thought summer people didn't arrive until closer to the Fourth of July."

She laughed, sounding like the tinkling wind chimes hanging in Martha's kitchen window. "My parents need to arrive early, so I get to come too. We work for a very important family, and there is much to do to prepare after the long winter season."

He adjusted his initial assessment. *Not rich summer people, but summer workers.*

"Where did you come from?" Another blunt question from out of the blue. "Your voice has a funny accent."

"I grew up in Oklahoma. But I live here now."

"Why?"

He sucked in a deep breath and held it for a moment, before blowing it out. "There was a tornado. My dad died," he said slowly, carefully, as if the words themselves might hurt him. "Gramma is the only family I have left."

"I'm sorry about your father." She touched his arm. Under her gentle hand, his skin tingled, radiating warmth through his body. He felt himself relax, glad he'd told her the truth.

The girl touched her other hand to her neck and suddenly, a sharp jolt ran from the base of Shea's spine down one leg, as if he'd received an electric shock. Lucky jumped to his feet and began to bark at the girl. Startled, Kae quickly

53

released her grasp of his arm and took a step backward. He squatted to scratch behind the dog's ear. "It's okay, Lucky. Just static electricity or something."

"I hope we can be friends." She blinked her eyes finally. He noticed how long and thick her eyelashes were.

"Me too." Shea returned her smile, his eyes rested on the length of black cord around the girl's neck. Her fingers wrapped around the stone dangling from the end, a round black stone with a hexagonal hole through its middle, identical to the one he'd plucked from the waves the previous morning. "Where did you…?"

"Hey, you kids!" A loud, crackling voice interrupted his question. Shea turned toward the parking lot and saw a police cruiser parked there with blue lights flashing. "No dogs on the beach," boomed the amplified voice from the cruiser's loudspeaker.

Hurriedly, he bent to clip the leash to Lucky's collar. When he stood, the girl was gone. Wondering how she disappeared so quickly, he tugged the dog's leash and ran across the sand, stopping for a second to grab the bag of garbage.

When they reached the parking lot, Shea dropped the full bag into the barrel. The police cruiser sat at the front edge of the parking lot, lights silently flashing blue and white. Shea approached the car warily. His experience with police was limited to the day of the tornado. "I'm sorry, officer. My grandmother said it would be okay if we got off the beach before eight."

"The sign says no dogs, May through October." The officer wore mirrored sunglasses despite the fact the sun barely crested the horizon. "That means no dogs on the beach. Period. The fine is a hundred dollars."

"I'm sorry, officer," Shea repeated. He realized he was staring at his own reflection in the mirrored glasses, but seeing a very different scene. A scene in Oklahoma, where a similar cop walked into his history class to excuse him from school. For the rest of the year.

He tore his eyes from the mirrored lenses and tried to see this police officer and not the Oklahoma trooper. "Officer L. Tandy, Harwich Police Department," he said, reading the shiny brass nameplate hanging on the uniform pocket, right over the shiny silver badge.

"What's your name, boy? I haven't seen you around town. You visiting from somewhere?" Officer L. Tandy's voice had lost some of its edge, but the crisply ironed uniform still made Shea uncomfortable.

"MacNamara, sir. Shea MacNamara. I live here now."

The officer gave him the once over, pushing the sunglasses to the end of his long beaky nose. "Tom MacNamara's son, I assume. I went to school with your dad and your Uncle Rick," the officer said, nodding his head. "Wasn't there someone else on the beach with you? I thought I saw two of you by the jetty."

Shea shrugged his shoulders. "She left."

"You'd better get home, too, before you miss the school bus." Officer Tandy pushed his glasses up his thin nose and made no further mention of the fine.

"Yes, sir," Shea agreed, as if getting on that bus were important to him. "Thank you, sir."

"And no more dogs on the beach," the officer called after him. Shea didn't acknowledge that last order but broke into a run, heading to his grandmother's house.

****

Kae peered from behind the rock jetty. The boy and dog left the beach, and the big black and white land boat was also leaving. "Not a boat, but a *car*," she said experimentally, recalling the name of the thing from her previous encounter with humans. A good memory was essential when things couldn't be written down. "The girls in Florida called those machines by the name of *car*."

She climbed onto the jetty, and walked carefully to the end of the rocky outcropping. The sky above her already changed from the hesitant pastels of early morning to a brilliant shade of blue, the few clouds evaporating like morning mist on the ocean. Seagulls wheeled overhead in slow lazy circles.

At the jetty's end, she clambered nimbly down the algae-covered boulders. Sitting on the one lowest to the waterline, her feet dangled ankle deep in the lapping waves. One hand wrapped around the stone medallion hanging at her neck and she closed her eyes, reciting the words her mother taught her long ago. "*A pedibus usque ad caput mutatio.*"

Suddenly, the sun seemed to shine more brightly on the water at her feet, orange and yellow sparks dancing on the blue-green surface. Kae watched the sparkles slide soundlessly along the surface straight toward her, to where her feet made contact with the lapping saltwater. The dancing lights ran up both her legs, shimmering along the skin as they twined up her thighs. Sitting very still, she kept her hand on the *transmutare* stone, rubbing her thumb in slow circles around its rim. The whole process took mere seconds until the twinkling lights receded to the water's surface, leaving behind a glittering green mermaid tail where once two separate legs had been.

Smiling to herself, she slid into the ocean, submerging in the cool depths. The codium weeds grew thick near the base of the jetty, dancing in the dappled sunlight that penetrated the waves. The seaweed parted easily as she swished through the undulating underwater forest. She wanted to hurry home to tell her mother about the encounter with the boy. She knew she might get in a bit of trouble, but she had to tell her. Secrets were too hard to keep in their small community, let alone within her own family.

Just as she reached the far end of the weedy patch, she heard a large splash and an unfamiliar voice. Kae froze, sinking to the sandy ocean floor, hiding within the edges of the spongy field of seaweed.

"I can't believe the rumors are true." An unfamiliar merman swam right past the spot where Kae hid, his expression so intense it raised bumps along her bare arms. Although clean-shaven like a young boy, his hair was completely white, flowing behind him as his tail fin fluttered at high speed. "After all these years..." He swam so quickly that in mere moments he was miles beyond where Kae could see the flick of his tail.

She shivered, pushing aside the weeds. The clean shaven face, the speed at which he swam and the bulging chest muscles all pointed to one conclusion. The merman belonged to the Adluo clan. She'd never seen an Adluo up close before, but had heard all the tales of their blood-thirsty and savage fighting skills. Shaking stray bits of the seaweed from her curls, she started swimming deeper into Nantucket Sound, wondering why the merman was in Windmill Point. Everyone knew Adluos hated the humans.

"Maybe it's something to do with the peace accords?" The upcoming accords were the hot topic in the kitchens of the Summer Palace. The servants discussed the treaty at length while cleaning the signs of winter's neglect from the building and unpacking the supplies they hauled with them from the south. Kae listened with interest when the older merfolk discussed the whys and hows of the war, and whether the peace treaty would stop the Adluos from invading more of the northern Atlantic. And how the servants planned to handle the influx of Adluo soldiers for the Solstice celebration.

Her own father didn't think King Koios should be negotiating at all. "They're terrorists making a grab for power," she heard her father argue. "Their purity of race proclamations make me sick."

The Adluos despised all things "drylander," their derogatory slang for humans. Their clan's territories were based in the Southern Ocean around Antarctica, far removed from land creatures of any type. At least, that's the way it had always been. Until Prince Demyan rose to power. He stirred the anti-human prejudice of his own clan to a fever pitch, even though other clans tolerated and even traded with the land dwellers. Angry words gave way to skirmishes between the clans along the southern border, which quickly escalated to all-out battle. King Koios had no choice but to negotiate a peace. Most Aequoreans were farmers, not fighters.

The current rumor was that the victorious young king demanded a royal marriage between the clans, in return for ending the war. She couldn't even imagine how the princess must feel about having to marry a cousin young enough to be her own child. Kae knew royal marriages were about politics instead of love, but that was ridiculous. What Kae didn't know was exactly what the marriage meant for her family, whether she and her mother would follow the princess to the Adluo palace in the cold Southern Ocean or stay with King Koios in the Atlantic. She had no doubt her father would stay with the king, and hated the thought of their family splitting up.

I can't worry until I have something to worry about, she told herself firmly, and swam faster. Finally she spotted the peaks of the castle's roofline rising in the distance. She needed to tell her father about the Adluo soldier she'd seen by the shoreline. Her tailfin froze in mid-flutter. If she told him about the merman, she'd have to tell her reason for swimming so close to land. She wasn't ready to tell him she lost her first medallion and took a second out of the storage closet.

I'd rather tell Mother the story, she thought. *She's more lenient with her consequences. And she can decide whether to tell Father about the Adluo.*

She swam toward the gardens in search of her mother, thoughts of Shea MacNamara filling her head.

Chapter Eight

Shea knew nothing about coastal geography. He'd spent his whole life in Oklahoma, after all, far from the coast. It wasn't something they talked a lot about in his old public school. Tornadoes, yes. Oceans? Not so much.

He knew his compass points and was a fast learner, since his brain instantly absorbed and remembered everything. From the oversized book on Gramma's lobster trap coffee table, he studied the geography and long and storied history of Cape Cod. The Pilgrims first landed on the tip of the Cape, in Provincetown. They eventually decided to sail north to seek safer harbors, finally landing at the famed Plymouth Rock. But Cape Cod was first.

The Pilgrims also encountered their first Native Americans on Cape Cod. And many famous pirates sailed in these waters, going around the arm-like stretch of

Massachusetts that juts into the Atlantic Ocean. According to the book, lots of U.S. presidents vacationed on Cape Cod and the surrounding barrier islands over the years, including John F. Kennedy, Bill Clinton, and Barack Obama.

He read all this and more, but was still dissatisfied. Martha didn't have a computer or an internet connection, just a pile of books on the area. Nothing explained the shifting sands of the beaches themselves. Nothing talked about the ocean in all its beauty and mystery. Nothing helped lessen his nightmares.

Maybe Martha could take me to the library, he thought as he made his way home from the beach. Kae hadn't been there this morning, and he felt restless. Somehow, having met her the other day made him feel even lonelier than before, which was crazy. He'd met her for all of five minutes, but he couldn't stop thinking about her. Her smile, her laugh, her golden curly hair… if he had to describe the perfect girl, it would pretty much be her. Except if she was truly perfect, he'd know where she lived and how to find her.

As he wandered the streets of Windmill Point, he wondered which house belonged to Kae's family. He decided it had to be one of the big summer mansions along the waterfront, and not one of the smaller cottages. But which one? They all looked empty, with the shades drawn closed, except the windmill house. That one at least had lights on, the rest seemed abandoned. Empty homes with pristine gardens and lawns, thanks to the landscapers who zoomed in and out of the neighborhood once a week.

He wondered if the windmill house could be where the strange girl lived, but it wasn't a true "McMansion" like the rest of the waterfront homes. It was more of a large sprawling farmhouse, and in serious need of a new roof, judging by the missing shingles. Someone rich enough to have live-in servants wouldn't need roof repair.

As he passed one of the older, smaller homes on the corner of his street, he noticed the empty rocking chair creaking back and forth on the porch, almost like a ghost had taken up residence. "That's odd," he said out loud, pausing in the street to stare at the empty chair. Lucky stopped, too, cocking his head to one side. "No, boy. It's okay," he reassured the dog, rubbing the top of Lucky's head. "I've never seen that chair empty. And here it is two mornings in a row."

According to Martha, the man who lived in that cottage retired to the Cape some years before and was one of the few other year-round residents of the Point. Although his grandmother said he was harmless, Shea thought Mr. Guenther was a pretty creepy old guy who wore his hair a little too long. He always sat in the same chair, in the same spot, dark eyes staring, no matter what time of day Shea walked past the house.

Except Shea hadn't seen him in that rocking chair yesterday. And he was absent again today.

"Maybe he's away on vacation," Shea told Lucky. The dog squinted his grey eyes. "Okay then, maybe he's sick and stuck inside drinking tea. Either way, it's kind of nice not to see him!" The dog whimpered in agreement and they continued home.

In the solitude of his small room, Shea sat on the edge of the twin bed. Martha said the room belonged to his father, Tom, and there were certainly signs that a teenage boy might have once lived here. Faded posters of classic rock bands covered one wall and dusty baseball trophies lined the top shelf next to a row of framed swimming medals. College textbooks and well-worn paperback science fiction novels filled the rest of the bookshelf.

Not one single thing reminded him of his dad.

The Tom MacNamara he knew was a no-nonsense guy. Something either mattered or it didn't. There wasn't a lot of emotional middle ground. In fact, there wasn't much emotion at all. Everything was black or white. The dad he grew up with didn't have time for playing sports or listening to music. Shea sighed as he flopped on the bed, wondering what happened to take all the fun out of his father.

The faded blue comforter smelled of detergent and bleach. Martha firmly believed in the importance of cleanliness. She told Shea that after being married to a fisherman for so many years, she liked the smell of bleach because it meant things were truly clean. No matter how much the chlorine might fade things.

As the shower down the hallway turned on, the old water pipes groaned in protest. Shea wondered cynically if his grandmother washed herself with bleach as well, her Irish skin so pale for someone who lived right next to the shore.

Rolling onto his side, he opened the drawer of the bedside table and took out the stone from the beach. The sparkles were gone. It looked like an ordinary black rock. Even the strange hexagon-shaped hole in the center seemed smaller than he remembered. Less defined.

"It still resembles the one on Kae's necklace," he said, trying to convince himself. Without the shine of water on the surface, it was hard to think there was anything special about this particular rock. He'd tried to run it under the tap in the bathroom last night, but it remained dull and lifeless. Not that Shea was into glittery things in general, he reminded himself, embarrassed by his thoughts and glad there was no one here to tease him. But the sparkling rock looked... magical before. Now it looked like a plain old rock.

"Maybe it needs salt water to shine," he decided, and slipped the stone into the pocket of his cut-offs. He felt the weight of it flat against his thigh. He'd take the rock to the beach and test his theory after breakfast, and see if he could get the sparkle to return.

Maybe he'd find Kae again.

Toenails clattered on the wooden stairs and Lucky pushed the bedroom door open with his nose. The dog spotted Shea and wagged his tail as he trotted across the small room. "Hey, boy." Shea scratched the dog's ears with both hands. The wagging grew faster until Lucky's entire backside swayed to the rhythm of his tail and Shea couldn't help but smile.

The sound of running water stopped and the sudden silence was louder than the noise had been. He heard the door to the bathroom creak open, and moments later another door slammed shut. The dog whimpered, his grey eyes looking toward the window. Blue sky and bright sunlight shone through the thin curtains.

"You can't come with me to the beach every time," he told Lucky, shaking his head to answer the dog's unspoken question. "The lifeguards will be showing up soon." Martha warned him the lifeguard stands would be manned on weekends through Memorial Day, and then on a daily basis

66

after that. Beach walks would have to be an early-morning-only kind of thing.

When he told Martha about his run-in with Officer L. Tandy, she laughed and told him not to worry. "Officer Tandy's more of a cat person," she explained, but Shea didn't want to push his luck too far. The officer let him off with a warning that first time, but Shea thought it wiser to avoid a second confrontation. It didn't mean he'd stop taking Lucky to the beach – as far as Shea was concerned, that particular rule was meant to be broken.

The dog walked to the window. Putting his paws on the sill, Lucky gave a short bark. Shea rose from the bed, and went to stand next to him. Down on the street, a bicycle whizzed around the corner, out of sight. Could it be Kae? He took the stairs two at a time, Lucky close on his heels. His hand was already on the brass handle of the front door when his grandmother called from upstairs. "Shea?"

"What is it, Gramma?" He crossed to the bottom of the staircase.

"What's all that racket?" Martha now stood at the top of the stairs, a faded terrycloth robe tied tightly at her waist.

"Lucky needs to go outside," he answered, which was true. But not the whole truth. He hadn't told Martha about his new friend yet, and wasn't ready to do it now. Not when he needed to run after her and catch up.

"Don't be long. I'm coming downstairs in a few minutes to cook breakfast. The most important meal of the day, remember." He heard her bedroom door snap closed, and headed out the front door, Lucky following.

The street was empty. He stood on the grassy part of the yard between the house and the street, looking in both directions. Tilting his head to one side, he listened for clues as to where the bicycle might have disappeared. Lucky stood watching the boy, and cocked his head the same way. The dog took off running, headed toward the end of Pine Street away from the beach.

"Lucky! Come back here right now!" He ran after the dog and caught him in a yard farther down the street. The dog skidded to a stop at the base of an oak tree and barked. Shea spied a small orange and white cat clinging for dear life to one of the lowest branch. He let out an exasperated sigh. The dog was chasing cats, not bikes. "That's enough, Lucky. Leave the little guy alone."

The dog wagged his tail in triumph. Seeing the disapproval on Shea's face, Lucky's tail slowed. He walked over and nudged Shea's hand with his nose.

He couldn't help but laugh. "It's okay, I'm not mad." Lucky wagged his tail faster. He lay in the fallen leaves at Shea's feet as the door to the house swung open with a bang.

"What's going on out here?" An elderly woman stood in the shadows of her doorway. The orange cat yowled, and the woman stepped out into the morning sun.

She looks older than Gramma. And that faded dress must mean she shares Gramma's obsession with bleach. "I'm sorry, ma'am," he said. "I think my dog chased your cat into the tree."

"Well? Get him out." The old lady's head nodded with each word, loose grey curls bobbling in agreement.

Lucky thumped his tail on the ground. Shea sighed and turned to the oak tree. The small orange creature stared at him, eyes wide. "What's the cat's name?"

"Gingersnap," the woman replied, scuffing her furry slippers along the graveled walkway. The cat mewed loudly.

"Come here, Gingersnap." He raised his arms. The cat looked on with disdain. *Make me*, he could practically hear it thinking.

The woman cocked her head to one side. "You must be Martha's grandson," she said, nodding. "You have that MacNamara look about you. I'm Ann McFadden, a friend of Martha's."

"Nice to meet you, ma'am."

"You'll need to climb up there. Gingersnap can never get down by himself."

"Has this happened before?" He circled the tree searching for a way up. There was a broken branch on the other side to grab onto. The oak's bark was thick and rough, offering a good grip for his bare feet against the trunk. He grabbed the stubby branch with both hands and pulled himself up.

"I usually call the police department, and they send over a cruiser, especially when Mr. McFadden is out at sea like he is today. The police aren't busy in the off-season, and Officer Tandy is such a sweetheart. I was good friends with his mother, God rest her soul."

"Officer L. Tandy?" Shea swung his legs to the higher branch in the front of the tree. The cat eyed him warily.

"Do you know Leslie?" Mrs. McFadden smiled broadly. "The Tandy family used to live over on Sea Lane. He took your mother out for ice cream a few times, but I think she was trying to make young Tommy jealous."

Shea smirked at the officer's name. Leslie. Wasn't that a girl's name? Then the rest of the old woman's words sank in. "You knew my parents?"

"Of course, dear. Mr. McFadden and I have lived here forever." She patted her grey curls, looking lost in her memories for a moment. "I remember when your grandparents moved into the neighborhood." She paused. "I

70

am sorry to hear about your father. Such a shame. Such a good boy he was."

He swallowed the sudden lump in his throat. "And my mom? You knew her family too?"

Mrs. McFadden shook her head. "Never met the family, really, just your mom and one of her friends. She said her father traveled a lot, for business or some such. I still see her friend in the neighborhood occasionally, when she visits Martha for tea. But I heard your mother had to go into the family business, so I assume she's the one traveling now."

"But Gramma has tea with Mom's friend? When…"

Just then, the cat yowled. Mrs. McFadden put her hands on her hips. "Young man. Can we please focus on getting Gingersnap out of this awful situation?"

"Yes, ma'am." He pulled himself all the way onto the low branch, and sat still for a moment, letting the cat get used to his presence before petting him. The cat started to purr.

"That's the same way Leslie does it." Mrs. McFadden nodded as he picked up the animal and held it against his chest. He jumped down and handed the cat to its owner. The woman snuggled the orange furball against her cheek. The cat closed his eyes and continued to purr. "Now, young man, how did you come to meet Leslie?"

He shrugged his shoulders, feeling his cheeks burn a little at the memory of being caught breaking the law. "Lucky and I were on the beach yesterday talking to this girl…"

"Oh! So you met the new owners of the windmill house?" Mrs. McFadden's grey curls bounced excitedly. "I hear the husband is some Wall Street bigwig! I hope they're going to renovate that old place. It deserves a second chance."

He opened his mouth to reply, having already decided Kae couldn't live at the windmill house, but the old woman barreled on. "The moving van blocked that end of the street for two days last week. So they have children, you say?"

"Actually, I'm pretty sure this girl doesn't live in the windmill house." He wanted to hear more about his mother. But the dotty old woman already turned away, heading up the walkway toward her front door.

"Thank you for rescuing Gingersnap," Mrs. McFadden said over her shoulder. "And remind your grandmother we have bridge this afternoon at the Community Center. It's her turn to drive, since Mr. McFadden is away."

Shea's eyes opened wide, remembering breakfast would be on the table any minute. He could ask Martha these questions directly. "You're welcome, ma'am. Have a nice day." He sprinted down the road, Lucky at his heels. His hand was already on the doorknob when a voice from behind stopped him.

"Good job with the cat. I'd give you a B minus."

He tensed, spinning around to see who that voice belonged to. A girl on a too-big bicycle rested on the street in front of the house. Dark hair poked from beneath her bike helmet in two long woven braids. A brown t-shirt sported orange block letters screaming, "I do my own stunts." A liberal dose of freckles covered her nose and cheeks and most of her arms, in stark contrast to the pale skinny legs that poked from below her blue satin gym shorts.

"Thanks, I think. I didn't know anyone was grading me."

"My brother and I grade everything." She smiled. "I'm Hailey. We're new to the neighborhood. And you are?"

"Shea MacNamara." He realized he still held the doorknob in a death grip, and let his hand fall to his side. "I'm kind of new around here myself."

"Cool name, like the old Shea Stadium back home, right? I'm a big Mets fan. Are your parents Mets fans, too? Do you like baseball? I'll bet you're a Red Sox fan, here in Massachusetts? Do you even like baseball? Of course you do 'cuz you're a boy, right? How old are you?" Hailey flung the questions at him rapid-fire, squinting her chocolate-colored eyes as if trying to read his mind.

Maybe she'll grade herself on how well she guesses. "Fifteen."

73

Hailey nodded. "I knew you were close to my age. I'm actually only thirteen, but my birthday is at the end of June. My brother Chip's sixteen. Teenage boys are such a pain. Present company excluded, of course. Unless you turn out to be a pain, because then I'll lump you in with him and all the other rotten teenagers I already know but I'll give you a pass for the moment. At least until we get a chance to be friends. Or enemies. Do you have brothers or sisters?"

"Shea, is that you?" Martha swung the front door wide open, startling him with the sudden movement. He'd been completely transfixed by the barrage of words coming from the brunette on the bike. Martha nodded her head toward the girl. "Who's your friend?"

"Hailey Thompson, ma'am." She flashed a wide smile and dismounted from her bicycle, wheeling it across the lawn. Dropping the bike to the ground with a thud, she shook the older woman's hand. "My family bought the windmill house at the other end of the neighborhood. Just moved to the Cape, too. This is all brand new to me, and so far so good."

Martha smiled at the chatty girl. "Welcome to Cape Cod, Hailey. Have you eaten breakfast yet this morning?"

"I had half a banana before I got on my bike. And then I ran into Shea, and..."

"That's not breakfast!" Martha waved her hand dismissively. "You can't skip the most important meal of the day! Come inside, we've got plenty of pancakes and bacon."

"Thanks!" Hailey unhooked her helmet and tossed it onto the grass next to her bicycle. "I'd love to, ma'am, if it's okay with Shea."

He shrugged. "Whatever," he agreed, and followed Hailey and his grandmother into the house.

"So, Hailey, where did you move from?" Martha placed heaping plates of pancakes on the table in front of Hailey and Shea. She bustled around the kitchen, grabbing juice glasses from the cabinet and silverware from the drawer.

"New York City." Hailey made a fast grab for the syrup bottle before Shea even settled in his chair. She slathered her plate with the sticky brown sweetness, talking while she poured. "Mom's an interior decorator. She had some really important clients in the City. She didn't want to move at all. But my dad worked on Wall Street, and with all the ups and downs in the market this last year, he gave himself a heart attack. The doctor told him he needed a quiet environment and less stress. Or else." She passed the almost empty bottle across the table to Shea. "It was kind of like 'Move or Die.' So we moved."

Shea stared at the plastic bottle, at the residue of syrup dripping down the sides to pool on the bottom. Barely enough left. Not that he'd actually eaten any maple syrup since arriving on Cape Cod, but still. "My father is dead. That's why I'm here. He died. I moved."

His grandmother's hand flew to her chest. "Shea! Don't be rude to your guest!"

Hailey's fork clattered to her plate, her freckled cheeks reddening. "I'm so sorry. I had no idea." She pushed away from the table, the chair legs scraped loudly along the linoleum floor. "I never know when to shut up. That's always been one of my problems. Everyone says so. Maybe…maybe I should go."

He instantly regretted his words. He glanced at his grandmother's stern expression then turned to Hailey. "Please stay. You're only the second kid I've met since moving to Cape Cod. And I know where you live. It would be good to have someone to hang out with other than Gramma."

"Second?" Martha asked, ignoring the slight jab and raising an eyebrow. She poured orange juice into his glass and gave Hailey a smile. The girl settled into her chair.

"I met one of the summer people on the beach the other morning." The frown on her face made him uncomfortable. "But I don't know which house she lives in."

"It's kinda spooky how most of the houses are empty." Hailey stuffed a whole pancake in her mouth, and was blissfully silent for an entire minute while she chewed.

Swallowing with a loud gulp, she turned to Martha. "These are the best pancakes I've ever had, Mrs. MacNamara! You get an A-plus!"

Martha beamed. "You've earned yourself a standing invitation for breakfast, my dear. And you can call me Gramma. Now if you'll excuse me, I need to check on the washing."

There was silence for a few moments as Hailey filled her mouth with more of the sticky sweet pancakes while Shea watched. He poked his fork into the tops of his own golden cakes, making a line of tiny holes across the flat surfaces, but couldn't bring himself to eat. *Will I ever want to eat pancakes again?*

Hailey washed hers down with orange juice and wiped the back of her hand across her mouth. "You are so lucky, Shea!"

"Why is that?" He narrowed his eyes. He couldn't think of much of anything lucky in his life at the moment.

"My mom doesn't cook, you know? I mean, literally, she can't. Everything burns to a crisp. Seriously. We used to order out or go to restaurants every, and I do mean every, night back home, before we moved. I'm not sure how we're going to survive out here in the boonies without 24/7 takeout! Do you think there's any food delivery around here? My friends told me they don't have bagels or pizza on Cape Cod.

How could there be no bagels? And I already saw two pizzerias on the drive into town so I know that's not true. I mean, who can live without pizza, right? So where'd you used to live?" Hailey ended her questioning by stuffing another large pancake into her mouth.

He paused for a moment to let her torrent of words recede before answering the last question. "On a farm in Oklahoma." He pushed the food around his plate with his fork. He wondered how she could eat faster than Lucky and stay so skinny. Passing his bacon strips under the table to the waiting dog, he asked, "What's New York City like?"

"A lot different from Cape Cod!" Hailey grinned, bites of pancake filling one cheek. She looked like a chipmunk gathering nuts. "It's so quiet here! No traffic, no sirens, just like nature and stuff. And there're no people. It's really strange."

"Gramma says the neighborhood gets busy in July and August. It's mostly summer people. Maybe you'll know some of them from New York."

She swallowed quickly and laughed out loud. "You are too funny, Shea MacNamara. Like I would know everyone in New York or something. Ha! Have you ever even been to a big city? Do you realize how big a city really is? And especially New York!" She snorted, laughing harder.

"What?"

"It's just that New York is like the biggest city in the whole entire world!" Hailey wiped tears from her eyes. "Look at me, I'm laughing so hard I'm crying, too!" That started her on another gale of giggles and snorts. This time, Shea couldn't help but grin, and soon laughter filled the kitchen. He wasn't completely sure what was so funny but it felt good to laugh. Lucky stood and bumped his spine against the underside of the kitchen table, nosing his head into Shea's lap and whipping Hailey's knees with his tail. For some reason, this too struck the pair as hysterically funny.

"I love your dog," she said, wiping her eyes again with the back of her hand. "He's so big! There was a twenty pound limit on pets in our building."

"We always had farm dogs, but they were working dogs and they slept in the barn. Gramma lets Lucky sleep in my room with me at night."

"Really?" Hailey sounded jealous.

He nodded, smiling. "He's awesome." He placed his breakfast plate on the linoleum. Lucky eagerly slurped the pancakes and syrup.

Hailey put her plate on the floor next to his. "Maybe my mom will let us get one, now that we have a yard and everything. Then Lucky'd have a playmate."

"Lucky has me. But you can hang out with us whenever you want."

"Really?" Her eyes locked with his.

"Really." He decided he liked being around this quirky girl who talked too much and too fast. He hadn't heard from John in more than a week now, although he still hoped his friend would visit Cape Cod over the summer, like Mrs. Hansen promised. But it was time to start making new friends, too.

"Hey, do you have a bike?"

Shea cocked his head, knowing he'd seen a bicycle somewhere around. "I think there might be some old ones in Gramma's shed. I haven't really checked them out yet, you know, to see if they still work or if they're hunks of rust."

"Let's go figure it out." Hailey picked the plates off the floor and carried them to the kitchen sink. He followed with the juice glasses and silverware. "Then we can explore the neighborhood. Maybe we can figure out which house that other girl lives in, the one you met on the beach. Do you think it's one of the big ones on the water? That would be cool to see inside one of those, to see if they're as fancy inside as they seem from outside. I mean, our new house is big, but my mom has her work cut out for her. And, of course, I wouldn't mind a girl to hang out with. No offense, you know. But you are a boy and all."

Shea was grinning from ear to ear, listening to her running commentary as they walked through the kitchen door into the backyard. The screen door slammed shut behind him, stopping him in his tracks. "Oh, hang on a minute! I almost forgot." He ran inside and opened the door to the basement laundry room. "Gramma," he called, "Mrs. McFadden said to remind you about bridge today at the Community Center. It's your turn to drive since her husband's out at sea."

"You must've misheard," Martha called. "Or maybe she's confused again. The poor woman has dementia of some kind, which is why she's not allowed to drive."

"What do you mean?" Shea was sure he'd gotten the message right.

"Mr. McFadden died a few years ago. Mr. Guenther took his place at our bridge table. I think the two of them might have a little bit of a thing going on between them, but they certainly aren't married."

He frowned at the thought of his grandmother hanging out with that creepy old man, or that Mr. Guenther might be having a "thing" with anyone, even the dotty old lady with the orange cat. "Whatever," he muttered under his breath and hurried out the door to catch Hailey. He'd ask Martha the questions about his parents later on, maybe at dinner or something. He had plenty of time. After all, he was stuck here on the Cape for good.

At least now he had someone to hang out with.

Things on Cape Cod were finally looking up.

CHAPTER NINE

The warming ocean currents of late spring meant planting season in Nantucket Sound, and Kae enjoyed helping her mother work with the seedlings in the castle's many gardens. Even if her mother thought of it as punishment for breaking the rules.

Kae enjoyed the slow pace of planting, gently coaxing the baby greens to grow alongside the algae-covered walls surrounding the underwater castle. She moved carefully down the rows of tender new growth, concentrating on slowing the flutter of her tailfins so as not to stir the sand and loam from the ocean's bottom. She didn't want to dislodge the seedlings before they had a chance to take root.

Using a clamshell trowel, she worked her way down the row, lost in her concentration and her thoughts. In her younger years, she spent hours in muddy clouds stirred by her childish enthusiasm. Her mother used to set aside a small patch on one end of the gardens, calling it Kae's Corner. The rows never looked as straight or neat in that area, and there would inevitably be a strange plant or two growing tall in the middle, a stray she'd brought home from one of the other fields. Over the years, having her own patch of greenery to tend taught her to appreciate the cycles of life in the summer months, and she learned new respect for her fellow farming Aequoreans.

In more recent years, the war with the Adluos pressed deep into the waters of the Atlantic, making summertime travel more and more dangerous. Kae spent the last few summers stuck in the South Atlantic at the heavily fortified Winter Castle, tending the needs of the princess, while the king and a smaller entourage traveled north for the traditional observance of the Solstice. Her parents accompanied King Koios on these journeys, leaving her behind, wistful for the calm beauty of Nantucket Sound.

With the Oceans finally on the brink of peace, the king decided to relax some of his wartime mandates, including lifting the ban on free travel within the regions of the Atlantic. In a few weeks, dignitaries from all five of the world's oceans and many of the minor seas would arrive for the Solstice ceremonies, thankful to celebrate the end of the war between the Atlantic and the Southern oceans.

Kae knew the end of the bloody conflict meant good things, but every time she thought about the upcoming wedding her stomach clenched as if gripped by octopus tentacles. There was something wrong with making the princess wed a stranger, let alone a six-year-old orphan. It shouldn't matter that he was heir to the Southern throne. He was a mere guppy next to her princess, a grown woman.

Even more pressing to her mind, she wondered if she'd be allowed to finish her schooling, or would the princess expect her to travel to the Adluo court and stay there? She shivered at the thought of having to live among the deep blue shadows of the cold Southern Ocean. Scary rumors floated along the current, about the cruelty of Prince Demyan, the regent for young King Theo.

Some claimed the prince himself murdered his royal uncle and aunt in order to inherit the Southern throne. That his cousin might not live long enough to attend his own wedding. *If Demyan has the audacity to kill royalty, will my princess be safe in the Southern Ocean? Would he hesitate even a minnow's breath to kill a mere servant like me?* The peace was supposed to quell the uncertainty, and yet it wove its own net full of questions.

Worries scuttled through her mind like darting fiddler crabs poking in and out of their burrows. Rumors concerning her own princess nagged at her as well. Rumors that Princess Brynneliana secretly married a human when she was young.

84

And that they had a child whom prophesies foretold would one day rule the Atlantic.

Her mother appeared at her side, interrupting Kae's buzzing thoughts. "When you are finished with this section, I need you to swim to the oyster bed to check if any there are ripe. The princess will need fresh pearls for the engagement ceremony, and the Cook will need plenty of hors d'oevres to feed the foreign royalty."

"After I have done that may I swim to the shoreline? I could gather more of the wild scallops that grow along there." Kae hoped Shea would be on the beach. Her heart beat faster at the thought.

Kira put her hands on her hips, tailfin fluttering faster. "I don't want you going back to Windmill Point. The king forbade contact with humans, especially the ones along those beaches. You must not break his rules again, Kae." She turned away and swam to the end of the row, grabbing a tray of fresh seedlings.

"Why can't I speak to him, for Neptune's sake?" Kae's tail swished from side to side, stirring a cloud on the sandy ocean floor. Several hermit crabs scuttled out of the mermaid's path as she moved to follow her mother. Telling her mother about the cute human had not gone as well as she hoped. "The war is over. And he's only a boy, Mother, not some kind of spy. What danger could there be in talking?"

Kira looked from the tender plants she held in her hands, her eyes searching the area. Kae glanced over her shoulder to see what it was her mother sought. There was nothing. They swam alone in the gardens. Her father, Lybio, was out of sight on the far side of the castle, still at work clearing the last of the debris from the cobblestone courtyard where the trash tended to accumulate during the long winter months.

"You must not talk to him, Kae." Kira's voice grew low and urgent as she swam up the row toward her daughter. "Not this boy. Especially not this boy."

"But why? He seems harmless. And he cares for the ocean. Every day, he clears debris from the shore, just as Father is doing now in the courtyard. In fact, it's probably the same exact trash, since Father merely dumps it on the land where it belongs. Shea simply carries it a step further, away from the ocean…"

"You will not talk to that boy again." Kira pulled an extra scallop-shell clip from her own long hair. "I'm your mother and I forbid it. And you must not talk *about* him, either. His name will only cause trouble. Now, pull your hair away from your face and let's finish the planting. The King's entourage will arrive any day now."

Kae frowned, reaching for the hair clip her mother held, a thin stream of bubbles rising when she exhaled. "You don't understand."

The pair began to dig, now side-by-side. A school of small shining dartfish swished eagerly toward the seedlings, their zebra stripes flickering in the sun-dappled field. Kira swatted them away with her hand. "There seem to be more and more of these silvery pests each year, moving northward with us as the oceans warm."

Kae said nothing, preferring to stew in her anger. *Why would the name Shea cause trouble?* Her mother was being unreasonable and overprotective, trying to keep Kae sheltered in childhood. *I'm no longer a youngling, for Neptune's sake.* Why couldn't her parents understand?

The pair worked in silence for hours. The garden covered the vast expanse of the rear courtyard, just beyond where a ring of boulders marked the edge of the formal patio. As they worked among the swaying greenery, Kae's anger ebbed slowly, replaced by the serenity of the garden. Kae found the graceful green fronds and thin beige reeds much more beautiful than the stubby multi-hued anemones growing on the hard coral reefs which surrounded the winter palace.

The two castles were different in so many ways, both small and large. She wondered if the other clans had such variety in their summer and winter residences. She'd heard tales of the Pacific King building new summer residences every few years, scattered all throughout the wide expanse of his domain, one for each new prince or princess born into the already large royal family. She wondered how many servants they must employ to keep all those buildings maintained, and felt glad that her own clan was more traditional.

The Aequorean summer castle in the depths of Nantucket Sound had been in the royal family for many generations. The sprawling building stretched for more than a mile in each direction from the central courtyard. Long and low to the ocean's floor, the castle consisted of many open winding corridors and countless guest rooms, all grouped in twos or threes to accommodate summer visitors.

Where the winter palace was a tall, imposing fortress of a structure built of glistening marble blocks, glinting with golden touches, the masons built the summer castle of local granite, the same as the human jetties which jutted out from the shoreline. Kae's family lived in one of the servant cottages, which were separate two-room homes built with more of the stone and clustered off along the edges of the main structure.

Algae and seaweed grasses covered entire sections of the buildings, helping them blend into the surrounding landscape and go undetected in the comparatively shallow waters of the Sound. Although the castle had been built to go unnoticed, the proximity to the shore made humans impossible to ignore.

Kae finally broke the silence. "Why are humans bad?"

Her mother sighed, a slow stream of bubbles rising from the gills behind her ears. "Not everyone considers them evil. The purity of blood arguments spouted by the Adluos have been around a long, long time. But this utter hatred of the so-called 'drylanders' is a new twist on an old story."

"What do you mean?"

"Mermaids and humans have a long history of interactions. It's nothing new, nor is there anything wrong with it."

Kae rolled her eyes. She already knew her parents and most of her clan disagreed with the negative views of humans held by other merfolk. But her mother's next statement made her heart skip a beat. "Your father himself was born above water. His name, Lybio, actually means 'born in a dry place.'"

Kae realized her mouth hung open at this unexpected revelation. She caught herself and tried to make sense of her mother's words. "I didn't know… I didn't know such a thing was even possible. How can a mermaid and a human have a child together?"

"Just because a thing is possible, doesn't mean it should be allowed." Lybio's deep voice startled both mermaids. They turned to find him standing at the edge of the garden. His muscled arms folded across his torso, his dark grey hair and beard waving in the slight current. "Kira, what tales are you telling our daughter?"

"This may be her…her last Nantucket summer with us." Kira held her head high even as Lybio glared. "Whether she travels to university or stays to serve the Princess, she deserves to know her own history before she hears it from others who would use it against her. Especially if she is to travel south."

Kae was quick to read between the lines. If she were indeed even part human, she would be an outcast among the Adluos. Wasn't it said their own Queen Jessamine was murdered for having traces of human blood?

Lybio pressed his lips together, his mouth a barely visible line. Finally, he nodded in agreement. "So be it. But this part is my tale to tell." Kira turned and with a few quick flicks of the tail was gone from the gardens, leaving father and daughter alone.

"Is it true?" Kae's eyes traveled the length of his body, looking for some outward sign of his birth father and finding none. Lybio gave a sharp nod of assent. "So I'm…part human?" She glanced at her own hands. They suddenly felt different to her, like they belonged to a stranger.

"This is no one's business but ours," Lybio warned. "There are those even among the Aequorean clan who despise anything tainted by the touch of humans."

"I don't understand."

"Times were different under the kings of old." Lybio's deep voice took on the rhythmic pulse of a storyteller. "The oceans cleaner, the food more plentiful. For hundreds of years, the clans were at peace with the land creatures and with each other."

She listened intently while he talked of the past. She wasn't quite sure how old her father actually was but knew he was ancient even for a merman. Merfolk could live for a century without ever appearing older than twenty, unless they spent a lot of time above the surface. Everyone knew air was bad for the skin, causing wrinkles and ugly brown spots.

"Legends exist in every clan, and in every dryland culture, of mermaids falling in love with humans, foregoing their lives in the ocean to become land creatures." He focused on the edge of the garden, unable to meet her eyes.

Kae smiled. "Surely, those are make-believe stories. Who would give up eternal youth and life in our beautiful oceans?"

"All legends are based on some truth." Her father swished his powerful tail. The sand rose in a cloud below him. "Else how would the humans tell the same sorts of tales about mermaids to their young ones that we do?" Kae hadn't considered it from that angle. "Unfortunately, many such unions ended in sorrow for the mermaids."

"Tell me," Kae urged, putting down her trowel.

"Long ago, when there was peace in all the worlds, the tradition of the Grand Journey began. When a mermaid or merman turned fifteen, they would leave their home to travel alone, visiting each of the world's five oceans. They would spend a year in each, living with host families and learning the knowledge of that clan."

Kae nodded. Over the years, she'd heard many bedtime stories based on her mother's own Journey, of the wonders Kira had seen in other parts of the globe. With the current war and the climate of distrust between the clans, Kae's own Journey would be limited to the university housed in the undersea city of Atlantis, neutral territory for all the tribes and the High Council's seat of power. If she was allowed to make any Journey at all.

"My mother fell in love with a Gaelic fisherman across the Atlantic. When I was but a small child, she decided to tell him the truth of her being a mermaid and not of the land, as he thought. He ran from her, and she never saw him again."

Kae stared, waiting for her father to continue. He seemed lost in some memory, so she prodded. "If he was human, how is it that you are a merman?"

"Mermaid blood," Lybio explained with a heavy sigh. "Many mixed offspring never grow gills, which is why their mothers choose to stay with them on dry land. Mermaid blood is a tricky thing. Poseidon, god of the seas, creator of us all, chooses who shall serve him and in what form. After my transformation, my mother went before the Aequorean king. In exchange for her return to the clan, she pledged me into his service. Her pledge binds me to the new king as well."

"I'd hardly call King Koios new, Father." She crossed her arms over her chest, tossing her blonde hair with the current. "He's got to be as old as you are."

Lybio's expression was stern. "He was crowned king less than a hundred years ago when his father died, gods rest his soul. Even a century is barely a drop in the oceans of time. King Koios has found it much harder to govern than his father ever did, between the problems above the surface and the bloodthirsty Adluos always anxious to battle."

"Problems?" Kae's mind flashed to the boy on the beach. *Shea wouldn't ever cause any trouble.*

"Humans have mastered many forms of technology, but not the wisdom or self-control to govern it properly." Lybio shook his head. "They create too much waste, spilling it into the seas without thought to the consequences. They turn from the easily renewable powers of sun and wind, choosing to burn carbon fuels that pollute the air and seas. This leaves the ocean's inhabitants to fight for what remains…"

Kae rolled her eyes, having endured this same rant against pollution several times during their long swim northward. Everyone knew pollution was getting worse. Personally, Kae thought if the merfolk explained the situation to the humans, they would stop dumping in the oceans.

Lybio's bushy eyebrows lowered over his steel blue eyes. "When I was a boy making my Journey, we had nothing to fear from humans or the other clans. The few boats upon the surface were powered by the wind alone, and posed no threat to our way of life."

"But why do they teach courses about land dwellers at the university if we are never to interact with them?" Kae touched the black stone hanging at her neck. "Why wear the *transmutare* medallions if we are not supposed to travel above the surface?"

Lybio explained that the *transmutare* stone held very old magic, mined from the deepest part of the ocean's floor where Poseidon himself buried it. "The stone channels the power and magic of the sea to do your bidding, allowing you freedoms such as passing a fishing boat unseen, or traveling upon land, or staying in touch with your family when you are oceans away."

"I know these things." Her tailfin fluttered more quickly, stirring the sand and knocking down one of the freshly planted seedlings.

"Only a finite number of these stones remain. Some clans hoard them for their magical powers, seeking to use them to harness the weather. If the stones fall into the wrong hands they can be very dangerous."

"Wrong hands? Like the Adluos?" Kae echoed, her tail frozen mid-flutter. What if that soldier she saw in Windmill Point already found her stone?

Lybio nodded. "There are rumors of an Adluo sorcerer named Zan who is so powerful he doesn't need to wear the *transmutare* to influence others. He drains the power from the stones and can use it to influence humans and merfolk alike with a simple touch."

Guilt swept through her. "I should confess... I lost my original *transmutare* while gathering scallop shells. I found this one in the King's storeroom."

Lybio smiled and patted her shoulder. "Do not fear. The magic fades if the medallion washes ashore. Without a mermaid's touch the hole disappears in the drying air, and with it the magic. It becomes yet another stone upon the sand."

"But...there's something more, Father. I saw an Adluo soldier enter the water from Windmill Point. I meant to tell you right away, but I thought you'd be angry. What if...what if he took my *transmutare*?"

"What were you doing at Windmill Point?"

She glanced away from him, unable to meet his stern gaze. This was the part that would make him angry, but there was no way to lie about it since her mother already knew the truth. "Talking to a human boy named Shea MacNamara."

Lybio exhaled forcefully, sending a burst of bubbles streaming upward from both his mouth and the gills behind his ears. His mouth had thinned into a straight, unforgiving line as he growled orders. "Tomorrow you will search for your stone. You will stay away from that boy. The less said about humans the better. Especially once the king and the Adluo delegation arrive."

She nodded, again casting her head downward and picking up her trowel. She watched her father swim to where his fishing net lay on the ground next to Kira. Though they were on the far side of the grounds, the current carried their words to Kae's ears.

"What?" Lybio's voice sounded gruff. Kae watched him lift the fishing net he'd already filled with debris and swing it over his shoulder. He liked to dump the garbage onto the shore, where it belonged, but it always bothered her to see it among the seaweed at the strandline. She felt better knowing Shea was there, to finish the job.

Kira's hands fisted on her hips. "Do you not feel the least bit of guilt? Lying to our daughter about your own father? You know he loved your mother, you told me so, many times over the years. He did not run screaming from her because she was a mermaid."

Kae turned her head away. *They don't know their words are floating down current and I can still hear them talking!*

"The truth is too scary. Humans can be frightening creatures."

"You are a half-breed," Kira reminded him. "I've never had reason to fear you."

"So you think I should tell her how the townspeople killed my father and tried to drown my mother and me for witchcraft? That I had no idea of my mermaid blood until that fateful night when they threw me off a cliff?"

Kae gasped, clutching at the kelp seedling until the fragile stem broke in two. No wonder her father kept his past a secret!

"Drylanders can be every bit as cruel as those Adluo fear mongers who stir the clans against them. All of us fear what we do not understand."

Kira slapped his arm, the sound reverberating on the current. "Don't use that slur, not when it's part of your own heritage. And I still think it's always best to tell the truth."

Derisive laughter filled the castle's courtyard. "You? Tell the truth? You always tell whatever truth best suits your friend the princess."

"You keep the king's counsel and do not enlighten me as to your secret missions," Kira countered.

"Those tasks I perform for King Koios have nothing to do with you. And the clans are still at war until the treaties are signed and sealed."

There was silence, and Kae dared to look over at her parents again. Kira had her arms crossed over her chest and Lybio was leaving the court, dragging the fishing net in his wake.

Kae released the crushed seedling from her hand, watching it settle to the ocean floor. Her parents had more secrets than she ever imagined. Bigger secrets than talking to a boy along the shoreline.

Her world suddenly seemed a lot more complicated than it had been. And more than a little dangerous.

Chapter Ten

Four empty water bottles, three green shotgun shell casings, a green plastic shovel, two green plastic army men, three apple flavored NutriGrain wrappers, and a length of green plastic rope.

"Not a lot of trash, Lucky." Shea trudged along the shoreline, the dog by his side. "Not like yesterday. But today's theme seems to be 'green.' Even the water bottles are green from the algae growing inside them." He swung the plastic garbage bag, the wide arcs keeping time with his slow strides. He decided to keep one of the army men. The second plastic soldier already lost its head and one arm, so he tossed it in the bag with the rest of the day's trash.

Two hundred yards ahead, he spied a familiar figure walking along the water's edge searching the strandline, the line where the high tide leaves its row of seaweed, shells and other natural debris. Any thoughts of playing it cool went right out of his head in his excitement. He waved an arm to draw her attention. "Hey! Wait up!" He ran down the beach toward her, Lucky keeping pace.

She turned her head, smiling as their eyes met. "Hey there, Garbage Boy."

He skidded to a stop in front of her, panting to catch his breath, feeling a little foolish for sprinting. It's not like she'd disappear into the ocean without saying hello. He swallowed his embarrassment and smiled. "Hey, I've been looking for you. Where've you been?"

"Helping my mother plant the garden, while the ocean is calm." She stared out at the water's flat surface. His eyes followed hers, not understanding what gardening and quiet seas had to do with one another. "What did that angry man want with you the other morning?"

"The policeman?" When Kae nodded, he shrugged. "He wasn't angry. He wanted to tell me Lucky's not allowed on the beach." He bent to scratch the dog's head. A wave soaked the cuffs of his blue jeans before receding into the ocean, his feet sinking a little deeper beneath the surface of the sand.

"But… you didn't listen to him?" She tilted her head to one side.

"I don't always do everything I'm told." He waggled his eyebrows.

100

She laughed and broke into a sunny smile that warmed him all the way down to his toes. "So you came searching for me?"

"Yeah." His smile mirrored hers. "A new girl moved into the neighborhood this week and she wants to meet you."

Her eyebrows lowered, smile gone. "A new girl?"

"Yeah." The sudden chill in her attitude left him feeling like he was on an emotional rollercoaster, not sure what she was thinking or if she liked him. "Her name is Hailey. She moved into the windmill house this week with her parents and older brother. You know, the house at the end of the street with the windmill attached?" Kae glowered, the rollercoaster still plummeting and his stomach beginning to feel unsettled. She gave no indication whether she knew which house he meant. "She and her brother have their bedrooms inside the windmill itself. Pretty cool, right?" Still nothing from Kae, except that glare. "So, umm," Shea continued, finding it hard to complete his thought while her eyes shot daggers at him. "We, umm, rode bikes around the neighborhood trying to find your house because she wants to meet you, like I said. And then we came to the beach, even, but we didn't see you."

"Bikes?" The anger disappeared, replaced with curiosity. "What's a bike?"

"Haven't you ever ridden a bicycle before?" When Kae shook her head, he explained, getting back onto more solid ground as her anger dissipated. "Two-wheelers, you know, to get around faster? Tires, gears, brakes... Bicycles. I mean, how can you summer on the Cape and not know what bikes are?"

She turned again toward the ocean's barely undulating surface. "I spend most of my time on the beach or in the ocean." She put her hand to her neck, wrapping her fingers around her medallion. "Tell me more about these bikes of which you speak." She looked straight into his face, her green eyes widening under her long lashes. His heart did a little leap as a tingling jolt ran through his body...and he forgot how strange it was for Kae to know nothing about such an ordinary thing.

"I'm not sure how to explain bicycles, but I'd be happy to give you a lesson. John, my friend back home, taught me in one afternoon when we were nine. It's pretty easy."

His eyes rested on the medallion at her neck, reminding him of the stone in his jeans. He slipped his hand into his front pocket, against the stone, and rubbed his thumb in a slow circle around the surface, mimicking Kae's movements.

A crackle ran up his spine, like a flash of lightning exploding behind his eyes. He pulled his hand quickly from his pocket as if he'd been stung. A woman's surprised face flashed into his head, surrounded by a halo of floating blond curls. It was the woman in the silver frame on Gramma's mantle. His mother.

"What's the matter? Got a stingray in your pocket?"

His hand still tingled from touching the stone. The vision of his mother's face faded. He flexed his fingers, making a fist and then releasing. The burning sensation traveled up his arm, as if sparks of fire swam in his bloodstream. "That was totally weird," he said to himself, forgetting for the moment that Kae stood right in front of him.

"What?" Kae laughed, hands now on her hips. "Don't try to change your mind about the bicycle lesson. You've already promised."

"No, I..." he began, and looked into Kae's laughing eyes. He had to ask. "Where did you get your necklace?" Before she could answer, he plunged his hand into his pocket and brought out the other black stone. "I found one just like yours the other day on the beach." He held it on his palm, careful not to rub his fingers against it, afraid to start the fire searing through his veins all over again. He noted the shimmer had returned to the stone's surface, even though it was dry.

"My *transmutare*!" Kae grabbed for it.

"Your what?" He pulled his hand out of her reach.

"It's the medallion I lost the other day." She held out a hand. "Return it to me."

"You have the same thing hanging from your necklace. I found this one."

"The stone in your hand belongs to me, Garbage Boy. I lost it while I was swimming."

"My name is Shea," he reminded her, and slipped the rock into his pocket. He decided if she was going to tease him with the nickname, he could tease her a little too. Fair is fair, right?

Her eyes widened in disbelief. "What are you doing? I told you it's mine, you jellybrain."

"I'll return it when you ask nicely. Now let's go."

"Go where?"

"Lessons. You're a teenager, right? It's high time you learned how to ride a bike." He pushed his hair out of his eyes and grinned before turning away and headed for the dunes. Lucky sat on the sand next to Kae, watching him leave. He looked at them over his shoulder, suddenly nervous that she wasn't going to follow him. "Are you coming or what?"

"I guess so. Wait for me."

Lucky jumped up, wagging his tail as he followed Kae through the dunes.

Chapter Eleven

They walked along the street in silence, but Kae worried with each step at how far from the water he led. *This is not the smartest thing I've ever done. Especially since I was told to stay away from humans, and from this boy in particular. But... I need to get that stone back.*

She wondered what kind of creature a bicycle was, and whether she would be able to ride it. She already knew how to ride a dolphin by holding on to the dorsal fin with one hand. Giant leatherback sea turtles were different, riders gripping the front edges of the shell with both hands. But how do land creatures swim without water? And were land creatures tame like dolphins, or wild like sharks? Finally, Kae asked, "Are bicycles dangerous?"

Shea smiled, shaking his head. "Nah, not dangerous at all." He stopped in front of his grandmother's house. "Here we are. Wait while I put Lucky in the backyard and grab the bike." He left her by herself as he went through the wooden gate.

Her nerves jangled, not sure she was comfortable so far from the water. Her feet ached from walking on the pavement, so much harder than the sand on the beach. She turned to stare at his dwelling, and realized the building was made of wood. How impermanent! She remembered her father telling her those who lived on the land didn't live as long as those who lived in the oceans. *Probably all that exposure to the harmful air. Maybe that's why they don't build their homes to last very long.*

Except now she knew *she* was part human. *What does that mean? Am I not fully a mermaid? Is my father less of a merman because of his human blood?*

Shea emerged through the fence, pushing a metal contraption with both hands. It seemed to glide along two turning wheels made of rubber. Blue cloth dangled over one of his forearms as he steered the machine toward her.

"It's not a living creature after all," Kae murmured under her breath. She recognized the round rubber wheels, having helped her father clean similar, if rusty, debris from the courtyard earlier in the week. Now she understood their purpose.

He wheeled the bicycle to a stop in front of her and narrowed his eyes. "What'd you say?"

"Never mind." She nodded at the fabric draped over his arm. "What's that other stuff?"

"I pulled jeans off the clothesline for you." He held the material toward her. It looked similar to the cloth covering his legs. "They're mine so they'll be a little baggy on you, but you and I are almost the same height so they should be long enough. In case you tip over, you don't want to scrape your knees into a bloody pulp."

"My knees?" Kae looked at the bare legs stretching under her bikini bottoms. "Oh, right. The knobs on my legs where they bend."

He shook his head, laughing. "You girls are strange creatures sometimes, you know that? C'mon, put these on and we can start the lesson."

Hesitantly, she held the jeans in front of her, staring at them. She'd never worn such things. She'd never even had to put clothes on her legs. When she went ashore, she conjured clothing with her *transmutare*, as part of the transformation process.

Two tubes of rough blue material hung from a single opening with a metal button at the top. She noted Shea had one leg in each of the tubes, and the metal button was near his belly. *How did he get his legs inside, though? What am I supposed to do?*

"What's the matter?" He frowned. "They're clean, you know. Don't you think they'll fit? Or are you afraid the fashion police will arrest you?" He took the jeans out of her hands and held them against her waist. "See? They totally look long enough."

It suddenly dawned on Kae that if she lifted one of her legs, she could put it through the larger opening at the top and into one of the tubes. She lifted her leg high, grabbing onto his firm shoulders with both hands to steady herself, and put her leg into the jeans. Her toes emerged from the opposite end of the tube and touched the grass.

Shea dropped the pants, staring at her with his mouth hanging open. The jeans slid slowly down, pooling around the one leg already inside. She stared into his eyes, their faces so close together they were almost rubbing noses, her mouth suddenly as dry as a sandbar. Her stomach did a back flip like a baby whale learning to breach for the first time. Jumping jellyfish! What was happening to her?

He took a deep breath and ducked his shoulders out from under her hands, keeping his eyes glued to her. Under his watchful gaze, Kae stepped her left foot into the other leg tube now scrunched into a heap on the ground and let go of his shoulders, bending to grab the top of the pants he'd been holding a moment before. Sliding the blue jeans over her long legs, she wrinkled her nose at the scratchy feel of the rough material against her bare flesh. She tried to ignore his stare, hoping she was acting like a human girl would.

Glancing at the metal teeth in the vee of the opening, Kae wondered how they fit together, forgetting for a moment that the boy was watching her so intently.

"Don't you know how to zip a zipper?"

"It's my first time wearing...jeans." She rubbed her thumb in a circle around the medallion stone. "Could you help me?"

A dazed expression crossed his face. He tugged the zipper pull and buttoned the jeans for her. His warm fingers brushed against her bare belly, making her stomach do a mother whale of a flip, then turned away as if nothing strange happened. Kae was glad Kira showed her some of the other uses for the *transmutare*, besides the transformation of mermaid tail to legs. The stone could be used to gain help from humans, dazzling their minds so they forgot what happened. *A very useful bit of magick. I'll have to ask mom if it works on other merfolk as well. That would be truly helpful at university. Unless having your own transmutare makes you immune to the magick. Well, at least it works on humans.*

"This is a bicycle," Shea explained, wheeling it forward. "Basically, you straddle it between your legs and push the pedals with your feet. That turns the gears which makes the wheels spin." He demonstrated as he spoke, lifting one leg over the machine, and resting his bottom on the small cushioned triangle. He kept one foot on the ground and put the other onto one of the hard square pads attached at the center. Kae decided those pads must be the pedals he mentioned. She watched him grip the metallic bars at the front.

"Why don't you ride first?" She brushed her thumb around the *transmutare*. He nodded and pushed off from the ground with his other foot. The bike moved off the grass and onto the pavement. Fascinated, she watched his feet move the pedals in small circles, which in turn moved bigger metal circles – the gears, he called them – which made the bigger circles – the *wheels* – spin around. The bicycle rolled forward in a straight line until he leaned to the left, turning the bike in a semi-circle and heading toward her.

He stopped right in front of her, planting both feet on the ground. "The pedaling part is easy, you kind of pump your legs up and down. The tricky part is balancing. If you lean too far to the left or the right, the whole bike tips over. Know your center of gravity." He lifted one leg over the machine so that he was no longer astride it, and leaned the whole thing toward her.

"My father tells me my balance is excellent for someone so young." If it was only a matter of balance, this might be easy. Shea certainly made it seem easy. If a human could ride a bike, then so could a mermaid. Right?

She put her hands on the grips next to his. He released the machine and she lifted one leg over the center of the bike, straddling it like he did moments earlier.

"Get a feel for it first. Walk along with your feet on the ground while you sit on the seat," he suggested. "The tires will roll the bike with you as you walk."

It seemed easy enough. Pushing the bike with both feet on the ground was no harder than walking. "This isn't hard."

Shea laughed, and something pulled tight in her chest. Was he laughing at her? Was she doing something funny? "You're not riding yet," he said. "Try putting your feet on the pedals."

When her weight leaned on the left pedal, the whole bike tipped in that direction, and she crashed to the ground. He rushed to her side, concern etched on his face and blazing in his deep green eyes. "Are you okay?"

"Fine, just embarrassed." And very glad to have the blue tubes protecting her legs. "Let me try again." He helped her to stand up, the bike still between her legs. "Balancing is harder with two legs."

"How else would you balance?"

"Oh, right," Kae answered quickly, hoping he wouldn't remember her words. She tried again to put one foot on the pedal, this time making sure not to lean too far to the side. She rolled the bike forward a little with the other foot still on the ground, and then put that foot onto a pedal as well. She balanced there for almost a full minute, before the bike began to tip to one side and she planted her feet onto the ground.

"Good, you're getting the balance part of it. Now let's try moving forward at the same time." He put one hand against her bare back below the bottom edge of her halter-top. With his other hand he grabbed the end of the handlebar, his thumb brushing against her knuckles as she squeezed the rubber grip. "This is the way my friend helped me."

"Okay," Kae said, feeling the heat from his hand warming the skin on her lower back. It felt strange to have this boy touching her. Strange, but in a good kind of way. Her stomach wasn't flipping out this time, but felt more like waves curling gently onto the shore in a soothing way, spreading warmth in their wake. She scrunched her forehead in concentration, trying to ignore the feelings twisting through her body. "Don't let me fall again!"

"I won't," Shea said with another smile. A smile that said, *Trust me.* And for some strange reason, Kae trusted him. Something in his eyes told her he was different.

"Now put both feet on the pedals." As she did, he began to push the bicycle forward, keeping a steady pressure on her back. "Pump your legs, one at a time. Push this one, now that one. See? You're doing it, Kae!"

She realized the bike rolled forward, her legs moving independent of one another. "Jumping jellyfish! I get it – it's like walking!" She kept her eyes straight ahead of her as she spoke, the bike wobbling underneath her as she pushed on one pedal and then the other. "The legs must move separately."

"I guess you can think of it that way if you want. Keep pumping. There you go. You're getting the hang of it. Try going a little faster now."

The breeze pushed her hair from her face. He let go of his hold on the handlebar when she pumped her legs faster, but still ran alongside to keep up. Suddenly his warm hand was gone and he wasn't next to her anymore as she glided forward on the bicycle, gaining speed and feeling the wind against her cheeks. It felt exhilarating and dangerous at the same time, riding along on the strange machine, slicing through the air as if it were water.

"Slow down! I didn't show you how to stop!"

"What? So how do I stop?" Kae panicked and looked over her shoulder to find him. The movement caused her to lean too far left and the bike crashed to the pavement, pinning her beneath the still-spinning tires. The black gravel dug into her flesh and she cried out in pain.

Shea rushed to help, yanking the machine off her body and tossing it aside. "Are you okay?" He took both of her hands and helped her to her feet. Her legs felt bruised and sore beneath the blue cloth. Bright blood oozed from her left elbow, where the rough pavement scraped the skin away. Small black pebbles clung to the raw wound like sea leeches.

"This looks kind of bad." Shea sounded worried. He cradled her arm, inspecting the scrape. "I guess I'm not a good teacher. Sorry."

Despite the stinging pain, Kae watched the blood pooling and dripping from her arm with detached interest. Open wounds are rare in the ocean and demand immediate attention. They attract scavengers. Like sharks. Luckily there were no such worries on dry land. "Don't be sorry. You didn't harm me, you clownfish. It was my own fault."

"We should clean this and get you a bandage." Shea released her arm, his brow knotted with concern, his green eyes the color of the ocean in the morning after a storm. Kae felt her knees weaken and her heart race, and knew it had nothing to do with the tumble she'd taken.

"I don't want you to get in trouble, going home injured." He cupped a warm hand against her cheek. Little tingles of excitement flowed through her body at his caring touch. His eyes held hers in their gaze. His other hand rested

114

at her waist, where it helped to steady her on the bicycle moments before. Now the sensation of his strong hand on her bare flesh caused feelings inside of her that felt anything but safe. He drew a slow, deep breath and shook his head. "It would suck if I wasn't allowed to see you again, you know, because of this."

Kae pulled away from his hands and tried to focus her jumbled thoughts. She had no idea what a human bandage looked like, but it would be a red flag to her parents. And would never fix the real problem.

She wasn't supposed to even *talk* to this boy. She shouldn't be this far from the ocean, alone with him, touching him… And yet, she didn't want to be anywhere else. She wanted to stay with this boy forever. Suddenly, she felt as if her heart would shatter into a million pieces if he didn't feel the same about her. The intensity of her feelings scared her. "I think… I think I'd better go home now," she whispered, shifting her eyes away from his to watch the blood dripping down her arm. She undid the button and slid the jeans off, leaving them in the middle of the street. "I need to go." She walked toward the ocean, leaving him standing alone in the road, the fallen bicycle at his feet.

"I thought you wanted your stone?"

Kae didn't look back.

****

Shea stared after her retreating form, wondering what he'd done wrong.

115

The whole morning was surreal in so many ways, and yet when he was with Kae, he felt like he was "real" in a whole different way than before. More real than he'd ever felt back home in Oklahoma. Like he'd figured out his purpose in life, and she was the key.

Part of him couldn't believe a gorgeous girl like that would waste two minutes on a guy like him, with no money and no family to speak of. He'd been friends with girls back in Oklahoma, but he'd never had a girlfriend. And he'd never kissed a girl. The thought of actually getting a chance to kiss Kae made him dizzy with excitement, but after today that possibility was looking pretty remote. He was an idiot. Bike riding lessons? He remembered how many times he wiped out when John taught him, how much those scraped elbows hurt and how much John teased him. What made him think he could do any better as a teacher? Just being with Kae made him think he could do anything.

What is it about that girl? He scratched his head and continued to stare down the now empty street, Kae's tall figure well past the point where he could see her. Someone appeared on the horizon. His stomach balled into an excited knot of anticipation until he realized it was Hailey walking toward him.

"Hey, MacNamara! What are you doing?" She pointed at the bike, still lying on its side, droplets of blood spattered on the ground around it. "Did you wipe out?"

Shea shook his head and reached for the fallen bicycle. "Nah. You just missed Kae. I was giving her lessons."

Hailey bent to pick up the discarded jeans, the ones Kae left in a denim puddle near his feet. She held them by the waist and raised an eyebrow. "What kind of lessons?"

He snatched the pants from her, feeling the heat flame in his cheeks, draping the discarded jeans over the handlebars. "Bike riding. She was in her bathing suit so I lent her a pair of pants."

Hailey crossed her arms over her chest. "C'mon. You said she was our age."

"My age."

Hailey rolled her eyes. "Whatever. Why doesn't she already know how to ride a bike?"

"I…I'm not sure." He shoved one hand in his pocket as he thought, the medallion rock silky smooth under his fingers. Some of the weirdness of the situation crept into his consciousness, as if touching the stone helped him remember things, like the way she asked him to zip her jeans because she didn't know how. *Was that some kind of line?* He wondered. As he kept rubbing his thumb around the rock, he remembered more of the strange things Kae said.

Who is she?

And when will I see her again?

CHAPTER TWELVE

Kae hoped she could sneak into the cottage unseen. She didn't want to explain where she'd been all morning, or talk about it at all until she had a chance to sort through her feelings. At least her stomach wasn't doing those weird flippity-floppity things anymore, now that Shea wasn't around. Or touching her. Her stomach gave one last flop at the thought. She concentrated on finding healing mud to cover her wound, since the blood had already seeped through the clump of eelgrass she tied around her arm before swimming.

She also needed to decide if she wanted to see the boy again. *Maybe it would be safer to stay away from Windmill Point.* Her treacherous stomach knotted at the thought of not seeing Shea again, and soon.

Drawing closer to the grounds of the castle, she came to an abrupt stop. Busy servants swam everywhere, creating a chaotic scene where tranquility reigned earlier in the day.

The king's entourage had arrived.

She veered off the main path and into the gardens, seeking a quiet place to think and some fresh loam to use on her elbow in lieu of the healing mud. Voices floated through the manicured patch of kelp, and she recognized them all too well. Kae froze, her tailfin rigid as stone. Quickly, she scraped mud from the garden bed and pressed it to her wound, stemming the blood before the scent gave her away. She peeked through the plantings and confirmed her suspicions. The king and his daughter swam in the next row, arguing.

The king's loud voice carried through the hedge. "I thought you'd be busy preparing for the arrival of your fiancé, or at least eager to see your chambers again. And yet here I find you moping in the garden. This castle used to be your favorite place."

The princess exhaled a huge huff of bubbles, and a school of tiny yellow sunfish came darting through the hedge, right past Kae's nose. She clamped a hand over her mouth to stifle her surprised cry, not wanting to interrupt the royal discussion.

"There are too many soldiers already, Father. I thought the peace negotiations would bring an end to the tension. Instead, it's brought them closer to home."

"Prince Demyan is doing his duty, protecting your cousin from threat. Once we sign the treaty and complete the marriage ceremony, everything will return to normal."

"I…I thought you scheduled the wedding for winter." The way the princess pronounced "wedding" made it sound like a deadly disease or some dreaded event. Kae didn't blame her one bit. It seemed ridiculous that Princess Brynn should be marrying someone so young, even if he was a king.

The tone was not lost on her father, either. "Your *wedding* will be held in the Southern Adluo court over the Winter Solstice, and you will do your duty to your clan." His voice softened as he added, "You know I had no real choice in the matter, Brynneliana. I had to stop the bloodshed. It was one of Prince Demyan's few demands. He insisted – and I concur – we need to bind the clans together with more than words."

"I know we Aequoreans are farmers, not fighters. We're no match for the Adluo soldiers, who train to kill or be killed. I also do not trust those Adluos. I fear nothing we offer will appease them."

The king chuckled. "You forget you have Adluo blood swimming through your veins. Your own mother,

Neptune bless her, came from the South so long ago." The king paused. "Falling in love with a human was never part of my plan for you, even if this treaty hadn't been made with the Adluos. Royal marriages are meant to be political, not romantic."

"But you loved my mother."

Kae had never met the Queen, who died giving birth to her daughter many years before Kae was even born. King Koios never remarried, the rumor being that he was so in love with his wife, no one could replace her.

"I *learned* to love her very much," the king agreed. "When your grandfather first arranged my marriage to your mother, so many moons ago, I too had misgivings. It's natural to fear the unknown. But I did my duty for the clan, and was rewarded with love and friendship, as you will be. Your cousin Theo is young, and has many years before him to grow into a leader the oceans will follow. You can help him, and help all of us find peace." The trumpeting of a conch horn interrupted anything more Brynn might have said. "I must attend this meeting with the Adluo delegation," the king said, his voice fading as he swam out of the garden toward the castle. "This Solstice celebration is your engagement party, announcing to the world that the Atlantic will soon become one ocean."

"The Atlantic *is* only one ocean, father." The king was already too far away to catch her words. Strange noises came from the other side of the hedge, now that the princess was alone. Kae wondered if Princess Brynn could be…crying? She thought only humans did that sort of thing. She was about to swim over the barrier to offer comfort, when a screech sounded from the direction of the castle.

"I told you the salad greens should be absolutely fresh!" Princess Winona's high-pitched wail drifted from the kitchen windows and carried into the garden as she reprimanded the kitchen servants. Even though Winona had been the first-born child, she could not inherit the throne because she was not marked by the gods. Needing an heir, their father remarried and her younger half-brother Koios was born, the Mark of Poseidon upon his back. Instead of Queen of the Aequoreans, Winona would forever remain an aging Princess.

"There you are!"

Kae looked up, eyes wide, frightened to be caught spying. She saw she was still alone in her hedgerow, and let out a small sigh of relief. Princess Winona was in the next row, yelling at her niece.

"I'm sorry, Auntie. Did you need something?"

"I need you to come with me to plan the Solstice ceremony. It's your engagement party, after all."

"I'm giving you and father the rest of my life, into a marriage I do not want, to my six-year-old cousin. Can I not have a few more days for myself?"

"Soon you'll be a queen. "You must start acting like one, not like some petulant lovesick guppy!"

Kae gasped and covered her mouth again.

"It is obvious you still miss your drylander...friend." Princess Winona lowered her voice. "Tales of your affair even reached the Adluo courts. The delegates asked about a child from your union. I assured them no such abomination exists, nor would an Aequorean princess ever swim to such depths. Now, come with me to meet the representatives, and make your own reassurances. And perhaps, my dear, you should finally take off that ring."

"I'll come with you and play nice with the delegation." Brynn's voice sounded devoid of emotion. "But my choice of jewelry is none of your business."

Kae watched the two Aequorean princesses swim toward the castle and took in a deep breath of the salty water. "How can she stand it all? I could never marry a merman I didn't love. To think, she always has to sacrifice her own happiness. For politics!"

From behind her, a deep voice rumbled. "It's lucky you're not a princess."

Kae whirled to find her father hovering on the path beside her. "Father! I...I was just..."

"Spare me whatever tale you're trying to weave." His eyes blazed and Kae's cheeks burned under his harsh gaze. "How long were you spying on the princess?"

"I'm not spying." Kae crossed her arms against her stomach, making sure to keep one hand over her wounded elbow. "I was tending the gardens when the royal family decided to argue in the next hedgerow. I didn't know what to do, so I hid."

Lybio raised one eyebrow. "And what know you of Princess Brynn's son?"

Kae felt the color drain from her face. The rumors were true? *The princess has a son who's half human?* "Nothing. I know nothing about any babies."

"He's no longer a babe in arms, my child. He was born in the same lunar cycle as you." He took her elbow with his large hand and steered her down the garden row, toward the castle.

Kae swam beside her father, eyes widening as her thoughts whirled. "If there is a child, is he in danger? I heard that Demyan killed his own uncle and aunt in order to claim the title of regent to his young cousin."

Her father exhaled sharply, his expression grim. "I have heard that told as well, and fear it is no rumor. These are

125

dangerous times, despite the talk of peaceful negotiations." He stopped and turned to face her. "I may need your help, my daughter."

"Me?" Kae's voice squeaked with anxiety, and she covered her mouth with her hand. She took a calming breath. "What can I do?"

"Come with me now. King Koios would like to have a word with you about your new human friend."

Kae's body suddenly felt cold. She didn't realize her mother told her father about her adventures in Windmill Point. "What does the king want to know about Shea?"

"Everything." Lybio took his daughter by the hand, and led her into the Summer Palace of the Aequorean King.

CHAPTER THIRTEEN

Zan sat at a large round table with three other delegates from the Adluo Court, waiting for the Aequoreans to join them. Not that he wished to spend any more time with King Koios and his entourage. The long, slow swim northward taxed his patience to the limit, negotiating the details of the peace settlement day in and day out.

He preferred his battles more straightforward.

But this was the mission Prince Demyan assigned. If the plan to take over both oceans had any hope of success, Zan knew he needed to play his role well. The Aequorean clan might be inept on the battlefield, but King Koios was a strong and thoughtful ruler. His only weakness was caring more for his clansmen than for his power, willing to negotiate peace if it meant an end to the bloodshed.

The shrewd king kept his distance from Zan, refusing to let the merman come within arm's length. He knew Zan's reputation as a wielder of magick, and the guards allowed no opportunities for Zan to influence the king's thoughts or decisions through touch.

The only good to come from traveling at a snail's pace was the extended opportunity to hammer out specifics of the arranged marriage. Prince Demyan would be pleased, even if the Aequorean Princess was not. Zan had yet to meet the bride-to-be.

The aging Princess Winona granted ample audience to the Adluo delegation, however, and did not take the same precautions as her younger brother. The bitter old mermaid needed little influence to turn her against the king, and make her consider a side agreement with Prince Demyan.

Zan scrubbed his hand through his hair, wishing the shortened stubble would grow out. More sorcerer than soldier, he resented Demyan for insisting on shaving everyone's head for battle, especially since the prince didn't follow his own rules. Admittedly, Zan's normal hair color stood out among the drylanders when he had to go ashore. His black hair shone with blue and green highlights in the sun, an odd combination even for a merman.

Winona's screeching complaints jolted him from his thoughts, her high pitched voice floating out the kitchen door as the servers swam in and out and the Adluo delegates stuffed their faces. Zan shook his head in wonder. Did the old jellyfish not understand that his clan was starving? Even the greens the mermaid threw away in disgust tasted better than anything Zan ate in the last year.

Anger clouded his thoughts and the current around him began to warm in response. Why did one clan deserve such overwhelming bounty while another starved? Where was the justice in that? How could the gods ignore the plight of the Adluos while blessing the Aequoreans with such abundance?

Zan did not always agree with Prince Demyan on his methods. Killing so many farmers made no sense in the grand scheme of ocean life. Yet the unjust distribution of wealth and resources gave credence to the prince's arguments.

Things needed to change.

A frightened whisper jolted him to the present. "Sir? Zan? You need to calm down. Before someone gets hurt."

Startled, Zan glanced at his companions and realized what his anger had done to the current flowing through the Great Hall. The other mermen at the table gripped the plates and bowls to keep them from sliding off the table as the water stirred faster and faster around Zan. They served with Prince Demyan long enough to hear all the rumors about Zan's magick, and note the effects for themselves. They knew well enough that the sorcerer's emotions were deadly, if they didn't quite comprehend the full extent of his powers. Or his failures.

His anger slowly dissipated, replaced with resignation as he clamped down on his emotions. The swirling heat created by his magick subsided, the water in the hall returning to a normal flow. He berated his lack of self-control, annoyed that it took someone else to point out his shortcoming. When the magick took control, it pulled everything into its maelstrom, sucking the life out of anything too close to add to its power.

More death was not the answer, not right now. Death would come to the Great Hall soon enough.

Conversation among the Adluo delegates was muted, the other mermen unsure how to treat Zan. He wondered what it would be like to meet someone new without his fearful reputation preceding him. Or without magical influence, as he'd used on Princess Winona. He wondered if anyone could appreciate him for who he was, without the magick.

When the door to the hall swung open, the old princess reentered with a flourish, dragging a blonde mermaid in her wake. Although the younger mermaid wore no crown upon her head or fancy jewels at her neck, Zan spied the golden flecks among her scales that marked her as a royal heir. He also noted the redness around her eyes, and wondered what kind of affliction ailed her.

"Zan, my dearest boy. I need to introduce you to my elusive niece. I found her wandering the gardens. Princess Brynneliana, meet Zan of the Southern Ocean, the lead emissary of King Theosisto's court."

Zan rose from his chair and bowed. "A pleasure to finally meet you, my Princess."

She gave a stiff nod before taking a seat at the table directly opposite from him. "I've heard the tales, my Lord. Your powers are legendary."

He acknowledged her words, choosing to take them as a compliment. "No need for the formal title, my Princess. I am but a humble servant of the Adluo Court."

"I apologize for my absence at the negotiations. I saw no point in allowing my emotions to cloud the already muddy waters. Too many have already lost their lives. All I lose is my freedom."

Zan's back went rigid, wondering at her veiled words. Had the mermaid heard stories of his own deadly emotions? Could she somehow know the secret he kept so closely guarded? He would need to keep an eye on her, and not underestimate her intelligence.

Princess Winona misinterpreted Zan's unease, and cast furious glares at her niece. "I cannot comprehend why you consider gaining a title such a horrible loss. You will be a queen, my dear. Isn't that the wish of every princess in our world?"

The younger princess fixed her gaze on the table. "The gods decided I would be a queen when I was born, Auntie. Poseidon's Mark on my back shows their intent. I do not need to marry to gain such a title."

"Not all are so lucky," Winona snarled. "And do not mistake the gods for all-powerful beings. Even gods make mistakes."

CHAPTER FOURTEEN

Six soda cans, three water bottles, a tangle of balloon strings with one lonely balloon still attached, a small gray sand shovel, four lids to Styrofoam coffee cups, an empty plastic container marked 'fresh bait' with black marker, and five wooden fishing lures in various hues.

Shea went over the list of the morning's trash again in his head, squinting his eyes against the glare. The bright sunshine sparkled on the river's surface as the water rushed back from the ocean, the swift current creating streams of light out of the reflected brilliance.

"I love watching the tide come in," Hailey said. The pair sat on the edge of the dock mesmerized by the flowing water, bare feet dangling inches above the rising surface. Fishing poles and sandals lay discarded behind them on the wooden walkway. "It's like the river went out to play in the ocean and is now rushing home for lunch."

He elbowed her ribs. "You think about food all of the time, you know that?"

She turned and grinned. "I'm food deprived. Have I mentioned my mom can't cook?"

"Only forty million times. And I've only known you about a week!" He paused, watching a seagull wheel overhead. "Finding all those wooden lures this morning made me want to go fishing. You didn't have to tag along."

"I wanted to." She turned her face upward to watch the same gull. "Fishing is a good Cape Cod experience, and it gets me out of the house. Chip has been awful to live with lately."

"He still doesn't like it here?"

Hailey shook her head. She stood on the dock and pulled her hot pink shirt over her head, revealing a plain, black one-piece bathing suit. "C'mon, Shea, let's jump in." She shimmied out of her shorts, dropped the clothes in a heap on the wooden dock, and cannonballed into the river.

He shielded his face with his arm across to block the splash. "Watch it! And no, I told you I don't know how to swim. I'll sit here and watch you drown."

With an exaggerated pout, she swam toward him. "It's no fun alone. Pull me onto the dock." He stood and bent to help her, but she tugged his arm instead.

He toppled into the river beside her. The blue-green coolness swirled as he tumbled through the water, arms and legs flailing. He struggled to hold his breath, his cheeks puffing like a chipmunk. Somehow he managed to right himself, head over kicking feet, but still he sank into the murky depths.

Millions of air bubbles traced the path of his body, the precious oxygen escaping from his clothing and through his nose. He hadn't been kidding when he told Hailey he couldn't swim. Suddenly, he realized he was inside a scene from one of his nightmares, except this time it was real.

He was drowning.

Eyes wide with panic, he clawed helplessly at the water. A huge school of minnows parted down the middle to swim around him, surrounding him like walls on either side of his body. Turning his face upward, he saw Hailey's legs kicking above him as he sank further and further under the water. He had no idea the river was this deep! How would he ever get back to the surface?

His throat and lungs burned from the effort of holding his breath. Darkness pressed hard against his eyes as he sank deeper, swirls of strange colors dancing in front of him as his whole body strained against the sudden lack of oxygen.

I need to breathe, he thought desperately, his whole body feeling like it was on fire. *This isn't a dream. I'm going to die!* His flailing limbs slowed their movements when his feet thunked onto the mucky river bottom.

His eyes squeezed shut, an image of his father playing in his mind. Next to his dad, he saw the face from his dreams. The blonde woman, the one he now knew was his mother. The one who looked like a mermaid. If he opened his eyes now, would she be hovering in front of him, like in the dreams? Fear of the unknown shivered down his spine and his eyes stayed closed.

Searing pain ripped through his throat, as if his entire body would explode any second from the effort of holding his breath. Finally he opened his eyes, expecting to see her there by his side. Smiling at him. Reaching for his hand, just like his dream.

Nothing.

Nothing but swaying fronds of seaweed grabbing at him, tangling themselves around his bare shins. There was no mermaid to save him.

He was going to die.

Finally, the pain overwhelmed him. He gave up trying to fight. Shea opened his mouth to exhale the stale air pounding like a jackhammer in his lungs. Large bubbles rushed to the surface in a hurry to escape. Water gushed in, filling his mouth and lungs. He struggled to breathe, but there was no air on the river bottom, only water.

Water that somehow acted like fresh air to his exhausted body.

I can breathe under water?

He took a second deep and satisfying breath. How could it be possible?

I'm breathing water! Maybe this is how drowning feels.

His head pounded and his entire body still felt like it was on fire, burning out of control. But he was breathing. Water. He sucked big mouthfuls in and out, faster and faster, realizing he wasn't going to die after all.

Not…going…to die…

His eyes rolled backward and he drifted into shocked unconsciousness.

CHAPTER FIFTEEN

Shea's eyes fluttered open, searing light burning into his consciousness. He squeezed the lids shut to block the sudden brightness. A shadow passed over him, and he cracked one lid to check his surroundings, his chest muscles tight with the effort to breathe. "Where am I?"

"Welcome back, buddy." Hailey's face hovered over his, her hand gripping onto his shoulder. Tears filled her eyes, tracing paths down both cheeks while her sopping hair clung to neck and shoulders in a wild mess.

"What happened?" His voice crackled from the effort of getting the simple words out. He lay flat on his back, sand under his hands and feet. He must be on the shore of the river, but how? The last thing he remembered was the horrible burning sensation of water filling his lungs. He drowned at the bottom of the river. Goosebumps raced across his skin as a chill ran through his whole body.

Somehow he survived.

Hailey swiped at her cheeks and sniffled. "You sunk to the bottom like a rock. I guess you told the truth about the not swimming thing. I had to pull you from the muck. You weigh, like, a ton. I was so freaking scared, Shea. You could have drowned!"

But I did drown. "I told you I can't swim." He grimaced, raising a hand to his forehead. It felt like someone split his skull open with an axe. The tide rushed in faster than before, creeping up the bank close to where he lay. He pushed himself into a sitting position and pulled his feet away from the water's edge, as if the lapping waves might cause him more pain. He wiped his cheek against his shoulder, and looked at his shirt in surprise. "I'm soaked!"

Hailey laughed a little hysterically and hiccupped, tears still leaking from the corners of her eyes. "No kidding, Sherlock. You fell in the river. I'm so totally glad you're okay."

"No, you don't get it. Gramma's going to be so pissed. I'm not supposed to go in the water. Period. I'll be grounded for the rest of the summer now, thanks to you." It was easier to focus on his grandmother's disapproval than the fact that he might be going crazy. People don't breathe underwater. They just don't.

Hailey's face hardened into a deep frown, the tears subsided as she stared at him before finally speaking. "It could be worse, you know." She rose stiffly and brushed sand off her knees and shins. "You could be dead."

He took in a deep breath, his lungs burning with the effort just as they had at the bottom of the river. Before he'd exhaled and breathed in the salt water. He closed his eyes and shuddered at the memory. Yes, he drowned. Except he could breathe water. None of it made sense. *So why am I not freaking out more than this?*

"We can borrow some clothes from my brother. And by the way, you're welcome."

He shook his head as he stood, putting a hand on her shoulder to steady himself. His body felt weak, like he'd been on a ten-mile run. His head felt funny. "Welcome? Do I need to thank you? For what?"

"For saving your life, dummy." Hailey eased herself out from under his hand and pushed her way through the tall sea grass growing up the riverbank.

He stood on the sand a few more moments, staring out at the sparkling water. Could she seriously be upset that he wasn't more grateful? "You're the one who pulled me into the water. Why am I supposed to thank you?" He knew she must have heard him, but she didn't answer or look back.

At the top of the hill she veered toward the wooden dock where their poles and the tackle box waited in the sun, passing the equipment to sit on the edge of the dock, dangling her feet in the water. He followed, the rough wood of the dock feeling solid and comforting under his muddy feet.

She cleared her throat. "So, umm, I hate to bring this up, but you were underwater for a long time. Probably five minutes. Or more. You're very lucky you didn't drown."

"What do you want from me? I told you I can't swim." He didn't know how to explain the fact that he'd been breathing underwater when he didn't understand how it could have happened.

"Hello? I saved you didn't I? Only..." Her mouth clamped shut, her sentence unfinished.

He didn't want to think about it anymore, or talk about it with anyone until he figured out why he didn't drown, and why he wasn't more upset about the incident. "I held my breath as long as I could and passed out. And I guess you saved me just in time. So thank you for saving me."

"Okay-ay." She looked at him dubiously. "You're welcome."

"Can we fish now?" He turned his back on her and opened the tackle box, taking out a Styrofoam container of sea worms. He wanted to focus on something normal. *Fishing is normal. Breathing underwater is not.*

Pulling one of the bristly creatures free of the writing mass, he squeezed the head so the worm's mouth gaped wide open. The worm's razor-sharp pincers glistened in the sunlight. "Those are so nasty," Hailey said, the disgust evident on her face. The ugly creatures succeeded in changing the topic of conversation away from Shea drowning. Or not drowning. "They don't look like worms so much as prehistoric hairy snakes."

"Yeah, but the river is salt water, so regular earthworms or night crawlers would be useless." He was relieved to talk about fishing and not about his near-death experience. He pushed the hook through the mouth. "Gramma showed me how to hook them the right way, so they don't latch on to your fingers." As if that were the most dangerous thing that could happen to him today. *Forget about drowning, who wants a sea worm biting off a chunk of finger?*

"How does she know how to fish?" Hailey took the baited rod from his hands. She held it carefully so the hairy looking creature dangled far from her body.

He shrugged, the gesture exaggerated by the wet shirt clinging to his torso. "She knows everything about the ocean." He dug into the bait container and started skewering another sea worm onto his own hook.

"You know, your hair already looks dry. Must be the bright sun. Maybe if you hang your shirt over the dock railing it'll dry fast, and you won't have to explain anything to your grandmother."

142

The worm successfully hooked, he touched his hair and realized Hailey was right. It felt dry.

She cast her line into the water, still talking. "I don't know what to tell you about the shorts, but if your hair and shirt are dry maybe your grandmother won't notice the rest."

"I guess so." He put his fishing pole on the dock to strip the shirt off, revealing chest muscles hardened from long hours of farm work. The last few weeks in the sun tanned his face, neck and arms to a warm brown, but the color stopped abruptly mid-bicep, where his sleeves normally hung.

Hailey's eyes widened and she laughed. "It's like you're wearing a white t-shirt now!"

"Ha, ha." He stuck his tongue out and hung the shirt over the railing. Picking up his fishing rod, he plunked down beside Hailey at the end of the dock.

"I didn't realize you had so many...muscles," she said, staring openly at his chest. "Did you used to work out, or play sports, or what? I mean, hey, I was on the swim team so I've seen plenty of shirtless high school boys but man! Look at those biceps and pectorals! You must lift weights, right?"

He shook his head. "No time. Running a farm takes a lot of work."

"Hey, what's on your back? Seaweed or mud?" She wiped the brown smudge.

"It's a birthmark." He flinched, pushing her hand away. "It's been there forever. The kids at school used to tease me."

"Why? If it's a birthmark, why should they tease? It's not like you can help it if you're born with it, right? Birthmarks are like freckles, some people have them and some people don't. It's like teasing someone for the color of their hair, just not fair."

He shifted, uncomfortable with the conversation. "It's not because I have a birthmark. It's because of the shape. They called it the mark of the devil, since it looks like a pitchfork."

"Let me see." He met her eyes but didn't turn. "I promise not to touch, I only want to see."

He finally nodded and shifted his shoulder to give her a better view. She craned her head and he flinched again under her intense scrutiny. He knew the six-inch long brown patch between his shoulder blades would be starkly visible against his white skin. He'd seen it in the mirror, and knew it clearly resembled a three-pronged fork.

"Maybe not a pitchfork so much as a trident, since the middle prong is longer than the other two. "See?" She traced the mark with a finger, sending a shiver down his spine. "Kinda cool. Since Dad told us we were moving to Cape Cod I've been obsessed with ocean mythology, you know. Sea monsters and sea gods and all that sort of thing, from Odysseus to Disney's Little Mermaid."

Shea slapped her arm away, frowning. "I thought you weren't going to touch. And my birthmark is not at all cool, it's embarrassing."

A long stretch of silence ensued before she apologized. "I'm sorry. For pulling you into the water. For messing things up. Can we still be friends?"

He debated whether he should go home. He thought about losing the one new friend he made on Cape Cod. Well, he also had Kae. Sort of. If she wasn't still mad about the bicycle thing. Finally he made up his mind. "Of course we're friends. Now shut up and fish." He cast his line into the water alongside Hailey's.

After fifteen minutes of sitting side by side, not talking, he asked, "What's a trident, anyway?"

Hailey turned to face him and squinted her eyes. "You know, from Greek mythology? Poseidon, god of the ocean, carried one around with him to zap the bad guys."

"We didn't do mythology in school." He shrugged. "They cover that in tenth grade English, I think."

"We learned it in eighth in New York." She closed her eyes for a moment, as if trying to remember what she'd learned. "Poseidon was one of the gods from Mount

145

Olympus. When the gods defeated the titans, Poseidon claimed the oceans for his domain."

"So he's king of all the oceans? And I have his mark on my back? I guess that's kinda cool."

"Way cool. My teacher said Poseidon was really powerful, and the Greeks totally worshipped him. He divided his underwater kingdom among his children, mermaids and mermen, marking them with the trident symbol. Maybe that's why you didn't drown."

"Because I'm marked by the gods? That's a good one. You'd better be nicer to me if I'm royalty." He reeled in his line to cast again.

"Don't let it go to your head. Once you get a real tan, no one will even notice the birthmark. All they'll see are these wimpy muscles." She flicked his bicep with a finger.

He shoved against her shoulder and laughed. She leaned too far to get away and lost her balance, but he grabbed her arm at the last minute and pulled her onto the dock. "It'd serve you right if you fell in the river."

"Yeah, but I can swim."

Shea smirked. "Maybe I'll ask the mermaids to pull you under so you can see how it feels. You know, since I'm marked by Poseidon."

"Don't even joke about stuff like that, Shea! What if mermaids are real? I saw this special on the Discovery channel about mythical sea creatures, and how science if finding out the reality behind the legends." Hailey babbled on about the documentary, Shea only half listening. Despite his nightmares, he didn't believe in mermaids.

They sat together on the dock for hours, lines dangling in the water. The only tugging came from the insistent current, still bringing the tide in from the ocean. A salty breeze stirred the air, flapping the drying shirt against the railing. Two gulls circled overhead.

Hailey broke the silence. "How come you don't know how to swim?"

"No oceans in Oklahoma."

"Give me a break. I'm sure there were pools and rivers and lakes and swimming holes, right?"

"Yeah, I guess so," he agreed, turning his head away from her.

"So how come you almost drowned today?"

He shrugged, raking his fingers through his dry hair, now stiff with salt and sticking out every which way. "There was never any time, what with running the farm and all. Besides, my dad said he'd had enough of swimming to last a lifetime. He grew up here, you know."

"Yeah, I figured that out for myself. Your Gramma lives here, remember? But it seems kind of irresponsible not to teach a kid how to swim."

147

He wasn't sure how to respond. He'd asked his dad lots of times over the years, but always got the same response. Now he wondered if there was more to his father's reluctance.

Silence stretched between them, each lost in thought. A sudden tug on his fishing line nearly jerked the pole from his hands. He clambered to his feet. "Whoa, I think I caught something!"

A large bluefish broke the surface of the water halfway across the river, flying into the air and jerking the line from side to side, trying to pull free. Shea waited while the fish struggled, and then reeled it in a bit. He paused again while the fish swam furiously from side to side, and then reeled it in a little bit more. "Hailey, bring in your line. I need your help to land this big guy."

She complied, pulling in her empty hook and putting her rod on the dock behind them. "What can I do? I have no idea how to catch a big fish!"

"Where's that net we brought?"

She searched the dock before spotting it on the shore next to their bicycles. She sprinted up the walkway and was back in a flash, net in hand. He reeled in the blue a few inches at a time. "Wow, that fish is a fighter!"

"I don't think he wants to be dinner." He pulled the rod so it bent nearly in half. Easing up on the pole, he quickly reeled in more line. The fish swam close enough to the dock now to gauge his size – almost three feet long. "The net," he directed. "You should be able to grab him soon."

She perched on the edge of the dock, balancing net above the waterline. "What now?"

"He's too big for me to pull out of the river on my own. The line will break if I try. When I get him to break the surface, scoop under him. Got it?"

"I – I think so." Her voice sounded less than certain. She lowered the net until it touched the water, and waited, gripping the pole until the knuckles on both hands turned white. The blue inched closer to the dock with every twist of the reel.

Suddenly, there it was, breaking the surface right beside her. Hailey scooped the net underneath the fish, catching it squarely in the basket. The blue struggled, but already used too much of its energy fighting the fishing line. Arm muscles straining, she tried to lift the net onto the dock. "This guy is wicked heavy!"

Dropping his fishing pole next to hers, he helped pull the net the rest of the way. He knelt next to the bluefish now flopping on the dock and covered the side of the fish with one hand, quieting his struggle. He watched the fish's jaw open and close, sucking at the air, gills wagging uselessly. In his head he heard a low voice, crying for help. He shook his head, trying to make the voice go away.

He pointed to the long, sharp needles lining the fish's mouth, many times larger than the razor pincers on the sea worm's mouth. ""Look at those teeth! How am I going to get the hook out of there?"

"Very carefully."

Surprised by the unfamiliar voice, they turned to find Mr. Guenther standing at the end of the dock, watching them. "Would you like help?"

"Sure, Mr. Guenther," Shea answered, giving Hailey a sidelong glance. He wasn't quite sure if she'd met the strange old man before. He widened his eyes, trying to tell her to bite her tongue about his strange appearance. "We can use all the help we can get, right Hailey?" She nodded in agreement, not taking her eyes off the struggling fish.

The old man extracted a pair of long thin pliers from his pocket. He approached and knelt on the dock beside them. "Now the thing about blues is you never want to get your fingers anywhere near those teeth."

"I can see that," Shea said as the fish snapped again. The rumble of voice in his head sounded frantic, begging to go back to the water, pleading to rejoin his school to lead them to the next feeding ground. Why on earth was he imagining an entire dialogue between him and this fish?

With a swift, practiced movement, the old man pushed the ends of the pliers deep into the fish's mouth and extracted the hook. Blood spurted out onto his hand and Hailey gasped. "Just a little fish blood," Mr. Guenther reassured.

"Will it die now?" Hailey's voice sounded very small as she finally turned her eyes to the old man.

Shea's hand hadn't moved from where it rested on the blue's side. It no longer struggled. The gill flaps behind its head strained open and shut with the effort to breathe.

"Only if Shea wants him to," Mr. Guenther said.

Shea continued to stare into the bluefish's unblinking eye, deciding to trust the voice in his head. "Throw him back."

"But he's bleeding," protested Hailey. "Won't he die anyway?"

"Minor mouth wound. It'll heal fast in the salt water. He needs to return to his group to lead them to the next feeding area. He's one of the oldest, one of the leaders." *TMI in the total sense of too much information I should have no idea about in the first place. How do I know all this about the stupid fish?* But he knew, just as surely as if the fish had spoken out loud to him. He reached into the net, past the sharp teeth to grab the blue's tail end. Lifting the fish out of the net, he swung it out over the water. It splashed into the river and disappeared. Moments later, it broke through the surface of the water, jumping more than a foot into the air and landing with another big splash.

Shea waved farewell, and turned to smile at Hailey. She stared at him, eyes wide and mouth hanging open. He glanced at the old man, who wore a mysterious smile upon his face. "Uh, thanks for your help, sir. We appreciate it."

Mr. Guenther stood from his kneeling position and then bowed at the waist before Shea. "Whatever you need of me, Sire, uh, I mean, Shea..." He straightened and walked swiftly off the dock and up the hill.

Shea stared after the old man's retreating form. *Sire? What was that all about? Just because he threw the fish back?*

"Well, that was a little freaky," Hailey said, breaking the silence. "What's going on with the old dude?"

He shook his head. "No idea. But can I tell you something a little freakier?" He paused for a moment, checking to make sure Mr. Guenther was out of earshot. "The weirdest part is when I was touching the fish? It felt like the fish was telling me stuff. And I could understand what he was saying."

Hailey smirked. "Yeah, right. Like fish can think and talk. You're too funny sometimes."

Shea shrugged, realizing there was no way he could make her believe him, or understand how freaked out he felt. Maybe it was just as well that she thought he was teasing. He grinned and gestured to their gear on the dock. "Come on. There's more fishing to do."

The afternoon wore on without another bite. The conversation steered clear of Shea's near-drowning and fish whispering, focusing instead on the merits of random television shows, and the sad fact that Martha MacNamara flat out refused to install cable television. Shea was more than happy to forget about the entire afternoon, because in his heart he knew he should have drowned. And he heard that stupid blue fish talking to him as clear as anything. How could he explain either of these things? He couldn't. Which kind of sucked.

At six o'clock they said goodbye, each heading home for dinner.

Shea's shirt and shorts dried, but the salty water left white lines along all the creases. He hoped to sneak into the house and avoid any confrontation or need for explanation. He managed to open and close the front door without a sound, but the stairs betrayed him, creaking on the second step. He winced, wondering if anyone heard him.

Martha's footsteps echoed in the hallway. "Glad you're home in time for dinner, Shea. Was fishing fun?" Her voice woke Lucky, who startled to his feet from his hiding spot behind the living room couch. Shea dismissed the idea of sneaking and pounded his way up the staircase. Lucky scrambled after him, toenails clattering on the wooden stairs.

"I put the fishing gear in the shed," he yelled over his shoulder. "I need to change because I stink of fish and sea worm slime. Be there in a minute." Lucky reached him before he could close the door.

"I want to hear all about your afternoon with Hailey," Martha called after him. The oven timer dinged and her footsteps retreated.

In the bedroom, he slammed the door and hit the light switch. Ripping the salty shirt from his body, he flung it toward the laundry basket in the corner. It landed in a heap beside the basket. He pulled a new shirt from the drawer and over his head, and spied Lucky licking at the salty white lines on the shirt in the corner. Sighing, he bent to retrieve it, thinking to push it to the bottom of the basket. Lucky licked Shea's neck instead.

"Cut it out, boy," he commanded, wiping the dog slobber from his ear. His fingers slid along the side of his neck and he froze.

He felt a row of small, parallel slits behind his ear.

His fingers flew to the other ear. The same thing.

Panicked, he ran to the mirror and leaned in as close as he could, pulling his ear forward to see behind it.

He wasn't crazy.

He had gills.

CHAPTER SIXTEEN

Beneath the undulating waves off Windmill Point's beach, Kae turned to her companion. "I know I saw tons of jellyfish here yesterday, Lailani. Let's search a little while longer."

The other mermaid wore a skeptical expression on her round face. "I don't know, Kae. I think there's too much of this spongy codium weed in this part of the Sound. The bigger swarms of moon jellies tend to like more open spaces."

"Why don't we spread out, and find the sandier areas?" Kae wanted to take another peek above the surface to check for Shea. Not that she could talk to him today, not with Lailani tagging along. But she wanted to *see* him. If she could only get away from the other mermaid for a few minutes…

"Your mom made me promise to stick close to you." Lailani crossed her arms over her chest, her left hand gripping two medium-sized mesh bags. "With the Adluos around, it's not safe for a mermaid to swim alone. Besides, we need to stay together to fill these nets. It takes two, you know."

Kae sighed, a rapid stream of bubbles exhaling from her gills. "Fine. Where is it you have in mind to seek moon jellies?"

"A little north of here there's a big, more open beach. There're always tons of jellyfish in those waters. And some of the cutest human boys you've ever seen, too! They come right out into the waves, floating on long boards."

"You know we're not supposed to talk to humans!" Her cheeks grew hot as she thought of Shea and her own rule breaking.

Lailani grinned. "Everyone does it. The war is practically over, you know. C'mon, what are you, a scared little cuttlefish? Let's have some fun!" She spun in the water and headed east with the current.

Kae followed Lailani away from Windmill Point. With a few sharp kicks of her tail, she soon swam abreast of the other mermaid. "Tell me. What humans have you ever spoken with?"

The other mermaid remained silent for a long while as they swam into deeper waters. "Well, none actually," she admitted. "But I heard Bella in the kitchen yesterday telling

Ciara and Juliet about a surfer she met. It sounded like such fun."

Kae shook her head. "Bella's older than we are, Lailani. She's already home from Atlantis." According to the kitchen rumors, Bella was sent home for disciplinary reasons. There were consequences for getting caught being friendly with humans.

"So? If she can do it, we can do it."

"I'll swim with you, but I'm not getting in trouble so you can one-up your cousin."

Lailani flashed a brilliant smile at Kae. "There's no harm in looking, right?"

After thirty minutes of swimming, Kae still hadn't found enough jellyfish to fill their nets. "Are you sure there are jellyfish swarms along this stretch of shoreline?" They veered further east to go around a series of barrier islands, where big furry harbor seals basked in the warm sunshine. Several curious creatures swam along with them, and one baby seal stuck by Kae's side when they continued northward along the coastline. "I think there might be too many seals for us to find enough moon jellies. They already ate them all!"

Lailani nodded, the current rushing through her short dark hair making it spike all around her head. "Bella gathered a lobster trap full of nettles yesterday. She said all the jellyfish were plentiful."

"Nettles?" Kae wrinkled her nose. "Aren't those the stinky poisonous ones?"

"Only if they're cooked wrong. Bella collects them for the King's sister. She says the old mermaid likes her food with extra stink." Both mermaids laughed and Lailani pointed toward the surface. "We should be almost there. Shall we take a look around again?"

Kae agreed. "Hopefully we see more than seals this time." The baby harbor seal swimming next to her snorted as if in full agreement with the mermaids. Slowly the three poked their heads up among the waves and gazed toward the shoreline. They could see humans sitting on colorful cloths along the beach. The young ones splashed in the shallow waters closest to the sand.

"Shall we watch from out here or go closer?" Lailani bobbed in the waves next to Kae. Now that she'd dragged them all the way up the coast, she sounded nervous at the prospect of talking to the humans.

"We can watch from out here. As long as those swimmers don't get too close to us, everyone will think we're just another bunch of seals playing in the waves." The baby seal barked in agreement.

This beach stretched so much further than the one at Windmill Point. The sand dunes pushed high into the sky, the long stretches of tall sea grass swaying and moving like green waves upon the land. A cacophony of seagulls wheeled overhead, calling to one another and occasionally diving for a fish.

It had been a long time since Kae ventured this far from the King's castle to explore the waters around Cape Cod. She knew there were many vast stretches of secluded beaches around the Cape and the islands of Nantucket and Martha's Vineyard, and many more teeming with life like the one they were observing at the moment. She wondered if she'd have time to explore them all after the Solstice celebration.

She smiled at Lailani. "Thanks for dragging me out here. It's such fun to see new places."

The other mermaid shook her head. "According to the whispers in the kitchen, you'll be seeing plenty of new places soon. Rumors are that the Adluos plan to bring our princess home with them this summer, after the Solstice."

The smile faded from Kae's lips. "This summer? So soon?" She gazed toward the humans along the shore, wondering how they could be so clueless about everything happening below the ocean's surface. She was about to tell Lailani they should turn around and go home, when she spotted a familiar figure by the water's edge. Even from this distance, she could tell it was Shea.

Her Shea. Walking with a short girl in an ugly shirt the color of dead seaweed. What was he doing on this beach, so far from his home? And what in Neptune's name was he doing with that strange girl? She needed to find out.

"Let's one-up your cousin for real. Let's transform and go ashore."

"Transform?" Lailani's olive skin paled a shade or two.

"Now who's the spineless one?" Kae wrapped her fingers around the medallion at her neck. "Coming with me or not?"

Lailani hesitated. "Can we swim in a little closer first? If we transform way out here, swimming all the way to shore will be hard."

Kae glanced toward the sand and saw Shea moving steadily away. She made up her mind. "Do what you want. I'm going to talk to that blond boy on the beach." She ducked under the water and swam several yards closer to shore.

When she surfaced, she waved to Shea and cupped her hand next to her mouth. "Hey! What are you doing here?" Her green mermaid tail swished beneath the waves, easily keeping her safe from the riptides.

"Kae? Is that you?" Shea stopped mid-step and shaded his eyes with a hand. His companion turned toward the water as well. "You're out pretty far." He took a step toward her, the waves washing over his ankles as he stood at the ocean's edge.

"I'll swim in. Wait for me." Kae concentrated on the *transmutare* hanging from her neck. Usually, she climbed onto the rocks at the end of a jetty to transform her tail into a pair of legs. The process took several moments to complete, during which time the lower part of her body was immobile. She knew it was theoretically possible to change while still in the ocean, but this was her first attempt at a water transformation.

Holding the medallion in one hand, she whispered the incantation. Tiny bubbles swirled around her tail, popping with effervescence as they rose to the surface making the seawater around her look like sparkling champagne. The bubbles forced their way through the middle of Kae's tail, the magic pulling it apart down the middle, cleaving it in two. The ocean around her warmed as air bubbles swirled swiftly to surround each of the sections, tingling like millions of tiny pinpricks as they smoothed the scales into the shape of legs.

With one hand clutching the *transmutare*, Kae struggled to keep her head above water for the sake of appearances, moving her right arm rapidly back and forth as the temporary paralysis gripped her newly forming legs. As her face dipped below the water line, she blew a stream of bubbles out of the gills behind her ears, hoping the paralysis would wear off before any lifeguards decided to swim out for a rescue.

After what seemed like forever, Kae felt the intense warmth of the transforming magic ebb away, leaving her with two legs and a yellow bikini bottom. She kicked her new legs to tread water. Lailani and the baby seal were nowhere to be seen.

When she was closer to shore, her feet touched the sandy bottom, feeling a crab scuttle across her toes as she walked the last few feet into shore. "I wasn't expecting to see you on this beach. I thought this was a spot for swimmers and surfers only."

Shea grimaced. "The water is way too chilly for swimming, not without a wetsuit at least."

Kae shook salty ocean from her wet hair. "The cold doesn't bother me."

"Well, the blues and stripers both feed close to shore this time of year. You could get caught in a feeding frenzy if you're not careful. I mean, you got hurt enough on the bike, right?"

"Fish don't bother me either." Kae ignored his slight against about her bicycle skills. She nodded toward the dark-haired girl. "Who's your friend?"

He looked surprised to find the dark haired girl standing so close. "This is Hailey. I told you about her the other day, remember?"

"Hey," said Hailey, a friendly-enough smile on her face. Dark sunglasses hid her eyes, but Kae felt the coldness of her gaze. This girl wasn't happy to see her.

An unfamiliar burning sensation churned in the pit of Kae's stomach. She turned to Shea, wondering how many more chances she'd get to talk to him before she left Cape Cod forever, for her new life in the Southern Ocean. She wondered if everything she'd been told about Shea was true. Her conversation with her father and King Koios replayed in her mind and a chill ran down her spine.

"See? You are cold." He untied a long sleeve shirt from around his waist and took a step closer. Slipping the piece of clothing over Kae's head, he stared into her eyes. This close, she could see how big and ocean-green his eyes truly were. *Jumping jellyfish*, those eyes looked so familiar, as if she'd known him all of her life. Of course they looked familiar. He had the same eyes as the princess. His mother. She blinked hard, turning her head away and taking a deep breath.

Trying to distract herself, she slipped her arms through the sleeves of the borrowed shirt and searched for a safe topic of conversation. "So, what're you doing here? This is pretty far from Windmill Point."

"My mom is meeting a potential new client in downtown Orleans," Hailey answered. "She dropped us off at Nauset to hang out. I would've preferred to walk along Main

163

Street but she wouldn't give me her credit card. My stupid brother tagged along and he wanted to check out the surfing scene. Mom figured there's a snack bar if we're hungry so we'll be okay on the beach for a while."

Shea laughed, stopping the girl's flow of words with a friendly slap on the back. "Hailey has to eat, like, every five minutes."

Hailey elbowed him in the ribs and grinned. "Can I help it if I have a super-fast metabolism? And a weakness for onion rings?"

Kae felt the churning in her stomach kick up a notch. She only understood half the words out of the girl's mouth, all jibberish as far as she was concerned. But Shea was so at ease with the girl, laughing and joking. As if everyone knew what credit cards and onion rings were. She tried not to let her jealousy show. "This is such a great beach. But you're not wearing swimsuits?"

Hailey threw an arm around Shea's shoulders, making Kae's stomach churn even more. "No swimming for this dummy. Says he never learned, which at fifteen is a mystery to me. I mean, he almost drowned the other day. I saved him." She squeezed him close. Too close for Kae's taste.

Kae's eyes narrowed as she stared at him, trying to see any difference. If the things she'd been told about him were correct… "Is that true, Shea? You were in the water? The ocean?"

He shrugged off Hailey's hug and took a step away from the girl. "It was no big deal. I fell off the dock into the river."

"Did anything strange happen?"

"Yeah," Hailey interrupted again, taking off her dark glasses and speaking slowly. "Didn't you hear me the first time? He. Almost. Drowned. Luckily I pulled him out of the water."

Shea's brows furrowed. He glared at Hailey and Kae felt a wave of hostility flow between the pair. "You also pulled me *into* the water. After I told you I couldn't swim."

Kae put her hand on his arm to reclaim his attention. "What did your grandmother say?"

"Are you kidding me? She'd kill me if she knew."

"You didn't tell her?"

He shook his head.

"I think you should," Kae said. "She…needs to know."

Hailey laughed. "Obviously, you've never met the woman. Nice lady, awesome cook, but I wouldn't want her mad at me."

Kae's eyes didn't leave Shea. "She won't be mad. But she needs to know." She wished she'd been there when he fell.

Been there to see whether his mermaid blood kicked in to save him, as it had when her own father first fell into the ocean as a boy. She brushed the hair blowing across Shea's face, and froze as her fingers touched his neck. *Gills.*

He flinched away, taking a quick step backward.

"I...I need to go," Kae stuttered, at a loss for what she should do in this situation.

He stared into her face for a long moment, as if memorizing it. "Can't you stay longer?"

She felt a thrill run through her. Could he have feelings for her? Her stomach fluttered at the thought.

Hailey snorted with laughter, breaking the spell of the moment. "The girl lives in our neighborhood, Shea. It's not like you'll never see her again. Give me a break. You can be so melodramatic for a fifteen-year-old boy."

"I don't think you understand," Kae said, frowning at Hailey.

The girl glared at her. "Oh, I understand just fine."

Shea placed a hand on Kae's arm. "Can't we all be friends?"

"I don't think so." She turned and walked south down the beach, angry with herself for losing her temper with the jelly-brained girl who called herself Shea's friend. She resisted the temptation to look at him one last time.

Thoughts whirled through her head as she stomped along the sand, hands clenched by her sides. He definitely had mermaid blood swimming through his veins. What should she do about it? What could she do? She reached a rocky outcropping jutting into the ocean and came to a stop. She turned slowly, hoping to find him close behind her.

She was alone.

He chose to stay with the other girl.

She swallowed the bitter taste in her mouth and turned to scan the waves. Her eyes found Lailani and the baby seal, their heads barely visible on the rolling surface. She raised an arm to catch their attention and walked straight into the ocean, ready to swim home.

"Kae, wait!"

She turned to see him running toward her. Crossing her arms over her stomach, she hugged herself as she watched him approach, his strong body moving fluidly along the sand. "What do you want?"

He planted his feet in the sand right in front of her, hands at his sides. "I don't want you to be angry with me. I thought we were friends." He dug into his pocket and brought out the black stone. It sparkled in the bright sunlight, exuding raw magic. "Here, take this. I shouldn't have teased you by keeping it." He held it out to her.

Kae looked at the stone, then into Shea's face. She saw in his eyes the same kind of uncertainty she felt within herself, and felt a lump of emotion rise in her throat. If he was truly the son of Princess Brynn, there was so much he needed to learn. And quickly. With gentle fingers she cupped his hand, closing it around the *transmutare* stone. "You keep this one. You may need it."

His unwavering gaze never left her face. "I don't know what I did to make you angry, but I'm sorry. I don't want to fight with you."

She squeezed his hand between her own, hoping the simple gesture would convey at least some of her feelings for him. The magic of the stone pulsed through their hands and she saw his eyes widen with surprise as he looked at his hands. *He can feel the magic!*

His voice didn't sound scared, just curious. "Did the stone do that?"

"I think it's because of who you are. I can't explain it all now. My friend is waiting for me."

He nodded his head slowly, not really understanding what she said, but trusting her. Her heart swelled at the thought. He trusted her! He cleared his throat. "When will I see you again?"

"Soon," she promised, taking a step backward. "I'll find you again soon." She pulled his shirt over her head and handed it to him. "You need to return to your friends now."

He nodded and she watched him walk away, her heart heavy as her mind swirled with questions. She climbed over the rocks to the far side, away from any prying human eyes, and dove straight into the next big wave as it crashed onto the shore. She swam underwater as fast as she could, her legs pumping together as one, until she reached the spot where Lailani and the baby seal hovered near the surface, their heads underwater watching Kae's approach.

The other mermaid seemed impressed. "I never knew you were so full of adventure! Who's the cute boy? Was that his girlfriend with him? You stole his affection from her, didn't you?"

Transmutare in hand, Kae ignored her friend's babble and chanted the words to change back. The tiny bubbles dissipated to reveal her bright tail. "Sorry that took so long. We need to hurry and get back to the castle." She needed to talk to her father about what happened to Shea.

Lailani grinned. "Speaking of the castle, we'd best find some more moon jellies, or Mariella will have both our tails!"

They swam south, Lailani keeping up a steady stream of questions and comments about the humans on the beach as the pair filled their nets with jelly fish. Kae answered when she needed to, but her mind spun too fast to concentrate on her friend's words. She needed to find answers to her own questions.

And fast.

CHAPTER SEVENTEEN

At the castle, preparations were well underway for the Solstice celebration. Kae's jellyfish hunting trip with Lailani was a distant memory even though it had only been a few days before. She now spent every second of her time serving the princess, which at the moment meant a lot of hovering at the edges of chambers, waiting to be needed.

This had never been the case in the past. Usually, the princess enjoyed spending time alone and only called on servants when she needed a task completed or wanted companionship. Since the final negotiation of the peace treaty and engagement, a pair of Adluo soldiers guarded Brynn day and night, which made the princess uncomfortable. She'd requested either Kae or Kira stay with her at all times. With so many important things to prepare and tend to prior to the Solstice, much of the hovering and waiting fell to Kae.

She desperately wished she could tell the princess what she knew about Shea, but there was never a good time. The guards were always there. It didn't seem prudent to try to talk about anything in front of the Adluos, when the princess herself went to such lengths to conceal Shea's very existence. The situation frustrated Kae.

The princess chaffed under the weight of the constant attention. "You may as well get used to it," Princess Winona sniffed, shooing some small silver fish out of her path. "Once you are queen you should never swim anywhere alone." The royal entourage made their way down a corridor to the Great Hall. A luncheon buffet was being served for the Solstice guests who'd already started to arrive. The king sent word for his daughter to join him in welcoming the visiting dignitaries.

"You know I like to swim by myself," Brynn argued. "My marriage should not alter my personal habits."

Winona let out an un-princess-like snort of laughter. "Should not alter your personal habits?" She wiped one hand across her forehead, tucking a stray hair into place under her jeweled tiara. "My dear girl, life in the Atlantic Ocean is about to change completely, your life most of all."

"But young Theo already sits upon the Southern throne, with Demyan as his regent," Brynn reminded her aunt. "Neither of them is replacing my father nor ruling the Atlantic."

"Things change," the older princess snapped. Kae heard the ice in her every word. "You know what they say: it is best to flow along with the tide, rather than be swept ashore."

Following in their wake, Kae stared at the two princesses ahead of her. She hoped her face did not reveal the dread she felt in her heart. Her mind reeled at the old mermaid's words. What could she mean?

Her mind whirled with possibilities.

None of them were good.

The two clans arranged this marriage to end the bloodshed. Kae didn't understand why a full grown mermaid would be forced to marry her six-year-old cousin. Kae's father tried to explain the intricacies of political maneuvering to his daughter. Promising some portion of the southern Atlantic along with Princess Brynn's hand in marriage seemed a reasonable compromise in return for a peace treaty between the Adluos and the Aequoreans. King Koios also hoped that with his daughter in place as Queen of the Southern Ocean, King Theo would dismiss Prince Demyan as his regent. Kae's father explained that King Koios perceived Demyan as the true threat, not the young king.

Kae felt sure Prince Demyan had something else in mind when he negotiated the marriage as part of the treaty. She knew a six-year-old king had no desire for a wife, except perhaps as a substitute for his dead mother. And now it sounded like Princess Winona might have schemes of her own.

The royal entourage entered the Great Hall. A handful of Aequorean and Adluo advisors accompanied King Koios at the largest round table. Kae spotted a dark-eyed merman seated to the right of her king, a thin gold circlet upon his dark head. His skin was slightly olive, and she could see that his tail was darkest green with not a fleck of gold shining among his scales. Not nearly young enough to be King Theo, she assumed he was the regent, Prince Demyan.

The merman looked young next to the elderly King, but she knew a merman's face could be deceiving. He could be the same age as she, or he could be over one hundred years old. Prince Demyan seemed too young to have done all of the terrible things he was rumored to have done, but there again, she knew looks could deceive.

King Koios arose when his daughter and her group entered the Great Hall. "Ah, here she is. Princess Brynneliana, the brightest pearl in the Atlantic." He gestured to the crowned merman at his table. "These good mermen bring greetings from your betrothed."

Laughter rumbled through the water, causing shivers to race along the length of Kae's tail. The Southern Prince rose, and swam to where Brynn stopped short. "Prince Demyan, at your service. I must say, you are even more beautiful than was described to me, Brynneliana, like a delicate sea flower."

His low, scratchy voice caused the back of Kae's neck to prickle uncomfortably. She watched him take Brynn's small hand with his larger one, bending to brush his thin lips against her skin. Kae imagined it took all of Brynn's royal training to resist yanking her fingers from that grasp, for despite the circle of gold on his head the merman seemed much more sinister than sincere. Kae took in the prince's dark eyes, his overly muscular forearms and his scales the color of dying seaweed, and swallowed the bile rising in her throat.

Princess Brynn's voice sounded stiff and formal. "It's good to finally meet you as well, my Prince. I have heard much about you."

He narrowed his eyes at her simple words, as if to decipher a hidden meaning. His face relaxed just as quickly, giving nothing away. "You can't believe every story swept northward on the current, the same way we in the Southern Court try to ignore those rumors that drift southward about you, my dearest Princess."

Keeping her hand gripped within his own, Prince Demyan turned and gestured with his other arm toward the table. "Join us for our midday meal, won't you? It's just been served, and I'm famished after my long journey."

"But my entourage," said Brynn, trying unsuccessfully to extricate herself from his grasp. "I see there's not enough room at the table for all of us."

Kae glanced around the King's table. Lord Marcus and Lady Tatiana were the only two she recognized, minor lords from the part of the Southern Atlantic now closest to the edge of the advancing Adluo armies. Lord Marcus was young and unmarried, probably hoping to find a suitable wife at the Solstice gathering. Perhaps from among the Adluo delegation, to further bind the clans.

Kae remembered hearing that Lady Tatiana lost her husband when their lands were attacked. Her husband, one of the king's own cousins, lost his life while battling Adluo soldiers. Those southern lands were part of the treaty and now considered Adluo territory. Yet she seemed happy enough sharing a meal with the leader of those who killed her husband. *How can she forgive so easily? The nuances of politics escape me.*

"Nonsense, my dear child," King Koios said with a smile on his face. "We're discussing your engagement party and the plans for the winter wedding." He patted the stone seat next to his own. "Of course you and my dear sister should join us and share your thoughts on these important matters. Your servants can attend you from a distance, if need be."

"No doubt you are correct, Father," Brynn conceded, bowing her head as the prince released his grasp. She took her place beside her father, and Winona took a seat on the far side of the round table next to a stiff young merman with the short dark hair of an Adluo soldier. Kae wondered why a soldier would be seated at the table, and whether he was actually the legendary dark sorcerer of the Adluo clan. At a nod from Demyan, his two guards stationed themselves at the entrance to the Great Hall. Kae alone was left not knowing where she should be. Slowly, she swam backwards until she hovered next to the wall of the chamber, forgotten by the royal gathering.

"As we were saying, Prince Demyan," the king continued, patting his daughter's hand. "The Solstice celebration will be an excellent time to announce the outline of the peace treaty we negotiated between our clans, as well as young Theo's engagement to my daughter. I personally invited royalty from each of the world's oceans, as well as the High Chancellor from Atlantis."

"I look forward to the celebration," Demyan said. Kae noticed the prince's black eyes had not left Brynn's face, and she shivered at their dark intensity. "In truth, good Sire, you must excuse my boldness. I did not expect to find your daughter so utterly captivating. My heart beats in a most unfamiliar way."

Brynn's cheeks turned bright red. "Such talk is quite improper, I'm sure," she said stiffly. "I plan to honor the commitments of my father, for the sake of both our clans, and marry King Theo. I hope you will be able to stay on in the Adluo court, perhaps return to your role with the army, now that your services as regent will no longer be required?"

The prince scowled in response and Kae's heartbeat quickened with fear. When a kitchen server patted Kae's arm, she startled, her hand flying to cover her mouth before she could cry out and embarrass herself. She recognized the mermaid as one of her mother's friends.

The servant nodded her head toward the double doors leading into the kitchen. "You should come into the kitchen and grab some food while you can. The princess won't be needing you for a while. The king ordered a seven-course luncheon, they'll be at it for hours."

Kae nodded, and followed the mermaid to the kitchen. As the double door pushed open, the cacophony of smells and sounds that usually filled the castle's busy kitchen assaulted her senses. In addition to the regular mayhem, several of the Adluo guards lounged along one wall eating their midday meal. Despite the swords hanging at their sides, the soldiers joked and flirted with the Aequorean mermaids as if it were a garden party. The soldiers were unconcerned by the constant flurry of servants swimming in and out, and Kae wondered if they were paying attention at all or simply happy to have plentiful food. She'd heard starvation was not uncommon in the Southern Ocean.

Relaxing a bit, she glanced around to see if either of her parents were nearby. She wanted to share her suspicions, but she could find neither Kira nor Lybio in the massive kitchen. She wondered if she should risk swimming to their cottage on the chance that one of them might be home.

And what would I say to them? That there's a plot hatching to dethrone King Koios? What proof do I have? She could tell the southern Atlantic wasn't enough for the dark-eyed, dark-hearted prince. And he didn't seem to like the idea of Princess Brynn sending him to the army barracks, either.

Kae suspected he had bigger plans for himself. Did the king realize the full extent of the dangers posed by this Adluo merman? Or did he think all royals acted with honor because of their royal blood?

She needed to warn her father. She needed to warn the king! But who would believe her? She was merely a young mermaid who'd never been anywhere outside the Atlantic Ocean. She spent all her time inside the royal courts, with little idea how the world worked. Would she be a laughing stock for imagining such a far-fetched tale?

"What's wrong with this serving girl, Mariella?" One of the Adluo soldiers hovered over her, peering into her face. "She seems awfully pale."

"Kae, are you all right?" The head chef loomed over her, putting a hand to the girl's forehead.

Kae seized the opportunity being handed her. "I'm sorry, ma'am. My stomach does not feel well. But I must attend the princess." She sighed heavily, scrunching her forehead as if the thought pained her.

"You are in no shape to serve anyone. One of my helpers can fill your place at the princess's side." Mariella glanced around the kitchen. "Lailani? Please attend to the Princess Brynneliana at once." The girl bowed at the waist, and swam out through the double doors. Mariella turned her attention to Kae. "Straight to your cottage. I will let your mother know where you are."

Kae bowed her head. "Yes, ma'am. Thank you, ma'am." She swam out the kitchen's back door, but instead of turning toward the cottages, she swam toward the shoreline of Windmill Point. She needed to warn Shea. The Solstice was only a day away, and he still didn't know anything about what was really going on under the ocean's surface.

Prince Demyan was hatching some sort of plot, she was sure of it.

And if the Atlantic King was in danger from the Adluo Prince, then so was his grandson.

CHAPTER EIGHTEEN

The sky boasted a brilliant shade of blue. Yesterday's coastal storm moved further out to sea during the night, taking the oppressive clouds with it. The Summer Solstice was going to be a long, sunny day.

Twelve soda cans, eight beer cans, four water bottles partly full of water, three Styrofoam coffee cups, six more pieces of Styrofoam cups, an orange snorkel filled with sand, a cracked red shovel, and ten cardboard bits of various sizes that looked like pieces from exploded fireworks. Shea recited the day's list of trash in his head, trying to distract himself from his recently mutated status. He kept hoping the gills would disappear.

So far, they hadn't.

More than a week passed since the accident at the river dock. A long time to keep such a monumental secret. His grandmother kept giving him funny looks, but so far he hadn't told her a thing. Really, what could he say?

Hey Gramma, I've got gills.

Yeah, right.

He hadn't seen Kae since the day on Nauset beach, when she touched his neck. Maybe she knew something was wrong with him. Could she feel the slits when she touched him? *Who wants to be friends with a freak?* Which was why he knew he couldn't tell Hailey, either. He didn't want to lose another friend because of something he couldn't control. He glanced at her sideways as she walked beside him. Hailey wouldn't understand. He didn't understand it himself.

Humans don't sprout gills. They just don't.

Beside him, she bent to grab one more soda can, breaking the long silence. "I'm glad the weather cleared. Did you know tonight is the shortest night of the year?"

"The Summer Solstice," he said, nodding his head. "Gramma says my parents were married on the Solstice in Hyannis. Afterward, they all drove to Provincetown to watch the fireworks and pretend the celebration was for their wedding."

"Sounds nice," Hailey said, and clamped her mouth shut again. He noticed she wasn't talking nearly as much since their run-in with Kae at Nauset. In fact, she hadn't mentioned the beach encounter at all. They walked on in silence for a while before she spoke again. "I wonder why there's so much trash along here after a storm. Is it because you haven't been out here in a few days to pick it up?"

He stopped to watch the gentle waves washing toward the beach. "I think the storm's larger waves help bring it closer to shore. I read somewhere about these huge gyres of trash that form in the Atlantic and Pacific."

A puzzled look scrunched her face. "Where do you learn these things? I've never even heard the word gyre."

Shea stared out over the ocean toward the horizon, his fingers twisted in the long hair covering his ear, hiding the offending gills. His eyes unfocused as his mind dredged the definition out of his photographic memory. "A gyre is a pile of water pushed together into a large vortex by winds and currents. The North Atlantic has two large gyres in which garbage collects, but close to the Cape another, smaller gyre stretches from New Jersey in an elliptical pattern to Nova Scotia. Separated from the Gulf Stream current, New England's gyre keeps debris that enters the ocean here from being dragged out into the middle of the Atlantic." His eyes flicked to Hailey, who stared at him with her jaw hanging open.

"What are you, a walking encyclopedia or something?"

He froze, not sure what to say, sorry he hadn't kept his mouth shut. His dad told him to keep his photographic memory a secret. At the moment the unusual mental ability paled in comparison to his newly acquired physical attribute. What tops gills? Not much. He shrugged. "Once I read something, it's stuck in my brain."

"It sounded like you swallowed a textbook and threw it up." After another minute she asked, "Can you do that in school, too?"

"Yeah, it's not something I can turn on and off. But it's also not something I brag about. No one likes the smartest kid in the class." He kicked at the sand, memories of Plainville High School floating through his brain.

It was like she read his mind. "So you, what, get answers wrong on purpose?"

"Sometimes. To fit in. Not that it worked very well." He changed the subject. "Speaking of fitting in, how's your brother adjusting?"

She snorted. "Oh, you know. He barely ever leaves the windmill. Stays in bed until noon. Hangs out in those ratty flannel pants all day watching cartoons and playing Xbox. My parents haven't even noticed. Dad's busy organizing his office, and Mom's still coordinating the decorator stuff. She says it's hard to find good vendors here, whatever that means."

He made noises of sympathy while she ranted. It's not like he cared about Chip, but he cared about Hailey. So he listened.

"I haven't seen much of Mom or Dad since we moved. Not much different than New York City, really. Except Chip doesn't have friends on Cape Cod. At least I have you to hang with."

"He could come bike riding with us sometimes. You know, if he wants to hang out with us losers." Her older brother went with them to Nauset Beach for the day, and was a pain to hang around with. Shea didn't like the way Chip questioned him about Kae on the car ride to Windmill Point. *Who was that hot chick on the beach? The legs on her! Can you introduce me? How does a loser like you know a girl like that? Does she have any friends for me? Is she even your girlfriend or do I have a shot with her?*

No, Shea definitely hated the way Chip talked about girls. Especially about Kae.

Lucky's sudden barking startled them. A figure stood on the boardwalk, hands on hips, watching them. Hailey squinted against the glare of the sun. "Who could that be? There's never anyone here in the mornings."

"I think it's Mr. Guenther." *What's the old man doing at the beach?*

"What is he doing here so early?" Hailey's question echoed his own thoughts as they approached the boardwalk.

185

"Good morning, Mr. Guenther. What brings you to the beach today?"

"Keeping an eye on you two, of course," he chuckled, his tone light as his eyes scanned the beach. "Did you have another friend with you?"

They turned to see Kae making her way toward them. "Where'd she come from?" Hailey sounded mystified.

Shea waved to Kae. "She lives in the neighborhood, too, remember?"

Hailey refused to let go of her argument. "But she's dripping wet, like she's been swimming. Why didn't we see her in the water?" She shook her head, looking to Mr. Guenther for support. "There's something strange about that girl, and Shea refuses to admit it."

"What do you mean by strange?" The old man seemed interested.

Shea scowled. "Hailey's just being mean."

"He makes excuses for Kae, saying she's had a sheltered life, but it's like she lives on another planet. I mean, what fifteen year old hasn't tried to ride a bike?"

Mr. Guenther narrowed his eyes, watching the other girl approach. "I'm sure she's from this planet."

Shea ignored Hailey's complaints, waving again to Kae. "Hey! Where've you been? I've missed you."

"I was here yesterday, trying to find you. We need to talk right away." Kae's green eyes flit toward the man standing behind her friend, as if noticing him or the first time. "I'm sorry, I didn't mean to interrupt."

Hailey put her hands on her hips. "Hello? It rained all day yesterday. Why were you on the beach?"

"I'm sure the rain doesn't bother a girl like Kae," said Mr. Guenther, still squinting at her.

Kae focused her attention on him and her eyes opened wider, as if she'd seen a monster. Shea noticed her strange reaction. "This is Mr. Guenther. Maybe you've seen him before? He lives on the corner by my house."

"It's a pleasure, Miss Kae," Mr. Guenther said, an odd smile on his face.

Kae shivered and stepped closer to Shea, her voice low and urgent. "We need to talk. Now. Is there somewhere we can go? Alone?"

Hailey stomped her foot in the sand. "Hey, what about me? You're going to walk away and leave me behind like a broken sand toy?"

"I'll call you later." Shea took Kae's hand and led her off the beach. Lucky barked and galloped after the pair.

Ten minutes later Shea pushed open the kitchen door, prepared to introduce Kae to his grandmother. Instead he spied a note on the kitchen counter, reading it quickly. "Gramma is out for the morning with Mrs. McFadden."

"Who?" Kae glanced around the kitchen with open curiosity. She ran a finger along the pattern of interlocking circles on the Formica tabletop.

His mouth quirked into a smile. "How can you live in this neighborhood and not know any of the residents? I mean, Mr. Guenther is creepy so I understand, but everyone knows Mrs. McFadden. She's a total busybody." Kae stared at him wide-eyed and he felt his stomach twist into a knot. "Actually, never mind. Let's go upstairs and find you something warmer to wear. I saw you shivering on the beach." He led the way down the hallway and up the stairs to the bedrooms. She giggled when the stairs creaked under her footsteps, and he shook his head. Girls could certainly be odd. Different than guys, but not all the same either. He compared Kae and Hailey, both weird in their own ways, for sure.

Entering his bedroom he went straight to the closet and pushed hangers around until he found a hooded sweatshirt. "Where've you been, Kae? I haven't seen you in days. Even before yesterday's storm." He turned to hand her the hoodie and saw her pushing both hands on the mattress, watching it spring back into shape. "Umm, what are you doing?"

Her head jerked up, her cheeks flaming. "It looks so solid, and yet it's so pliant."

"Kae, what's going on? You're acting so...strange." He used Hailey's word for lack of a better one. "Have you been avoiding me?"

Her eyes returned to his face, fumbling for words. "I'm sorry I wasn't around this week. I searched for you on the beach yesterday, though."

Shea frowned. "It poured rain all day long."

"I've been... I had to... The family my parents work for returned and... My dad told me things about... Wait a minute. Let me start over with the important part." She took a deep breath. "I know who your mother is. And I know where she is."

Stunned, Shea dropped onto the edge of the bed, the sweatshirt falling to the floor. "What are you talking about?"

"I know who you are, Shea. What you are."

His fingers crept to his right ear, gently touching the slits hidden there beneath his shaggy hair. Kae took a deep breath and exhaled forcefully, her eyes darting around the room as if searching for the right place to begin. Finally, she asked, "Remember when you fell in the river last week?"

"How could I forget?"

"What do you remember, exactly?"

He stared at her, his fingers still covering the slits in his neck.

"It's normal, you know. It's your body reacting to being reunited with the salt water."

"Reunited?" He stared at her, not understanding.

"For example, did you ever wonder why you're able to see so well with very little light? Why you can remember everything you've ever read, or heard, or been told?"

He hadn't mentioned these things to Kae. Ever. He only just told Hailey about the memory thing on the beach this morning. "How do you know?"

"You can see so well because there isn't always a lot of light underwater. And a precise memory comes in handy when you can't write things down. Mermaids don't make lists."

"Mermaids?" He shook his head and laughed. "Who said anything about mermaids?"

"Your mother is a mermaid." Kae sat on the bed next to him, her leg pressed against his. Her shoulder bumped into his, her body heat invading his space. "You're only half human. Part of you belongs to the ocean."

"There's no such thing as mermaids. Or mermen." The words came out his mouth automatically even as his brain started to process the possibilities.

"I'm a mermaid. Are you going to tell me I don't exist?"

"No, but…"

"My parents are servants to the King of the Atlantic Ocean. Your grandfather. That's who they work for."

"My mother's a…mermaid princess?" This was too unbelievable. His fingers ran along the gill lines behind his ear again. A boy suddenly growing gills was also in the category of unbelievable events. "But what about my dad?"

"Only human, as far as I know. But it's not uncommon for a mixed race child to favor the mother."

"How could this be real?" He noticed again that her large green eyes were identical to his own. Was that a mermaid thing? He rubbed his hand harder against his gills, trying to rub them away and erase this whole fairytale. *It's another strange dream. Wake up, Shea, wake up.*

"Here, let me see." She reached toward his head. He flinched away from her touch. She stopped, hand in midair. "I'm not going to hurt you, Shea."

Reluctantly, he moved his hand away from his ear and allowed her to brush the hair away from the slits. Kae nodded, then leaned her own head closer. She pushed her golden curls to one side, revealing matching slits behind her own right ear. "See? Me too. It's normal."

"Normal?" His voice cracked, his words edged with sarcasm. "I'm not sure there's anyone else on the planet who would call this normal." Yet he couldn't resist running his fingers along the gills on her neck. She shivered under his touch, but didn't move away.

"You'd be surprised. There are mermaids in every ocean of the world."

He considered her words. Could any of this be real? Could he be part mythical sea creature? Was his mother a real live mermaid? That would explain his dreams. His mind whirled. Finally, he asked, "Tell me about my mother?"

"She arrived ten days ago with the royal entourage. She's always surrounded by guards, but I'm one of her attendants so I've been with her all week. This is her first visit to Nantucket Sound since you were born, and I'm not sure if she knows you're here. But the king knows. He asked my father to keep an eye on you."

"Royal entourage? Arrived from where? Why are there guards?" Questions tumbled from his mouth even as his mind raced forward to the next big one. "Can you take me to meet her?"

Kae hesitated. "There are guards because of the war. The royals plan to sign a peace treaty tonight, but everyone is still taking precautions. I'm not sure it's safe for you to be so close to Nantucket Sound right now, let alone meet the princess."

"Not safe? You need to explain."

She told him about the takeover of the Southern Ocean kingdom, and the bloody war that raged undersea for the last two years, pitting clan against clan, Adluos against Aequoreans. About the fragile peace treaty that included his mother marrying her young cousin, at the insistence of a certain ambitious prince, who seemed to have his sites set on conquering the whole of the Atlantic Ocean.

Shea was outraged. "We can't let him get away with that! It sounds like Prince Demyan's nothing more than a big bully. My mom shouldn't be forced to marry anyone, let alone her six-year-old cousin. That's not right."

"Prince Demyan may be a bully, but he has an army of soldiers to do his bidding. The Aequoreans are farmers, not fighters. The princess is doing what she thinks is best for her clan."

He scrubbed his fingers through his hair, frustrated. "There must be another way. There's always an alternative. You say part of the negotiated peace treaty is the wedding?"

"Yes, but the marriage won't take place until the Winter Solstice. Today's Solstice celebration is for the formal signing of the peace treaty, and the announcement of the engagement. There hasn't been a big gathering like this one in several years so all the pageantry moves along at a moon snail's pace."

"Then there's plenty of time to stop it. Let's go."

Kae blinked. "Go? Go where?"

"To meet my mom."

"But…"

He rested a hand on her shoulder. "We can't let this Demyan guy win. There must be something we can do." Her body shivered under his touch and he remembered the reason they'd come upstairs in the first place. "You're still cold?" He put his arm around her and hugged her. She felt warm against him, her body radiating heat like a bonfire. Her hair smelled of salt air and sunshine.

"I'm not cold," she whispered and shivered again. "Just scared."

He cupped her cheek with his hand and tipped her face, looking into her wide eyes. "Don't be," he whispered. He swallowed hard, and decided it was now or never. He'd never kissed a girl before, but he'd never wanted something this much in his entire life.

He lowered his mouth gently to hers, her soft lips tasting of salt and sweetness, and irresistible combination. He wound his fingers through her golden locks, her hair silky and fine like spun sunshine and he pulled her head closer, pressing his lips more firmly to hers, letting his tongue slide along the seam of her mouth. His heart hammered, the blood pounding in his ears drowning out the world around them. His body tumbled headlong through time and space... until a sharp bark brought him back to the present and he opened his eyes. Lucky stood next to the bed, prodding Kae with his black muzzle.

Kae drew away, her cheeks flaming a darker shade of red than before. "Oh," she said, jumping to her feet. "Oh, I'm so sorry!"

"Sorry?" Shea stood slowly, his brow knotting with confusion. "What is there to be sorry about?"

"I...I... Maybe we'd better get going. My father will know what to do to help your mother." She turned and walked into the hallway.

He felt like all the heat left the room with her, his heart still pounding with a rapid, steady sharpness that made him think it might burst from his chest at any moment. *Sorry? Why would she say that? Did I do something wrong? Does she already have a boyfriend I don't know about? Or am I just a bad kisser?*

Lucky stood next to Shea. He frowned at the dog. "Way to go, dog. Rule number one? Never interrupt a first kiss."

Lucky gave another sharp bark and wagged his tail.

"Stay here," he commanded and followed Kae. The dog whined. "No, boy. You've done enough." He shut the bedroom door behind him. The dog thumped against the door and barked a frantic warning. Shea ignored the noise and followed Kae down the stairs. He had no idea where they were headed, but after that kiss he'd follow her anywhere.

CHAPTER NINETEEN

"I don't know about this." Shea stood at the edge of the dock, eyeing the rapidly flowing river. "The last time I went in the water, it didn't work out so well."

He left a note on the kitchen table for his grandmother, explaining he was going to a friend's house for the afternoon and would stay there for dinner. He didn't go into the minor details, like his friend being a mermaid and her home being underwater in the middle of Nantucket Sound.

Standing on the dock, contemplating what he was about to do, he wished he waited to talk with his grandmother about it first. Doubts swirled through his head. Maybe he shouldn't be trying to swim off with a girl who claimed to be a mermaid and claimed to know his mother, who was also a mermaid.

Mermaids belonged in movies, not in real life.

The craziest part of it all was he didn't doubt a single bit of the story. Right down to the part where he was also a merman and could grow a tail at will.

"Don't be a jellyfish." Kae nudged him with her elbow, her touch sending a faint tingle up his arm. "Swimming will be different now that you know you can't drown."

"But I still don't know how to swim. So I can breathe underwater, but I'll still sink and rot at the bottom of the river."

"Don't be so dramatic. You can always walk along the bottom and get out on the beach. But really, swimming will be easy once you transform. Much easier than riding a bicycle."

He eyed her skeptically. "I guess I have to trust you. But I'm nervous about this whole transforming thing. Are you sure it's going to work?"

"Absolutely. Since you already grew gills, you must have the merman genes. You just need the magic." Her hand wrapped around the *transmutare* on her necklace. "You have your medallion, right? Oh wait, yours is just the stone."

He took the black rock from his pocket. Looking around the dock, he spied a rope tied to one of the pilings. It dangled into the water, attached to a floating crab trap. "Wait a sec! I've got an idea."

He pulled the trap onto the dock. With a hard tug he snapped the rope loose and looped it through the *transmutare*.

198

He tied the ends of the cord into a square knot and put it over his head. The stone hung from his neck similar to Kae's, but on white rope instead of leather cord. "Now I'm ready. How do I work this thing?"

"First we need to jump into the water. You might want to take your shirt off, too, since mermen don't wear t-shirts."

He raised both eyebrows. "What about my shorts? I'm not about to strip in front of you!"

Kae laughed. "The magic will take care of that. You'll see."

He shrugged and lifted the shirt over his head. When he turned to hang it over the dock's railing, Kae gasped. "You have the Mark!"

He whirled to face her. "You mean my birthmark? Yeah, it's always been there. Kinda weird, now that I know my mother's a mermaid."

"It means you're an heir of Poseidon, the first king of the oceans." She blinked and bowed her head. "Whatever you need of me, Sire. I am yours to command."

The words tickled something in his memory, but the sight of Kae bowing to him was too much to handle. He put a finger under her chin, lifting her head to meet his eyes. "Kae, I need you to be my friend, not some dumb royal subject."

She nodded her head, but the look on her face was unreadable.

"Besides," he continued, "You already knew my mom is a princess. What difference does a royal birthmark make?"

"It's not merely a birthmark. Not every royal gets the Mark of Poseidon, only the ones whom the gods choose as leaders."

"So how many get chosen? One in five? Every other one?"

"In the whole of the Atlantic Ocean, your grandfather has the Mark, as does your mother. And now you."

"Wow." The reality of the situation began to sink in. "What do you think it means?"

"It means you *are* the boy that the rumors talk about."

"What rumors?"

"It's been rumored since long before I was born that a human boy would rise up to end the bloodshed between the clans and unite all of the oceans in lasting peace."

He laughed. "I don't know anything about your clans or your wars. I just want to stop my mom from marrying someone she doesn't love." He paused for a moment. "Why would marriage be part of a peace treaty to begin with?"

"The king said that the oceans need to be bound with blood."

Shea frowned. "Sounds painful when you say it like that."

"We should hurry now, my Prince, and swim with the outgoing tide. It will make it easier for you."

He grabbed her arm. "Wait. First of all, call me Shea. Not Garbage Boy and certainly not *my Prince*. Just Shea. Second, I need to understand something. Does this Demyan guy know I exist? Or does he think the rumors are wishful thinking?"

"I don't know. I know my father believes in you. He always says all rumors have some truth to them." She paused, inching closer and taking his hand. "Others believe but would celebrate your death. I would rather you were safe. I don't want to lose you."

He stared into her wide green eyes, feeling more sure of himself than he had in a while. "I'm not running away to hide. And I don't have to fight them to save my mother. I just need to outthink them."

She inhaled sharply and took a step backward. "Very well."

He glanced at the surface of the river rushing by the dock out into the wide Atlantic, and took a deep breath. Clutching the *transmutare* hanging from his neck, he asked, "What now?"

"Jump." Kae plunged into the flowing river. Her head soon popped up above the surface. "Come on, Shea. Jump."

He closed his eyes, took a last deep breath of salty air, and jumped feet first into the water, the *transmutare* closed within his fist, tingling in his palm. His breath blew out from his gills in a stream of bubbles, his body breathing the water without any conscious thought or effort.

He opened his eyes and realized he was again sinking toward the river bottom. This time, however, he had no fear. Only curiosity. He noticed all the details he'd been too panicked to see when Hailey pulled him into the river. The way the sun filtered through the water in a constantly moving stream of light fascinated him, the shadows dancing in the always-moving water.

Shiny black mussels covered the dock pilings, clinging in clusters with tiny, almost see-through shrimp scuttling amongst them. Down among the rocks on the river's bottom, green crabs of various sizes shuffled out of his way, claws snapping anxiously as he planted his feet solidly in their midst, feeling the muck ooze between his toes.

In a moment, Kae hovered by his side speaking to him. He was amazed to discover he understood her words underwater as clearly as he had on the dock moments before. "You need to rub your thumb in a slow circle around the outside of the stone." She demonstrated the motion. "And repeat after me. *A pedibus usque ad caput mutatio.*"

His eyes widened as tiny bubbles appeared out of nowhere and swirled upward, starting at Kae's feet and circling faster and faster up her body until so many bubbles swirled around that he could no longer see her legs. The water churned into a tightly seething circle, until suddenly the bubbles stopped their frenetic movements and dissipated, rising slowly past the rest of her body upward to the water's surface.

The whole process took less than a minute.

Where there were two legs before, he now saw one bright green mermaid tail, its scales glittering in the dancing light filtered from the river's surface.

"Wow." The seawater filling his mouth when he spoke. He panicked for a second before realizing he could push the water right out again, as if it were air. A small part of him hadn't believed any of this could be possible, even when Kae explained it to him. Now he knew it all to be true. He couldn't deny the mermaid swimming right before his eyes.

The sparkling scales mesmerized Shea, and she blushed, putting her hands on her hips. "You're staring, you know. Is my tail that awful?"

Her blonde hair swirled around her heart-shaped face, her green eyes glittered as bright as her tail. Shea struggled to find adequate words and finally gave up. "I've never seen anything or anyone so beautiful."

Kae's cheeks turned an even darker shade of crimson. "Thank you, my Prince."

He rolled his eyes. "Quit with the royal title stuff. What are those magic words again?"

She moved her hand away from her own medallion. "Rub your thumb in a circle on your stone. Like that, good. Now say *a pedibus usque.*"

"*A pedibus usque,*" repeated Shea.

"*Ad caput mutatio,*" finished Kae.

He repeated the last part of the spell, and felt a hot tingling sensation zing through both legs, from a spot right behind his bellybutton to the tips of his toes. Tiny bubbles creeped their way up his legs, starting at the soles of his feet and swirling ever faster. He tried to wiggle his toes and was shocked to find he couldn't move his lower body at all. Panic filled him. "I can't move! Something's going wrong!"

With a swish of her tail she was right next to him, putting a comforting hand on his arm. "Paralysis is normal during transformation. Trust me." Her wide green eyes held his in her gaze. "Don't be afraid."

He stared into her eyes, trying hard not to freak out, feeling the heat move further up his legs. Each moment seemed like forever as the tiny bubbles zoomed around his body, binding his legs together.

After what felt like hours, the froth began to dissipate and float away from his body. He squeezed his eyes shut when the rising bubbles swirled around his face, the surrounding water warm from the transforming magic. "Did it work?"

"See for yourself."

He slowly cracked one eyelid. There, where he always had two separate legs, was now one big green fish tail, similar to Kae's in size and color but with flecks of blue and gold scattered along its length.

"How does it work?" Even as he asked the question, the tail flicked back and forth, stirring the sand on the river bottom. A school of tiny silver minnows darted past him, hurrying away from his shining scales, the sound of tinkling wind chimes in their wake.

"A tail is much easier than legs. You'll see." With one shimmering flick she put several yards between them and motioned for him to follow.

Taking a deep breath of water, Shea concentrated on moving his new tail from side to side by wriggling his hips back and forth. His fins flickered every which way along the sand, sending the green crabs scuttling to find shelter under nearby rocks, grumbling as they fled.

A stream of bubbles burst forth from Kae as she bent over with laughter. "You move like you have a squid on your back that you're trying to get loose," she said between giggles. "Or like my father when he thinks he's dancing!"

"Maybe you could help me instead of laughing at me." He hadn't moved forward even a foot. "It might be easier than riding a bike, but you still need to explain how it works."

"I'm sorry." A smile danced in Kae's eyes as she swam to his side. She placed her hand over his bellybutton. "This is your center of gravity." She pressed against his bare skin. "Your movements should come from here, not from your hips."

He put his hand over hers and pressed against his belly. His tail flicked out behind him backward, and his body moved forward in response, closer to Kae.

She nodded, her cheeks flaming red again. "Umm, yeah, kind of like that. Swimming is more of an up-and-down motion, rather than a side-to-side one, see?" She withdrew her hand from under his and turned to swim away, her whole tail undulating slowly upward and then down again.

"Kind of like a wave on the ocean's surface, how it rolls?" He tried to imitate her slow-motion swimming. He kept his hand pressed flat over his stomach to remind him to focus on his center of gravity. Kae returned to swim by his side. His tail flicked as he moved forward into the middle of the river.

Pretty soon, he felt more confident in his movements and removed his hand, putting both arms in front of him and pumping faster. Kae kept up as his speed increased. "This is fantastic!" he cried, rising upward. His head broke through the water's surface, and he laughed out loud. Seagulls whirled overhead against the backdrop of pure blue sky. Everything looked the same, and yet his whole perspective changed. It was like things suddenly snapped into place.

He had a mom.

He had mermaid blood.

He had a tail.

Nothing felt impossible. Not even saving the ocean.

Kae surfaced next to him, smiling. "See? I told you it was easy, once you get the hang of it."

"I can't believe how wonderful the water feels! I never understood why my dad never let me swim, but maybe he was afraid I'd never come out again!"

"My father said your parents moved to Oklahoma to be far away from the ocean. The king didn't approve of the union, so your mother wanted to keep your birth a secret. After the king's guards captured her, your father was supposed to keep you away until you were old enough to handle the truth."

His chest tightened. His father couldn't be with the woman he loved because of him. The whole thing was so unfair. He turned away from Kae, not wanting her to see the tears burning his eyes. Facing the riverbank, he realized he could see all of the windmill house from this vantage point, and remembered the conversation he had with Hailey on the dock about his birthmark and her mermaid obsession. Never in a million years would he have guessed he was one of those legendary creatures himself.

Kae's hand tapped his shoulder. "What are you staring at?"

He nodded at the windmill. "That's where Hailey lives."

Kae scowled. "Your human girlfriend?"

"She's my friend, not my girlfriend. Why, are you jealous or something?" Shea licked his lips and pulled her closer. With a short flick of his tail, he raised himself in the water, and then lowered his mouth onto hers. He felt the beat of her heart against his skin as if they were one. The sudden heat burning inside him had nothing to do with the *transmutare* stone's magic, and everything to do with Kae.

She pulled away from him, a dazed look in her eyes. "We shouldn't do this. You're a royal. I'm just…"

"After Lucky interrupted our first kiss, I wanted a do-over."

"Do-over. I like that concept." Her eyes locked on his lips again, before she backed away and shook her head, blonde hair flying around her face. "But we should get going if we want to be at the castle before the Solstice ceremony begins. Now that you can swim, are you up for a race?"

"You're on!"

He dove under the water and sped down the river toward the open water side by side with the blonde mermaid, all thought of Hailey forgotten. Kae and the open ocean beckoned him onward.

CHAPTER TWENTY

"Everything is in place, Sire." Zan's tailfin fluttered faster than usual, betraying his irritation. Too many players in this scheme meant too many things to go amiss. He liked to have more control of situations, especially when his own life could be at risk.

The prince hovered before a mirror, dragging his razor along already smooth cheeks. Always the soldier, Demyan's short hair and lack of beard set him apart from many of the other royals gathered for the Solstice Celebration. He caught Zan's eye in the reflection. "How many times must I reassure you, Zan? My plans are fool proof. Don't act like a damned squid licker."

Zan's tamped down on his anger at the insult. Long ago, Demyan made him take a magical vow to never harm anyone with royal blood ever again. To do so would immediately backfire on the sorcerer himself. It was part of the prince's price for keeping Zan's secret. If he betrayed the prince, Demyan would turn him in to the High Court for his crimes. If he tried to kill the prince, he would also die. He had no option that let him swim away without consequences.

Demyan finished his primping and swam across the room. His gleaming golden sword sat on top of the chest of drawers. He picked up the massive leather belt. "Help me strap on this scabbard. I should wear the Adluo royal sword for the Solstice ceremony, don't you agree?"

"As you wish, Sire." He busied himself with the myriad buckles while Demyan stared out the window into the courtyard. Technically, King Theosisto should wear the sword with the rubies on the hilt. The former king wore it every day of his life, until that fateful shark hunt. But the sword was too long and too heavy for the six year old.

"Any word yet from the spy? Has he secured the drylander boy?"

Zan frowned and shook his head. "No communication since he received his orders, Sire. How hard can it be to capture one useless drylander?"

Dark laughter rang through the room. "Trust me. Those wily creatures are harder to kidnap than to destroy. Killing them is easy. Keeping them alive, there's the hard part."

Bubbles huffed from Zan's gills. "Why bother, Sire? Why go to the trouble of capturing him when his mother obviously cares so little?"

Demyan cocked his head, amusement in his eyes. "What makes you think that? Do you feel my fiancé is a bad mother?"

Zan chose his words carefully, keeping an iron fist around his anger. "She is betrothed to your cousin, King Theo. Take care your words do not betray your intentions. I do not wish to end the night in chains."

"Apologies, my overly cautious companion. Let me rephrase. You think the princess ill-suited to bear children to her wedded husband?" Demyan smirked. "Are my words shadowed enough for your liking?"

Zan's frown deepened. "I want what's best for the clan, Sire."

"I decide what's best for the Adluo clan, my sorcerer."

"I merely meant to point out that the fickle mermaid left a child in her wake before. Mermaids can only bear one true child."

Demyan's laugh sounded dark. "Dryland bastards don't count. According to legend, mermaids can bear as many half-breed whelps as they desire."

"My point, Sire, is that she abandoned the one she already has. Who is to say she actually wants or desires a baby? Mermaids so often die in childbirth, as did her own mother. She may not be willing to bear another."

Demyan waved a dismissive hand. "Of course she wants offspring. That half-breed bastard of hers is an abomination. My spy says he cannot even swim. What mermaid could care for a child who doesn't share her love of the ocean? Her true child will be a full merman and bear the Mark of Poseidon."

"Correct as always, Sire." Zan tried to veil his lingering doubts about the plan.

The prince stroked his chin, his eyes darting back to his reflection in the mirror. "I assume you've spoken with the battle commanders and the soldiers are encamped in their positions. So what has your tail in a twist, my good sorcerer? I feel your anger warming the room and don't think you're truly worried about my future progeny."

Zan blew out a long breath. "I should be at your side throughout the Solstice. My magick can't protect you from outside the castle walls."

A smile stretched across Demyan's face, not reaching the glittering black eyes now focused on the sorcerer. "Tsk, tsk. You know how I like to have contingency plans. It may never come to the point where you must rally the troops, but if the first plan should fail…"

"It will not."

"Do not interrupt. If the first plan should fail, I need insurance. I trust you, my dear Zan, to insure my success." He waved off any further protest. "Come. Let us join the others. The procession begins at sunset." He swam from the room leaving bubbles stirring in his wake.

Zan took a last look in the mirror at himself. His stomach churned with uncertainty, his magick warning him that something was not right with this plan, but he saw no way out of his situation. Demyan always achieved his goals, and it usually proved safer to be on his side than pitted against him.

"I owe him my life," Zan reminded himself for the millionth time, speaking to his reflection in a stern voice. "He believed in you when no one else would give you a chance. You owe him your loyalty *forever,* whether bound by magick or not."

He'd told himself this same mantra time and again over the years. But this was the first time *forever* felt like it might last too long.

CHAPTER TWENTY ONE

Having never even been in the ocean before, or any large body of water for that matter, each new sensation amazed Shea. Every new sight, every new smell, every unusual texture that he ran his fingers across... Everything was so completely different than anything he ever imagined.

Each nuance of his new appendage, the shimmering tail that was suddenly a part of him, continued to fascinate and distract him. All five of his senses threatened to overload from the sheer pleasure of the cool ocean current caressing his body. He felt like the ocean was running its fingers through his hair, welcoming him home. He wondered if he'd ever be able to get used to the feeling enough to ignore it completely.

The smell of the water as he breathed in through his nose and pushed it out through his gills was salty, but not in a bad way. *Not bad at all*, he thought, becoming aware of the

215

subtle differences in scent of the various streams of currents. He could taste the salt in his mouth too, every time he opened it to speak with Kae, to ask questions about their surroundings.

Algae covered rocks lay strewn across the ocean floor, amidst wildly growing beds of kelp and seaweed of different colors, sizes and varieties. Some rocks were lined in a deliberate pattern, marking the underwater road they followed along the ocean's floor. Small schools of brightly shimmering minnows darted across their path, startling Shea with their quick movements. He heard their silvery voices in his head like the tinkling of tiny wind chimes.

Maybe the thing with the bluefish wasn't a one-shot deal. Maybe merfolk could hear what other sea creatures were thinking and saying. Kae hadn't mentioned that among the attributes of mermaids, but it made sense. Otherwise, how would he know the minnows were making fun of his hair, calling it yellow seaweed?

As yet another school of tiny bright grey fish darted in front of them, he asked, "Are there larger fish in this area?"

"It's still pretty shallow along here." She pointed to their left, adding, "There's a deeper trench over that way where most of the big fish like to hang out during the day. They prefer the dark. You might see one or two, but they don't like the sun so much. When it gets closer to dusk, they'll come out to hunt for dinner."

He shuddered, remembering the sharp, pointy teeth on the blue fish he and Hailey caught from the dock. He was glad to see the strong sunlight filtering through the water around them. "We're not on their menu for later, are we?"

Kae laughed, and even underwater he thought her laughter sounded beautiful. "Of course not, you clownfish. We have nothing to fear in these waters, except perhaps humans."

Off to their right they passed a field of scallops. He stared at the hundreds of fluted shells sitting in neat horizontal lines along the ocean floor. On three sides of the bed were rows of large stones, covered with green, fingerlike branches of algae stretching upwards three feet toward the surface, forming a waving green barrier. "Wow, look at the scallops all nestled together. It's like they were planted there somehow, like the rows of corn on our farm in Oklahoma."

"Of course we grow crops! We Aequoreans are a farming clan. That tall greenery on top of the rocks is spongy codium, to discourage the fish from poaching in the beds. Beyond the scallops are a few fields of oysters, then the greens, and then the castle's courtyard. We'll be there soon."

They swam in silence while Shea marveled at the aquaculture propagated on both sides of the rocky pathway, thinking how impressed his father would have been with the underwater farm. He wondered if his father ever knew about all this cultivation at the bottom of Nantucket Sound. For a moment his heart felt heavy, thinking of his dad and the farm he'd been raised on. So different than the fields he now swam past, and yet in a strange way so similar.

The Aequoreans cultivated the ocean floor in the same way he and his father farmed their land, taking advantage of every available space. The sandy fields of oysters were even bigger than the ones with the scallops, stretching out beyond where Shea could see, into the vast shadowy areas. "You Aequoreans sure eat a lot of oysters."

"Mostly we raise them to harvest the pearls. They're good for trading, both with the other clans and with the humans. We should keep our voices low from here on, in case they posted guards along the road."

They soon passed another wall of the tall codium, growing atop a foot or so of neatly piled slipper snail shells. On the other side of the living fence, lanterns sat on pilings, their large glass globes filled with tiny flickering jellyfish. The phosphorescent green glow illuminated the broken white clamshells now lining the edges of the path. A tallish structure loomed in the distance. "Is that the castle?"

Kae nodded and reached for his hand, squeezing his fingers. "Yes, and I see they've already started to light the lanterns. We should hurry."

They passed another of the glowing globes. "Why do mermaids need to light lamps? I've always been able to see pretty well in the dark. Didn't you say that's a mermaid thing?"

"The jellyfish lamps out here along the road are more for show than anything else. It's a tradition to light the way to a celebration, kind of like proclaiming that everyone is welcome."

"So they're like decorations?"

Kae nodded. "There are times when even mermaids need to use lights, though. Like when you're inside the castle at night. If you're in a room without windows, you need some kind of light source in order to see."

He smirked. "The cartoons usually make use of electric eels in those situations."

Kae scrunched her forehead and frowned. "What's a cartoon? Is it like a car?"

"No, silly, a cartoon is…"

"Hush! Someone's ahead." Kae grabbed his arm. "Act normal."

There was a group of eight young merfolk swimming along the path toward the castle, laughing as one of their number continued to gesture wildly with both hands. Kae and Shea slowed their pace, staying behind.

Shea's eyes opened wider as took in the multi-hued group. "Are they all Aequorean?"

219

Kae shook her head to indicate no. "The one with the blue hair? He's obviously from the Pacific somewhere."

Shea's mouth quirked into a grin as he squeezed her hand. "Oh, right. *Obviously.*" She elbowed him in the side as they swam slightly closer to hear the conversation.

"So I said to the guard, I'm sorry, officer, but I told you my stingray doesn't like strangers!" The merman was big and blond and reminded Shea so much of his friend John Hansen that it startled him. Swimming in Nantucket Sound now with Kae, it felt like Oklahoma was a whole different world. He didn't expect things to seem so familiar.

The other mermen laughed at the stingray story, but the young mermaid next to the storyteller folded her arms across her chest, bunching her woven-hemp shirt. Her blue eyes glared at her partner as the current tossed her long, blood-red hair behind her. "You're lucky you aren't in the dungeons right now, Dereck."

"Or being fed to the Adluo pet sharks," added another pale-skinned mermaid, this one with hair the color of lemons and eyes that matched. "You shouldn't tease soldiers. It isn't safe."

"The war is over," scoffed another of the mermen, who wore a seaweed vest over his muscled chest. His hair was short, spiky, and blue, in a shade that blended with the water around him. "With the King's announcement at the Solstice feast tonight, the hostilities will officially end."

"Don't count your scallops before they're hatched," the redheaded mermaid continued. "I don't trust those Adluo ruffians as far as I could throw them onto the shore."

"Which isn't very far at all," teased Dereck. "Come on, Gwendy, lighten up. The war is over. Don't we deserve a little peace?"

"Deserve has nothing to do with it," she countered. "All I'm saying is be careful, please? I want to travel to the University of Atlantis this fall with you by my side, not stuck in some dungeon."

"Fair enough." Dereck planted a kiss on the mermaid's cheek. "Let's hurry now, before we miss the procession into the Great Hall." The group swam a little faster toward the castle. Shea and Kae stayed in the back, keeping pace easily. As the young merfolk swam under the elaborate marble arch marking the entrance to the courtyard, Shea grabbed Kae's hand and pulled her off the path.

"We shouldn't go into the courtyard," Shea whispered. "Someone may see my birthmark."

Kae's eyes opened wide. "Oh my gods! You're right!" She grabbed his hand and swam to a field on the side of the well-worn road. "Why didn't I think of this before?" She started tearing large fronds of seaweed from the ocean's sandy floor.

"What are you doing?"

She concentrated on the fronds in her hands, weaving them together. "Didn't you see the vest that merman was wearing? I hear they're all the rage among the western clans in the Pacific." She didn't look away from her task, fingers flying through the water so fast he could barely see them. After a few minutes, her hands slowed and he could see the green vest she made.

He smirked. "You want me to wear that? That's not a vest, it'll barely cover my chest. I'll look like a Las Vegas cowboy."

"I'm not sure what a Vegas is, but this'll hide the Mark on your back. That's all that counts at the moment." She held it out to him. "Put it on. Now."

He complied, the woven seaweed sliding along his arms and back as Kae adjusted it making sure his birthmark was hidden from view. "This may be what all the cool Pacific mermen are wearing, but the slime factor is just gross. Give me plain old cotton any day." He started the shimmy out of the vest.

Kae rolled her eyes and put out both hands to stop him. "Think of your safety instead of your comfort. At least now we can enter the courtyard without raising suspicions."

She started to swim for the entrance, but Shea grabbed her hand.

"Let's hang back. We can watch from behind these statues."

Kae shook her head, a short quick movement that sent her blonde hair floating wildly around her face. "I think we should blend with the crowd. If we lurk out here on our own, we'll seem suspicious."

"Not if they don't see us. I don't want to get too close to those guards." He nodded his head in the direction of the Adluo warriors who lined the pathway inside the courtyard. The guards stood stationary, almost like statues themselves. They wore decorative blue sashes across their chests, but their scarred faces were those of battle-hardened soldiers.

He tugged again on her hand, leading her away from the path and the marbled arch and over to a shadowy spot behind a large carved-rock statue. He recognized the statue as a fat Buddha, the giant rock carved into a pyramid shape with a huge round head at the top. "This is a bad idea," she whispered.

"Better than walking straight into the tiger's den."

"What's a tiger?"

"Okay, not a good analogy for a mermaid," he said with a smile. He kept forgetting she had a different perspective on things than he did. "How about better than swimming into an octopus lair?"

"Oh, I get it now." She peered out from the shadow toward the palace doors. "See the door on the far right? That's where the procession will exit the castle. The king and your mother will come out first, followed by the other dignitaries. This year there will be representatives from all five oceans. Then come those representing the lesser bodies of water and someone from the University of Atlantis. This year I think the High Chancellor himself is here, to observe the peace accords. The magistrates and chancellors have their fingers in everything political, or so my father tells me."

"Then what?"

"See that door at the far end of the gardens, over there on the left?" She pointed across the courtyard. Shea poked his head from behind the statue. "That leads into the Great Hall. The king leads the procession along the garden paths while people cheer, and then he and your mother stop at the door to greet each of the guests when they enter the Great Hall. On the Solstice, it's tradition that everyone in the crowd gets to meet the king face-to-face and then take part in the feast. Similar ceremonies take place in every ocean around the globe, but this year the Atlantic ceremony trumps them all."

"Why?"

"The peace treaty and your mother's wedding announcement. Royal weddings are a big deal. Being present for the official announcement guarantees an invitation."

They watched the crowd gathering, the noise level gradually increasing as more merfolk filled the courtyard. After a while, he couldn't see either of the castle's doors. "Will we be able to see anything from here?"

"I hope so," she said. "It's too late to choose a new vantage point, but there's nothing that says we have to stay close to the ocean's floor." Grabbing his arm, she pulled him upward, swimming toward the large head of the Buddha. "Good thing you chose a big statue."

From this new perspective, they looked out over the heads of the other merfolk. Shea was surprised to see the gathered crowd came in an even greater variety of sizes and colors than the university students they'd been following. It was similar, in a way, to any large gathering of humans, but different. *Humans don't generally have yellow eyes...or green skin. Or tails.*

Slowly the filtered light began to dim as the sun settled to the horizon, the longest day of the year drawing to a close. At the moment the sun touched the edge of the Atlantic, the liquid gold of the sunset on the water changed the light in the courtyard to a warm honey color. By some unseen signal, the guards all stood at attention. A second later, a conch horn sounded a long, low note, hushing the crowd into complete silence. Shea watched the door on the far right creak open. The merfolk gathered in the courtyard let out a great cheer as the king stepped into the open waters, the jewels on his crown glittering brilliantly in the golden light.

"That's your grandfather, King Koios," she whispered into his ear. "Your mom should come out next."

Servants carrying glass globe lanterns appeared on either side all along the pathway, serving to both illuminate the procession with a brilliant green light and keep the onlookers at arms length from the dignitaries. As the cheering continued, the king held out his hand and Princess Brynneliana emerged from the doorway, resplendent with glowing emeralds around her neck and beaded through her long, flowing blonde curls. Her entire head glittered with twinkling green lights as the gems reflected the glow of the lanterns. The crowd roared its approval once again, as the king and the princess made their way forward along the path.

He couldn't take his eyes off his mother. She looked exactly like the woman in his dreams, but also so royal and otherworldly. "She's like a faerie princess out of a movie."

Kae snorted, bubbles bursting from her nose and gills. "Are you kidding? Faeries are downright ugly. All pointy ears and sharp cheekbones..." her sentence trailed off as he stared at her with wide eyes. "What? You think merfolk are the only magical creatures in the world?"

He shifted his gaze to the courtyard without answering. The procession of dignitaries flowed out of the castle and around the glowing path through the courtyard. The crowd cheered and applauded, exclaiming over the fancy jewels and elaborate outfits from around the globe.

Close behind his mother, a burly, dark-haired merman escorted an elderly royal. The thin circle of gold on his head denoted royalty, but even from a distance the merman's sneering eyes looked black and evil. Despite the rainbow of colors represented in both the procession and the crowd, the merman's dark olive complexion and bulging forearms stood out oddly next to the fair mermaid at his side.

"Who are they?" He poked Kae to get her attention and pointed to the dark merman.

"The old mermaid is Princess Winona, the king's half-sister. The merman next to her is Prince Demyan, the regent from the Southern Ocean. Your mother is supposed to marry her cousin, King Theosisto, the one swimming behind Demyan with that dark-skinned Caribbean princess."

Shea absorbed this information and took note of Theo, but his eyes zoomed to focus on Demyan as he made his way around the courtyard. "She has to marry a little kid?

That seems so wrong. Why is he King of the Southern Ocean? What happened to his parents?"

"The king died on a shark hunt, an accident they say. Queen Jessamine…" Kae paused. "Officially they say she took her own life because of her grief when her husband died. But there are rumors."

"Rumors?"

"Some say she was killed for having…the wrong blood in her heritage. Another rumor says a dark sorcerer murdered her in his anger. Others claim Prince Demyan himself delivered the killing blow to make himself regent." She shook her head. "I can't believe the prince would slay a woman, though. Not his own aunt."

"I don't think murder would bother him one bit," he said, his attention riveted on the prince. The merman seemed to feel Shea's scrutiny, his black eyes darting among the crowd of faces as if seeking someone in particular.

"We're here to take a peek at your mother," Kae reminded him. "Don't waste your time worrying about the prince." She laid a gentle hand on his shoulder, but he wriggled away from her touch, dislodging several small pebbles from Buddha's shoulder.

The stones bounced down the front of the statue toward the ocean floor. The black head of the prince turn sharply toward the small movement. The moment seemed frozen in time as the two glared into each other's eyes, black and green locked together.

"Shea!" Kae grabbed his wrist and yanked him behind the statue's head. "Someone will see you!"

"Too late. Let's get out of here!" The pair swam into the open ocean, darting far away from the castle courtyard. After staring into the prince's eyes, Shea doubted anyone could swim fast enough to escape his wrath, but they had to try.

Two hundred yards away, at the far end of a field of oysters, the pair slowed their swimming to make sure no one had followed. "That was too close," Kae said, keeping her voice low. "I can't believe we got away without being seen."

"The prince saw me, that's the problem. Why am I such a klutz?"

Kae shook her head. "He has the Solstice ceremony to deal with. And finalizing those awful peace treaties. I mean, I'm happy for the end of war, but it's going to change my life so much."

"Are the clans always at odds with one another? Is that how merfolk are, always fighting, always at war?"

"I don't know a lot about politics, or about how the other clans handle disputes." Kae paused for a moment. "But I think this particular war is over resources. The Southern Ocean is pretty barren, and getting worse for some reason. I think the Adluos fight because they want what the Atlantic has to offer."

"Why can't everyone share the resources? Or trade peacefully? Did the Adluos fight when their old king was in power?"

"Not nearly as much. There were skirmishes, but not the bloodshed we've seen recently. The royal families used to be related by blood – the Adluo King sent his sister to marry King Koios. She died giving birth to your mom." Kae cocked her head to one side. "I guess that makes you part Adluo, too."

"You mean I'm related to that Prince Demyan guy? No, thank you!" Shea frowned and crossed his arms over his chest. "I think..." A rustling in the seaweed fence caught his eye, and he stopped mid-sentence. He turned just as a burly merman wearing a blue sash burst through the barrier, dragging a net behind him. "Watch out!" Shea grabbed for Kae's hand, but the other merman threw the netting over her head, pulling her backward. Furrowing his brow, Shea wound up to punch the soldier, but someone else grabbed both of his arms from behind.

"Got you," growled the second soldier as his fingers tightened their grip. "Thought you could escape, did you?"

A third Adluo swam into the oyster field, holding the ends of bright chains that harnessed a pair of six-foot long sand sharks. "Best hunters in these waters," the soldier said proudly, tugging the leashes on the grayish brown pair. The chains threaded through iron muzzles on their snouts, preventing the sharks from opening their voracious mouths. "Killers, my girls are," the soldier continued, "Trained them myself. The females are much better hunters, you know."

"Shut up, Griffin," yelled the soldier wrestling with Shea. "Why don't you help me with this prisoner?"

"No problem." Griffin moved in closer with his two deadly predators until the sharks' muzzles poked into the golden scales on Shea's tail. The sharks snorted, straining against their muzzles. "I'd stop struggling if I was you, boy. You wouldn't want me to let my pets loose, would you?"

The same way Shea listened to the thoughts of the blue fish he'd caught with Hailey, he could hear the frantic, jumbled thoughts of the sand sharks, seeing bloody pictures projected in his mind instead of words. He shuddered at the images of horror, then tried his best to tune them out. He straightened his shoulders, meeting the soldier's eye. "On what grounds are you taking us prisoner? We've done nothing wrong."

"You spied on our prince," growled the guard holding Shea's arms. He pushed him down as the other soldier pulled the fishing net wider. In moments, Shea and Kae were bound together, enmeshed in netting.

"We watched the procession," protested Kae, her front now pressed tight against Shea's back. "Do you plan to arrest everyone in the crowd for spying?"

"Ah, but you weren't in the crowd," said the soldier tying the ends of the net. "You hid outside of the courtyard. And you ran from us when we came to politely ask you to join the rest of the gathering."

"Politely?" Shea snorted, sending a burst of bubbles shooting from his gills. "You came after us with sharks and nets. Of course we ran away!"

"Only the guilty run away." Griffin stroked the dorsal fin of one of his trackers. "We'd better take the prisoners straight to the prince. Something about the boy's shiny scales is making my girls extra hungry."

CHAPTER TWENTY TWO

In one of the smaller buildings outside the palace courtyard, two Adluo soldiers waited with their newly captured prisoners. The third soldier swam off with word for the Prince. Despite his dire circumstances, the surroundings fascinated Shea. Everything in this underwater house seemed so similar and yet so different from his home on dry land. He focused on the curtains, waving in the current wafting through the open window. The same current carried hungry growls from the sharks caged right outside the door.

Kae's body pressed against his back. The pair remained tied together, the thick ropes of the net tangled around them. Shea could feel Kae's warm cheek against his neck, her body trembling. "Hey," he whispered to her, tilting his head toward his shoulder. "Everything's going to be fine."

Kae let out a nervous laugh and he felt her body tremble anew. "Sorry. This isn't the way I pictured things."

"Yeah." Shea smiled, despite the circumstances. "I thought I'd be facing you the first time we got this, you know, intimate."

"Oh." He heard her sharp intake of breath. He meant it as a joke, but her cheek felt even warmer against him, obviously embarrassed. "I'm not sure I know…"

The door flung open, banging against the wall, stirring the current in the room. "I must return to the Great Hall before I'm missed." The dark prince stopped in front of the bound pair, eyeing the thick ropes with disdain. "How can I question two prisoners if I can only see one of them?"

A guard sprang forward to untie the knotted fishing net. Prince Demyan rolled his eyes while the soldier fumbled with the rope. "Can't you move any faster, you insufferable wad of eel slime?"

"I'm doing my best…" the soldier's voice trailed off into a yelp. Shea turned his head to see the prince's knife slice through the netting that bound him to Kae, lopping off two of the soldier's fingers in the process. Thick blood oozed from the fresh wounds, clouding the water around the soldier's hand.

Shea's nose prickled, blood filling the water with a strong scent of iron. His stomach clenched tight, a twisted knot forming in his belly. *Death,* he thought. *This is what death smells like.* He could hear the excited thoughts of the sharks penned outside as the blood wafted out the open window.

"MY TIME is more valuable than you seem capable of understanding," the prince growled through clenched teeth.

The guard named Griffin rushed forward. "Let's keep the blood to a minimum. My girls get excited easily." He wrapped a kelp rag around his comrade's hand to stem the ooze of red. The sharks outside thrashed restlessly, banging against the side of their cage with a resounding clatter.

"Now then," Prince Demyan drawled, locking eyes with Shea. He pulled the net off his head and snapped the cord holding the *transmutare* stone. "No need to have you contacting any friends." He handed the medallion to one of the soldiers and motioned for him to take Kae's *transmutare* as well. "Tell me your name, you pusillanimous little squid, and WHY you felt the need to spy on a public procession."

Shea stared into the merman's dark eyes. He'd dealt with plenty of bullies in Oklahoma. The boys who played football and thought the world owed them everything. The kids who didn't have to rush home to do chores after school, the rich ones like B.J. who lived in town and thought they were so much better than a farm boy. Give them an inch and they'll take the whole farm, his dad always said.

Shea had no intention of giving this prince that inch.

Prince Demyan pressed his lips into a thin line. "Do you need further motivation to talk?" He scraped his bloody blade against the boy's neck. Shea shrugged, as if to say *So what? I dare you*, but kept his mouth closed.

The prince removed the threatening blade and wiped it along the left side of Shea's vest, leaving a dark bloody stripe on the green seaweed. "Perhaps I'm threatening the wrong *mermaid*." He grabbed a handful of Kae's blonde curls, yanking her toward him as she winced in pain, exposing her delicate neck. With slow precision he raised the knife and rested its shining blade against her skin, where the blood pulsed through her carotid artery.

Shea couldn't stand the fear in her eyes. "We couldn't see," he blurted. "We were trying to get a better view of all the royalty. Let my friend go." His hands clenched at his sides, helplessly. He knew he'd be outnumbered if it came down to a fight. That wouldn't help Kae.

Prince Demyan scraped the knife along Kae's pale neck until it came to rest on her collarbone. She bit her bottom lip when he pressed the blade deeper. A thin red sliver of fresh blood appeared along the knife's edge. "WHY did you flee?"

Abruptly, Demyan released Kae and shoved her toward Shea. He gave her a quick hug before pushing her behind him again. "Guards chased us. With sharks," Shea said through clenched teeth, his brow furrowed. "Of course we fled."

The prince seemed lost in thought, staring into Shea's face. "Those eyes," he murmured. "I've seen those eyes somewhere before…the blonde hair, the angry green eyes. It couldn't be mere coincidence, now could it?"

The dark prince's words made no sense to Shea. He turned his head slightly, to catch Kae's eye. She shrugged, shaking her head.

A thin smile slashed across Prince Demyan's face. "Could it truly be? The long lost bastard son of the Atlantic's beloved princess! And here I'd been told you were a mere drylander. I'll have to have that informant killed. And revise my plans." Shea's eyes shot open wide, and Demyan chuckled. "Yes, my boy, we've been expecting your arrival, although I must admit I didn't think it would be so voluntary."

He snapped his fingers at the guards. "Bind and gag these prisoners. I'll not have them spoil any of the surprises I've orchestrated for this fine Solstice evening." Those black eyes glittered in the faint light. The thin, calculating smile stretched across his face reminded Shea of a venomous snake about to strike.

A venomous *sea* snake.

"I've waited long enough to take my revenge over the Atlantic. I'm a man of action, and I shall have what I want."

237

Prince Demyan snarled. "King Koios shall pay for the death of my father, and you jelly-brained urchins shall not spoil my fun."

One of the soldiers spoke up, his voice quivering. "Shouldn't we kill 'em then? Get rid of the problem?"

"Of course NOT, you worthless son of a manatee," roared the prince, rolling his eyes as he jabbed his knife into its sheath. "I've always found hostages to be wonderfully motivating."

With that, he swam out of the room, a flurry of swishing bubbles in his wake. All three guards breathed heavy sighs of relief and gathered around the one who lost fingers, ignoring the prisoners. "You'll need to steer clear of my hunters for at least a week," said Griffin, nodding as he checked his comrade's ragged stumps. "Listen to those girls outside in the pen. Smell of blood drives them insane. They'll tear you to pieces, I tell you."

"Forget about me. Let's find fresh rope to secure these Aequoreans, now that the prince shredded my net."

"Pack this mud under the kelp to mask the smell. Stay on the far side of me until you get beyond the sharks. I won't be able to control them if you get too close." First aid complete, the three mermen exited, forgetting to leave a guard in the room with the prisoners.

"We need to get out of here and warn King Koios," Shea whispered. "Did you hear that prince guy? More than a little crazy!"

She stared at the floor, her hand covering the spot where the prince's knife had been. "I'm bleeding." She moved her hand to show the trickle of red seeping from her body and dissolving into the water. "I can't get by those sharks. Go without me."

"I won't leave you. What was it the soldiers used to stop the blood?" He spied the pot of mud and grabbed it, poking his index finger into the thick, black ooze. He wiped the mud across the red line at Kae's neck, and glanced around the room for another piece of kelp. Seeing none, he took off the seaweed vest Kae had woven for him. "Use this," he insisted, shoving it into her hands. "Hurry!"

Kae pulled two long strands loose and pressing them against her wound. She lifted her arm and he ran the seaweed around her torso, tying the ends together at her back. She glimpsed the trident between his shoulder blades. "You'll be in greater danger if Prince Demyan sees the Mark on your back," she whispered, returning the vest to him. "It's bad enough he knows you're the son of the princess. If he sees the Mark he'll kill you for sure."

He put the seaweed garment on. "Prince Demyan is going to kill me no matter what. We need to warn someone."

"How will we get away from the guards?"

"Leave that to me," said a gruff voice. They whirled to see a tall white-haired merman blocking the doorway, holding a wooden club in his left hand. In his right, he held a blue sash with a small bloodstain on it. He slipped the sash over his head.

"Mr. Guenther?" Shea couldn't quite comprehend what he was seeing. "What are you...? Why did...? How can...?" He couldn't finish any of his questions. His grandmother's strange old neighbor was apparently...a merman?

"You're Adluo," Kae said quietly, her eyes wide. "I thought I recognized you on the beach. But why would you help us?"

"Call me Gregor, please." The merman scanned the room. "Are you alone?"

"The guards will return any minute to tie us up," Shea told him. "We should get out while we can."

"I wouldn't worry about my old friend Griffin," Gregor said with an odd smile. "He and his comrades are taking a nap for the moment." He dropped the club to the floor. "But the mermaid was right about covering the Mark on your back. Prince Demyan will not leave you alive even for one more minute if he knew the truth."

Kae crossed her arms over her chest. "Why, in Neptune's name, should we trust you?"

Gregor smiled. "Do you have a choice?"

240

CHAPTER TWENTY THREE

They followed Gregor down the darkened path leading between the servant quarters. No glowing green lanterns lit this alleyway, but Shea's eyes adjusted easily to the darkness. When he thought they were far enough from where they'd left their captors, he asked Gregor if he had a plan.

"I'm taking you to Windmill Point where you'll be safe," Gregor whispered as he peered around the next corner. "I made a promise to your grandmother, Shea."

"My grandmother?" Shea grabbed Gregor's arm. "What does my grandmother have to do with any of this?"

The older merman turned toward Shea, a sad smile on his face. "Martha's a good woman. She's already endured so much loss, I couldn't let her lose you as well."

"Did you have something to do with her other losses?" Kae's tone was sharp.

241

Gregor shook his head. "Not directly. I was sent to Windmill Point years ago as a spy, by Prince Demyan's uncle, the last true King of the Southern Ocean. Shea's birth was but a rumor that the king wanted to confirm or deny."

"You're a spy?" Shea narrowed his eyes, still unable to reconcile the bent old man on his porch rocker with the muscled merman before him.

Gregor nodded. "I received word this week that I was to take you prisoner. I decided I couldn't be complicit with Prince Demyan's plans."

"You were sent to…capture me?"

Sand swirled below Gregor's tailfin. "Fifteen years is a long time to spend in your world. The MacNamaras were very kind to me when I moved to Windmill Point. I came to regard your grandfather as a friend, even if he was a drylander."

"But…"

"I was shocked when Prince Demyan told me he'd orchestrated the MacNamara deaths." He looked Shea in the eye. "You were supposed to die as well."

Shea stared at the merman. "Were you supposed to kill me?"

Gregor shrugged. "I was supposed to bring you before the prince. But I suspected your fate would be no better than your grandfather's."

"My grandfather's death was an accident. A hurricane killed him. No one controls the weather."

Gregor's mouth set into a firm line. "Prince Demyan has ways, Shea. No one is safe. Too many innocents have already died, both merman and drylander." Motioning for them to follow him, Gregor swam forward. "We must hurry to the docks at Windmill Point."

"No." Shea folded his arms across his chest. Kae stayed by his side. "We can't leave my mom and the king at the mercy of that evil prince. We have to stop him."

Gregor returned, shaking his head. "You're a drylander boy, barely a man even by merman standards."

"Are you taking Prince Demyan's side?" Kae crossed her arms over her stomach, mimicking Shea's stance.

"Prince Demyan has trained in the arts of war since the moment he was born. He thinks nothing of killing his own guards, his own family even. He won't hesitate to kill you both. What can you hope to do against such a ruthless, heartless soldier, when you just learned to swim?"

"I don't know what we'll do," said Shea firmly, "but we have to try."

"He's right," Kae said. "Prince Demyan practically told us that he's planning something terrible and wants to take over the Atlantic. We need to warn King Koios!"

Gregor sighed softly, a small stream of bubbles rising slowly upward. "I should expect no less. But I had to try, for your grandmother's sake."

"Gramma will be fine. She's safe in Windmill Point. It's my other grandparent who's in danger."

Kae still had questions. "So, you've been living as a human in Windmill Point? How did you stay in touch with the Adluos? With a *transmutare* stone?"

Gregor cast his eyes downward, swishing his powerful tail in the sand. "The prince required face-to-face reports prior to every Summer Solstice."

"You had to journey alone to the Southern Ocean? That's a long way to travel to make a report."

"It's a long way when there is nothing of interest to tell," said Gregor with a wry smile. "For the first ten years, I was sure the rumors of a child were false. When I knew the family better, I realized a second MacNamara son existed. I wasn't sure which twin was the princess's beloved."

"My dad," whispered Shea.

"Thomas never visited Cape Cod, except for the funeral of his father and brother. Adluo soldiers followed him home to find you."

Shea shook his head in disbelief. "My father was killed by a freak tornado soon after the funerals. I don't remember seeing any strange mermen in Oklahoma." Something gnawed at the back of his mind. Those strange sensations he'd experienced the day of the storm were similar to the way *transmutare* magick affected his body. "Can soldiers control the weather?"

Gregor nodded. "The sorcerer who accompanies Prince Demyan controls powerful dark magick. Anything is possible, but the objective of the mission was to find you, and that was before he knew of the Mark on your back. If he discovers it, he won't hesitate to kill you." Gregor looked over his shoulder. "Now, we must go, before my old comrades awaken and sound the alarm."

"How did you know?" Kae swam close by his side. "How did you know about him being the Aequorean heir?"

"I saw the Mark on his back one day when he was fishing, on the docks with the drylander girl. The same day I was ordered to capture him. It would be one thing to kidnap a drylander pawn, but quite another to anger the gods themselves."

Shea put the tragedy of the tornado out of his mind. There would be time to figure out the truth later. At the moment, he needed to focus on their current objective. "Your gods will surely be angered if the prince succeeds with his plans tonight. How can we warn the king without running into any guards?"

Kae's eyes lit up. "We can sneak in through the kitchens! It's always hectic in there, but especially during a feast. We'll find my mom or my dad and get a message to the king through them."

"Lead the way," said Shea. He saw the hesitation in Gregor's face. "What's wrong?"

Gregor spread his arms wide. "Even after so long on land, I still look like an Adluo soldier, not a kitchen servant."

"He's right," agreed Kae.

"I can escort you as far as the kitchens, but no further. I've already committed treason by helping you escape, and the penalty is immediate death."

Kae gasped, her eyes wide. She threw her arms around the older merman to hug him. "Thank you for freeing us. I never expected such sacrifice from an Adluo."

Gregor smiled sadly. "There's been too much killing. And I feel I owe this young prince a debt for my betrayal of his family. We are all ready for peace, Adluo and Aequorean alike."

"Yes," nodded Kae, her face serious.

"I'll keep Griffin and his men from sounding the alarm about your escape," Gregor said. "But you will need to be careful not to let Prince Demyan catch you. Neither of you will survive meeting him again, I guarantee it."

The dire warning didn't deter Shea. The king and his mother were both in jeopardy, and he could help. He glanced at Kae, wondering if she would risk her life for the royal family, or if he could stand putting her in that position. His chest ached at the thought of anyone hurting her again, but he had to give her the choice. "Kae, if you want to go with Gregor…"

She shook her head fast, curls tossing every which way. "I'm going with you to save the king. You'll never find your way through the castle without me, jellybrain!"

He smiled and grabbed her hand, decision made. "Lead the way."

The hustle and bustle of the busy royal kitchen was in high gear. Apron-clad mermaids zoomed around the sparkling marble counters, preparing elaborate trays of tiny hors d'oeuvres and finger foods. Another group of merfolk waited in a line to carry the silver bowls and trays out to the waiting guests. The mermaids worked swiftly, like a well-oiled machine, barely talking to one another. Shea wondered where the hum of noise came from, until the kitchen doors swung open and let in the full roar of the boisterous celebration in the outer room.

Kae held on to Shea's hand, pulling him along the wall of the kitchen as they tried to edge their way around the crowd of servants without getting in anyone's way. "You there! Kae!" barked one of the older mermaids, shaking a large shining butcher's knife in Kae's direction. "You and that boy! Get in line with the others to take the food out to the Great Hall."

Kae bowed her head in the mermaid's direction. "Right away, Mariella." Kae squeezed Shea's hand. "Stay close to me," she whispered. "We'll carry trays in together, and then exit the other end of the Great Hall."

"Okay," he whispered, glancing around uneasily. He followed behind Kae when she took her place in the line of servers. He watched a mermaid cook slice the tentacles off several jellyfish. Others lay tangled in a net on the table next to the chopping block, their scared thoughts a low buzz in the corner of Shea's mind, like a fly he couldn't swat.

The doors leading in to the Great Hall pushed open, the sounds of laughter wafting into the kitchen along the current. Shea peered through the doors as one server held it wide open for another. Guests gathered at round tables, their bright and various colors clashing merrily. Buffet tables laden with different seaweeds and sushis ran the length of the far wall. Young mermaids swished through the crowds with large silver platters piled high with delicacies, placing trays on each of the tables for the partiers to pick from. The door swung shut. He leaned closer to Kae and whispered in her ear. "Who all is out there at the feast?"

She turned her head. "Remember all the merfolk cheering in the courtyard?" He nodded. "All of them. Everyone is welcome at the Solstice banquet, from the royal families to the farmers. That's why most of the servers in here are young. Everyone of age gets to partake in the feast, even the servants."

"Wow." Shea tried to imagine how big the room must be to hold everyone. He could only see a small bit of it through the door. The doors pushed inward again, and a mermaid carrying an empty crystal bowl swam past the line of waiting servers, straight to where Mariella wielded her knife. "We're running low on the Eucheuma seeds, Mariella," the girl said. "The Pacific Prince said there were more somewhere?"

Mariella nodded her head toward some wooden crates by the door. "In one of those boxes," she told the girl. "I hope this doesn't lead to trouble."

Shea nudged Kae again. "What does she mean? Trouble? Is this something to do with Prince Demyan?"

Kae shook her head. "Eucheuma are fermented seeds from the Fiji Islands in the Pacific. The elders like to consume them because it helps them relax, but if they have too many they get a little…funny."

"Funny?" Shea eyed the blue and green seeds as the mermaid headed into the Great Hall with her full bowl.

"Intoxicated. One time some of the Arctic mermen ate too many, and got caught in the nets of a fishing trawler and started fighting with the sailors on board. To end the conflict, King Koios sank the boat. The fishermen were rescued, but luckily no one believed their stories about crazed mermen attacking their ship."

"So why serve them at all?"

Kae shrugged. "It's tradition, I guess."

The noise drifting into the kitchen from the Great Hall died suddenly. An eerie silence spread, as cooks and servers alike stopped what they were doing and turned their heads to stare toward the swinging doors. After several hushed moments, one of the mermaid servers pushed through the doors.

"It's King Koios!" she cried breathlessly. "He's been poisoned!"

Chaos erupted in the previously organized kitchen, as the mermaids dropped what they were doing and swam toward the Great Hall to see what was going on. The anxious servants swept Shea and Kae along with them, spilling into the Hall in time to see the unconscious king carried away by guards.

"Mom," Kae breathed, watching Kira follow the king out the door.

"He's still alive, praise Neptune," the mermaid next to Kae told her friend. "Let's hope the healers can find a cure for the poison."

"How do they know it was poison?" The other mermaid looked frightened. "Will the kitchen staff be blamed?"

"Over there!" Kae elbowed Shea's ribs and pointed toward a smaller crowd of merfolk, crouched on the floor next to one of the tables, calling for healers and wailing with distress. A merman with blue hair lay on the cold floor unmoving, his eyes unusually wide as they stared off into the distance, the whites of his eyes criss-crossed with blue lines. His lips were swollen and disfigured, as blue as his hair. A second body lay near his side, small and childlike, with raven black hair and staring eyes streaked with blue. Adluo servants surrounded the boy, holding back the crowd.

"Are they...?" Shea couldn't finish the question, riveted by the gruesome spectacle. His tail twitched nervously, stirring the water around him.

"Dead," Kae agreed, nodding her head slowly. "I hope King Koios will be okay."

"Who are those two?"

They inched through the crowd, closer to the bodies. Kae gasped with recognition. "The merman with the blue hair is Prince Azul from the Pacific. He traveled to the Solstice to find a wife. The boy is King Theosisto of the Southern Ocean, the cousin your mother is going to marry. Was going to marry. Oh my starfish! What's going to happen now?"

Shea's shoulders slumped forward. "We're too late. We didn't save anyone."

Kae whirled around to face him, green eyes blazing. She poked a finger hard into his chest. "You stop that talk right now, Shea MacNamara. King Koios isn't dead yet. There's still time."

"Time for what?"

"To find the antidote to the poison."

"Right." A new light shone in Shea's eyes as his shoulders straightened.

Kae pointed toward the table. "Let's start over there." The pair swam to where the blue-haired merman lay on the cold stone floor. Adluo guards ignored the larger body, pushing past to get to their boy king, lifting him gently and withdrawing from the Great Hall. Pacific servants hurried forward toward their prince, while the rest of the crowd drifted away, talking amongst themselves of poison, treason, and the suddenly fragile peace accord.

Shea tried his best to ignore the panic in the voices around him. He needed to concentrate. "What's this mess on the floor?" He stooped to pick a seed from a scattering of broken glass. He rolled it between his fingers. It was the size

252

of a small grape, but darker green in color and softer to the touch, as if overly ripe. As he squeezed, a trickle of blue juice escaped the thin skin and floated upward through the salty water, leaving a tangy sweet scent in its wake. "There seem to be a lot of them spilled here, and shards of glass."

"Eucheuma," Kae said, wrinkling her nose. She glanced around the Great Hall. "But there's a bowl in the center of every table, so that can't be the source of the poison."

Shea checked the crowd to confirm that indeed no one else was turning blue. He saw the crystal bowls on every table…including in the center of the King's table. Realization dawned. He grabbed Kae's arm. "The king had a separate bowl to eat from! Maybe the royals who were poisoned ate from a different stash of seeds! We need to gather samples, the ones scattered under the table. They must contain the poison!"

Many of the seeds had already been swept away by the crowd of onlookers and guards, but together Shea and Kae managed to find a handful left unbroken. He cradled the soft seeds between his cupped hands. "We need a quiet place to examine these."

"This way." Kae pushed open the swinging double doors, into the empty kitchen.

Shea dropped the seeds onto the chopping block where Mariella stood earlier dismembering tentacles. The seeds floated down onto the surface, their glistening green skins translucent under the bright kitchen lights. Mariella's butcher's knife sat gleaming on the table, next to the net of squirming jellyfish.

"What..." Kae started to ask.

Shea put his fingers against her lips. "Hush." His eyes focused on the wriggling net and he bent his head closer to the creatures. "I'm listening."

Kae looked at the netted creatures. After several long moments of silence, she asked, "Can you really hear their thoughts?"

He frowned. "Can't you? Isn't it a mermaid thing?"

She shook her head. "It's rumored that the king can hear the thoughts of all the creatures in his ocean. But most merfolk I know can only hear when you speak out loud."

"I guess I have something in common with my grandfather after all. Have you heard of something called an underwater lion?"

Kae shook her head, looking confused.

"These little jellyfish call themselves *nettles*."

"Obviously," Kae huffed impatiently. "Because that's what they are."

Shea rolled his eyes. "It's not as obvious to those of us who didn't grow up underwater. The nettles have poison in their tentacles, but they say it's nothing compared to a larger species they refer to as 'the lions.' Lions are big, with tentacles growing a hundred feet long."

"Oh wait," Kae said, her eyes widening. "Do you mean *Lion's Mane*? Those are the big jellyfish that come to this area to breed in the springtime. They're usually gone by Solstice, because they need colder water, like in the Arctic Ocean. My father has a story about one who…"

"Apparently," Shea interrupted, "If you grind enough of them, the poison is powerful. We need to tell someone, and fast."

"Who?"

"How about your mother? She'll know what to do."

Kae led the way through the swinging doors and into the Great Hall. "But we still don't know who put the poison in the seeds."

Shea pressed his lips together in a tight line. "Unfortunately, the only eyewitnesses have already ended up on the chopping block."

Kae frowned. "Jellyfish don't have eyes."

"Not everyone needs eyes to see what is going on around them." They swam through the thinning crowd. "Let me go first," he insisted, swimming ahead of her. "I'll check if the coast is clear."

Kae seemed puzzled. "We're underwater, Shea. There's no coast here."

He sighed and shook his head, deciding it would take too long to explain. They were almost out of the Great Hall when a hulking merman appeared out of nowhere, blocking their escape. He crossed his arms over his muscled chest. "And where do you two think you're going?"

Kae pushed forward and threw her arms around his waist. "Thank Neptune we found you!"

The big merman's face softened. "I've been searching all over for you, my daughter! I went to Windmill Point, but was told you'd already left with the son of the princess." He glanced at Shea again, this time with a less menacing expression.

Relief swept through Shea. "This is your father? I thought we were captured again for sure."

"Call me Lybio, my Prince. I serve the royal family. But what do you mean, captured *again*? Have the guards mistreated you?" He narrowed his eyes and touched the kelp bandage wrapped around Kae's torso.

When she didn't respond to her father, Shea spoke. "Prince Demyan tortured her. With his own knife. Now he's poisoned the king and we need to tell someone which antidote to use…"

Lybio put out a hand to stop the flow of words. "This sounds like a conversation better held in private." He motioned for them to follow him into the courtyard. They crossed the open expanse quickly and reentered the summer castle through another door. The passageway was darkened and silent.

"Father, there's little time," Kae blurted once the door closed behind them. "We can talk as we swim, but we must hurry to the king's chamber. His life may depend on it!"

"Very well, but I expect an explanation."

"You'll get one, sir," Shea assured. They swam swiftly down the long, empty hallway.

CHAPTER TWENTY FOUR

Shea saw no one, soldier or mermaid, as they swam through the empty hallways. The Solstice guests were either in the Great Hall awaiting word of the King's condition, or locked behind chamber doors, fearful of what might happen next.

Kae's father stopped in front of a wooden door, more elaborately carved and painted than all the others. No guards hovered anywhere nearby. "Where are the soldiers?" Kae asked as Lybio knocked on the wooden door. He shook his head in silence.

A very pale mermaid opened the door, throwing it wide when she saw them in the hallway. "Oh, Kae! You're safe! Praise the gods!" She wrapped her arms around her.

"Mom!" Kae hugged her tight. "We were prisoners! It was awful. But we escaped, and we're here to help."

"Why is this kelp stuck to your collarbone?" The mermaid drew a trembling finger along the bandage. Before Kae could answer, she turned her attention to Shea. "Is this him? The son of the princess?" He nodded and she bowed her head. "My name is Kira and I serve your family. I fear you may inherit the throne sooner than anticipated."

His stomach lurched. "We're here to save the king, not gain the throne."

Lybio swam to Kira's side and held both of her arms with his large hands. "Where are the healers? Why does no one attend the king but you?"

Kira shook her head. "I don't know, Lybio. Prince Demyan dismissed the soldiers who were guarding the king. The healers went away to consult their library and seek an antidote. Prince Demyan told us his soldiers are restless because of the poisoning, especially as their young king lies dead and King Koios yet lives. They felt there must be treachery afoot. He said he suspects it was the Pacific Prince, as the Eucheuma seeds came from Pacific territory."

Lybio snorted. "There's treachery afoot, all right. What else did the prince say?"

"He told Princess Brynn that rogue Adluo soldiers were holding her bastard son captive, and planned to harm him if the peace accords did not continue as planned. With the king near death, he insisted they speak with the High

259

Chancellor immediately, to do something official to quell the unrest." She turned again to her daughter. "How in Neptune's name did you escape from Adluo soldiers?"

"Mom, there isn't time to explain. Where are the healers located?"

"The poison is jellyfish toxin," Shea added.

Kira covered her mouth with both hands. "Blessed Neptune! But how…"

"There is no time. Go. Bring a healer to fashion the antidote," Lybio ordered. "The children and I will guard the king. Hurry." He put a hand against the small of her back and urged her into the hallway, closing the chamber door behind her. Lybio pushed a stone bench toward the door to block it from opening.

Shea swam to the king's side. Kae followed him. After staring at the sleeping merman for a few moments, Shea's hand found hers. "This is my grandfather?"

Kae looked from the sleeping figure to Shea's face. Her eyes widened as she squeezed his fingers. "Jumping jellyfish! You are so much like him! I mean, except for the beard, of course. But the rest of your face… No wonder Prince Demyan guessed who you are so quickly!"

Shea's eyes never left the king's face. "I'd like to meet him, you know?"

"I know." Kae released his hand and put her arm around his waist. "It's going to be okay."

Shea addressed Lybio. "You said someone told you we left Windmill Point? Did you talk to Gregor?"

Lybio shook his head. "The Adluos were not the only ones with spies on dry land. The king thought it wise to keep an eye on you. You are heir to his throne, after all."

"King Koios…knows…about me?"

Urgent knocking on the door interrupted them. The doorknob rattled. Lybio put a finger to his lips before calling out, "Who seeks to enter?"

"Lybio, it's me." It was Kira's voice. "I couldn't find the royal Healer, but I have Lady Kata, from the Caribbean, here with me. She promises to be discreet, and knows how to mix an antidote."

Shea helped Lybio move the bench. The chamber door swung open, and Kira entered, followed by a tall mermaid with a flowing mane of jet-black curls and brown skin shimmering like melted chocolate. Lybio closed the door behind them, and pushed the stone bench into place.

Lady Kata placed her voluminous silver bag on the table under the window, and pulled opened the drawstring. She withdrew several stoppered vials of thick liquid in brilliant hues, lining them carefully in a row. "I am told this is jellyfish toxin at work?"

"Yes," Shea confirmed. "Ground from a type called Lion's Mane."

"We don't have that species in my home waters, but I have heard tell of its powerful sting," Lady Kata said, her black curls waving wildly as she nodded her head.

Kira hovered next to her, hands clasped together. "What can we do to help?"

"You already did the most important thing. You discovered the source of the poison. Now you must let me work. And please, try not to stir the current." They watched in silence as Lady Kata chose three of the small colored bottles: one crimson, one deep blue, and one bright white. She poured five thick, fat drops from each bottle into a clear glass mug, the gooey liquids oozing out of their containers and through the salt water, to settle at the bottom of the glass. The healer swirled a glass rod through the mug to mix the colors until the muddy liquid appeared a uniform lavender color within the glass.

"There now," she pronounced when she had finished stirring. "King Koios must drink this, and then we must wait again. If you are correct about the source of the poison, he will awaken to rejoin us. If you are mistaken, he will stop breathing within the hour." She handed the mug to Kira.

Kira hesitated. "Should we wait for the princess to return?"

Lady Kata shook her head. "He must drink this now, before the toxins spread any further within his system. You saw what happened to the other mermen, the gallant Prince of the Pacific and the poor hapless boy who would be king."

"But what if it's not the right antidote?" Kira glanced at Lybio. "How sure are you that Lion's Mane was used to poison the food?"

"I'm positive," Shea interjected. "The nettles in the kitchen told me so."

"The… What?" Kira almost dropped the mug of the gooey formula.

Kae steadied her mother's hand. "Shea can speak with his mind to other creatures in the ocean. Trust him."

Kira placed the mug on the table. "I'm not sure…"

Lybio swept through the room with a flick of his powerful tail. He grabbed the mug and swam to the bedside. "We cannot allow King Koios to die today. This is our best hope for saving him." The gelatinous goo dribbled from the mug straight into the king's mouth and down his throat.

"Now we wait," Lady Kata said. Everyone in the room edged closer to the king's bedside. The tension rose with each passing moment. Seconds felt like hours. Minutes felt like entire days.

"It's no use," Kira said after several long minutes ticked by. "We must have been misled. And now the king will die!"

"No, look!" cried Kae, pointing. Eyelashes fluttered against pale cheeks. Faint blue streaks still traced through the whites of his eyes, but the king focused his gaze on the Caribbean princess by his side and smiled.

"Lady Kata," he said, his voice hoarse. "I must have dozed off during your tale. Would you please finish your story of how you met Prince Azul?"

Lady Kata smiled widely, her brilliant white teeth shining against the darkness of her skin. "He lives!"

The king furrowed his brow in confusion and glanced around at the ring of concerned faces. "What in Poseidon's name is going on? Why am I in my chamber? Why does my voice sound so rough?" His eyes connected with Lybio. "Lybio! What happened?"

"You were poisoned, Sire," Lybio said, bowing his head. "At the Solstice banquet. The Eucheuma seeds."

"Poisoned!" The king tried to sit up, but fell against his kelp pillow, raising a hand to massage his temple. "Is that why my head is pounding so?"

Lybio nodded. "Your grandson was the one to figure it out, Sire."

Shea watched as the king turned his head ever so slowly until their eyes connected. "Ah, we meet at last. I hope you have not had too harsh an introduction to our underwater world."

"No, sir." He opened his mouth to say more, but bit his bottom lip instead. He did not want to get into an argument with the king at their very first meeting.

King Koios studied him for a long moment, stroking his beard. "I'm sorry you grew up without your mother. Someday, when you are King of the Atlantic, you'll understand making hard decisions. I thought you would be safer on dry land, at least until we could be sure of your mermaid blood."

Shea rolled his eyes, unwilling to let the old merman off the hook so easily, but kept his mouth closed.

A slow smile spread across the king's face. "I can see you are reluctant to argue with an infirm old merman, but your eyes betray the fire in your heart. Just like your mother. I anticipate many interesting discussions when I regain my health." He glanced around the circle and frowned. "Speaking of Brynneliana, where is my daughter? Why does she not attend me?"

"She is with Prince Demyan, Sire," Kira said. "They went to seek the High Chancellor."

"I'm afraid the prince will try to force a wedding tonight," Lybio added darkly.

"Tonight?" The king turned to Kira. "How can she and Theo marry tonight? Isn't he as sick as I am from those infernal seeds?"

"King Theosisto is dead. As is Prince Azul. You are lucky to have survived."

"So who, pray tell, will be getting married?"

Kira put a hand on the king's arm. "Prince Demyan seeks the crown and your daughter's hand for himself. He said his soldiers were out of his control because of the treachery tainting the Solstice. He claimed the guards would kill Shea and everyone else in the castle unless the marriage happened tonight. With your life hanging by a thread, Brynn saw no other choice."

"It wasn't rogue soldiers," Shea said. "They were acting on orders from Demyan himself."

"That's a pretty big accusation," said the king, his expression grave. "How can you be so sure?"

"Demyan questioned us while we were bound. He threatened us both with a knife, and caused the wound at Kae's neck. He would have killed us both, but decided to keep us as hostages, once he recognized me."

"He knows you?" The king's eyes flew wider. "Lybio, does Prince Demyan know of the Mark on my grandson's back?" Lady Kata moved forward to stuff another pillow of seaweed behind him to help steady his still-feeble body.

Shea's eyes darted from the king to Lybio, wondering if everyone knew about the birthmark. He felt like a small chess piece in a much larger game he didn't understand.

Lybio shook his head. "No, Sire."

"Then there is still time."

"That is all well and good, Sire," said Lybio, "but what of the rest of the Adluos? Who will reign in their war-mongering ways?"

Kae's voice sounded small, as if unsure whether she should speak in the king's presence. "Most Adluos are as eager for peace as the Aequoreans. They are not all as evil as their prince. An Adluo helped us escape."

The king nodded slowly. "My wife's brother was King of the Southern Ocean. Brynneliana is half Adluo. They are not a bad clan. They only lack proper leadership."

"Perhaps that is the real reason the gods have marked both your daughter and your grandson with the trident," said Lady Kata. Everyone in the room turned to the Caribbean mermaid. "The gods don't make mistakes."

King Koios smiled, lifting a hand to touch Lady Kata's cheek. "I knew there was good reason to invite you to sit at my table. Your brilliance shines through the darkest of nights." He turned to focus on Shea. "The Lady is right. Your mother's destiny lies in the Southern Ocean."

"As long as she doesn't have to marry that evil prince guy," Shea said, swishing his tail. "She doesn't have to, right?"

"Not if I have anything to say about it," the king agreed. A sharp knocking resounded through the chamber. The room fell silent. King Koios nodded his head from where it lay propped on the pillows of seaweed.

Lybio swam to the chamber door. "Who seeks to enter?"

"Unlock this door at once, you sniveling sea worm!" a shrill voice rang out. "I heard my brother lies near death! I demand to see him!"

The king nodded again, his eyes twinkling. "Let's have some fun with my dear sister, shall we? Let her enter. Shea, stand in the shadows for now and don't breathe a word." He relaxed into his pillows and closed his eyes, pretending to be unconscious once again.

Lybio swam to the chamber door and pushed aside the stone bench. Princess Winona swept into the room, her golden scepter gleaming in her hand as she shook it in Lybio's face. "How dare you leave me standing in the hallway like a…like a mere servant? You are useless, you old jellyfish! You'll be mucking out the dolphin stalls by nightfall!"

"I apologize, my Princess," Lybio said, bowing his head. "Your niece thought it best to use extreme caution with the king, since there's an assassin on the loose in the castle."

The elderly princess snorted, her eyes sweeping the crowd gathered next to the king. She clutched her free hand to her chest. "My dear half-brother lies on death's doorstep, no doubt at the hands of that Adluo prince. In the interest of peace, I shall be forced to take over the Atlantic throne."

"You?" Kira put her hands on her hips. "Why would you become queen, when it is Brynn who bears the Mark?"

Princess Winona narrowed her eyes. "Isn't it obvious? Koios's wife was Adluo so Brynn bears the blood of their clan. She shall have to rule the Southern Ocean with her new husband by her side." Princess Winona let out an exaggerated sigh. "I never wanted the responsibility of ruling, but I shall bear it for the sake of my people."

"Not if the king survives," Lybio said.

"He won't." Princess Winona shook her head, her face filled with remorse. "I spoke to his healers earlier." She took the king's limp hand into her own, squeezing it gently.

Suddenly, the king grabbed Winona's wrist and opened his eyes. "What if the healers are wrong?" He chuckled, a big smile on his face. "Surprise!"

Winona's eyes widened to the size of giant clamshells. She screamed and tried to pull away from the king's grip. The golden scepter flew from her other hand, dropping to the chamber floor with a loud clatter, crashing to pieces with gems scattering across the tiles. All eyes turned to see a trickle of blue oozing from the scepter's head, through a hole where one of the gems had been.

Lady Kata pointed at the oily blue trail rising toward the chamber ceiling. "The jellyfish toxin! She poisoned her own brother!"

The king tightened his grip on Winona's wrist, his expression grim. "You? You did this to me? But, Winona, why?"

Her ensuing laughter sounded crazed. "Isn't it obvious? I should have been crowned Queen of the Atlantic long ago! Father thought you would be the stronger leader, but he was wrong. *Wrong!*"

Sadness filled the king's eyes. "Being a strong leader means making hard choices and compromises. The gods did not choose you, Winona." Lybio swam forward and grabbed both arms of the princess.

"The gods were wrong!" Her teeth bared in a feral grin as she struggled against Lybio's strong grasp. He tightened his grip and the old princess winced in pain. "How dare you handle royalty in such a way!"

"How dare you attempt such treachery?" Lybio countered. "How did you think to escape notice?"

She ceased her struggle. "The timing was perfect. One of Prince Demyan's soldiers, a nice young fellow named Zan, brought me the blue tincture and suggested the plan of action.

He told me the blame would fall on Prince Demyan and I would inherit the Atlantic."

"And you chose to work with foreign soldiers against your own clan? Against your own brother?" The king shook his head slowly. "Zan is no mere soldier but Demyan's second in command and a powerful sorcerer. He never intended for his master to take any blame. You, my dear, were used."

Shock registered on Winona's face. "But... But..."

Shea swam forward out of Kira's shadow. "Prince Demyan blames our king for the death of his father. He'll stop at nothing until he rules the whole of the Atlantic as well as his own ocean. You played into his scheme because you are a selfish old woman who cares for nothing but herself. That is why the gods didn't choose you."

Winona swiveled her head to stare at him, her lips curled to reply when her eyes widened with confusion and surprise. "You... You look like my half-brother...when he was a mere guppy of a boy. Who are you, a ghost?" Her trembling hand reached for Shea.

He pulled away from her touch. "Not a ghost. Not a rumor. I'm here to save my mother before it's too late." He turned to the king. "Now, Sire, how *do* we save her from Demyan?"

"I have a plan."

Chapter Twenty Five

Shea was out of breath by the time he and Kae zipped down the long corridor to the High Chancellor's chamber. As he rounded yet another corner, he slammed straight into Kae. "Stop," she hissed. "They're just up ahead."

He peered around the corner, trying to steady his breathing. Demyan's right hand gripped Princess Brynneliana by the elbow and another Adluo merman stood to his left. Two of his armed soldiers hovered at the far end of the hallway, keeping guard. "Shouldn't we go stop them?"

Kae shook her head and grabbed his arm with both hands. "The king said to wait. We're supposed to watch them and stall for more time if need be. Only the king can stop them."

"Where is the High Chancellor?" Demyan's voice carried through the hall. He banged his fist upon the door.

The merman at his side rolled his eyes. "Maybe he remained in the Great Hall with the crowd. I suggest we go seek him there."

The princess's voice sounded unsteady. "Perhaps we should return to my father's chambers to await the return of the healers. They may have found an antidote by now."

"Let us hope they are busy finding a cure for such evil treachery," sniffed Demyan. "Poison is the weapon of women and the weak. Who in Poseidon's name would ever wish harm upon poor helpless Theosisto? I fear the repercussions of our cousin's death."

The merman at Demyan's side started coughing, and Shea wondered if he was trying to hide his laughter. Shea snorted with disgust and turned to whisper in Kae's ear. "Yeah, right. As if that evil prince wasn't behind the whole thing."

Kae elbowed him in the ribs. "Hush!"

"In the meantime, my dearest Princess," Demyan said, "We must hasten to secure the peace between our oceans by binding it with our marriage. Tonight."

Shea heard his mother gasp and peered around the corner again. Brynn looked horrified. "I thought you meant signing the engagement tablet. You want to marry me tonight?"

"My dearest Princess, it is for the good of the oceans. Our oceans, Atlantic and Southern both. We need to reassure the Adluo soldiers that this Solstice celebration was not some elaborate trap to kill their beloved young king. We must present a united front to our friends and enemies alike, especially in light of the death of Prince Azul. The Pacific King will seek retribution."

"But no one could think the Aequoreans would purposefully poison our guests! Not when my father hovers on the edge of life from the same poison!"

"Desperate times call for desperate actions." Demyan banged one last time on the chamber door, and seemed startled when it swung inward. In the doorway hovered a merman with long white hair and flowing beard. Over his bushy white brows sat a verdigris circlet of metal shaped like a wreath of laurel leaves, the ancient symbol of both victory and honor. In one hand he held a stone tablet. "Forgive me," said the merman. "I was reading and must have been lost in thought."

Demyan's voice was smooth as an oil slick. "It's quite all right, High Chancellor. I hope we are not disturbing you too greatly by visiting your chambers."

"Not at all," the white-haired merman insisted. "Come in, come in, all three of you. Do you bring news of the king's condition? Has he yet awoken?"

"My father still sleeps," Brynn told him as she swam into the chamber. "But he yet clings to this life."

"*Clings* being the operative word," Demyan said. He signaled to his guards, who swam closer. "Stay right outside this doorway. Let no one enter." The pair nodded and posted themselves to either side of the chamber, staring straight ahead. Demyan entered and swung the door closed behind him.

Shea faced Kae, anxious about being shut out of whatever was going on behind that door. How could he keep his mother safe if he didn't know what was going on? "Now what do we do?"

"There's no other way out of the chamber," Kae said in a low voice, resting a reassuring hand on his arm. "So we wait here."

He frowned. "I hate waiting."

"I know, me too. But it's easier when we're together."

He pulled her closer and gave her a quick kiss on the lips, before she could object. Kissing underwater was a whole new experience, his gills pumping faster with excitement. He'd gotten used to the constant taste of the saltwater in his mouth, but tasting it on Kae's lips was somehow different and totally awesome. He leaned in to kiss her again, but she moved away.

"What's wrong?"

Kae shook her head. "We shouldn't. The king wouldn't approve."

"Why would he care? Because I'm his grandson?" His eyes flicked to her lips as she nervously licked them.

She cupped his cheek with her hand, her green eyes wide. "Because you're his heir. He knew about you this whole time. There are no secrets from King Koios."

"I don't want to keep how I feel about you a secret." Shea put his arms around her waist. "Besides, I can't really be his heir. I'm half-drylander, remember?"

"Don't use that word, Shea. Drylander is an ugly, insulting word that means you are no better than a jellyfish."

His mouth quirked into a grin. "You call me names all the time anyway."

Kae giggled. "Remember when I called you Garbage Boy?"

"I remember." He slowly lowered his mouth onto hers for a real kiss, giving her plenty of time to pull away if she really wanted to, but she didn't. Instead, her body melted against his and she returned the kiss. His blood pumped faster and his tailfin started fluttering all by itself. He could totally get used to this having a girlfriend thing, especially since kissing Kae was better than anything he'd ever experienced in his life. With her in his arms, he felt invincible, like he could do anything he set his mind to.

"Well, what do we have here?" One of the large Adluo guards towered over them, a leer on his face and spear in his hand. Kae trembled in his arms while Shea struggled for something to say.

"What'd you find, Clive?" called the guard still stationed at the door.

The Adluo looming over Shea smirked. "Two little lovebirds, hiding in the shadows."

Before Shea could put a coherent thought together, Kae spoke up. "Please, sir, we merely sought a quiet corner. If my father finds us he'll send me away to live with relatives and Neptune knows what else he might do…" she let the sentence trail off.

The guard narrowed his eyes and frowned. He shook a stern finger in Shea's face. "Do you have true feelings for this girl?"

Shea felt his cheeks burn. He tried not to look at Kae, but couldn't help but see her smiling. "Yes, sir, I do."

"Do you love her?"

Shea's eyes flew open wide at the question. "I…I don't know…"

The guard's frown deepened. "Then this is no way to treat a lady, you jellyfish. Ask her out proper next time, and get her father's permission. And decide how you feel about her before you go making a public spectacle of yourselves."

"Yes, sir." Shea bowed his head in deference, thrilled to realize the Adluo had no idea who they were, and better still – he was going to let them go! He grabbed Kae's hand and started to swim backward. "You're right, of course. I should go speak with her father right now."

The guard nodded his head. "Good lad. These may be dark times, but it's no excuse for that kind of behavior. You should always do the right thing, especially with a mermaid as lovely as this."

"Let's go find your father right now, sweetie." Shea tugged Kae along, swimming around the next corner where they stopped to regroup. Shea furrowed his eyebrows as he peeked around to see if the guard followed them. "He went back to his post." He turned back to Kae and found a strange smile lighting her face. "What is it?"

She poked him in the side. "So you have feelings for me, huh?"

He felt defensive and worried, all at the same time. What if she didn't feel the same about him? What if she made fun of him for declaring himself to that guard? "What was I supposed to say? Should I have told him we were there to spy on Prince Demyan?"

Kae's face fell. "So you were lying?"

"No, no! Not about that. It's just so…complicated." He didn't know how to explain, or what he wanted to say to

278

her. He certainly never felt this way about a girl before, but how do you put that into words without sounding like a jerk? "My whole life changed in so many ways today, I'm not sure what I think about anything. I do know you are very special to me, and I don't want to lose you."

Kae glanced over his shoulder. "Someone's coming. We need to hide. Quickly, through here." She grabbed his hand and pulled him toward the windows overlooking the courtyard.

She released his hand and swam right through the window, disappearing below the opening. He realized there was no glass and followed her out into the open yard as the voices grew louder in the hallway.

"Such a shame, marring the Solstice when it should be such a happy occasion. Over the last thousand years in Atlantis, I have seen many kings and queens come and go. Death is but another part of life and should not be feared. It is all in the hands of the gods. You should know that better than most, Prince Demyan."

"What do you mean, sir?" Shea recognized the prince's voice.

"I mean no disrespect, of course. But news of your father's death must have come as a shock to you. And then to lose both your uncle and aunt, and now your cousin in such quick succession. It is remarkable that you are holding up so well."

"We all do what we must for the good of the clans." The voices all got louder as they swam closer to where Shea and Kae were hidden.

"Tell me, is there anything I can do to ease the tensions of the gathered crowd?"

Demyan's chuckle sent a chill down Shea's spine. "Why, yes, High Chancellor, thank you for asking. I believe there is something you can do for us." Shea peered over the edge of the window and saw Demyan take his mother's hand and yank her to his side. "Something you can do for all of us, and change this day from a sad occasion into a happy one."

"Yes?"

"Marry us. Today, on the Solstice, so that our union will join our two clans and be blessed in the eyes of the gods."

The group stopped in front of the window, against the opposite wall. The two soldiers hovered at the rear of the small procession and looked surprised by Demyan's words. The High Chancellor pursed his lips. "It is still a Solstice holiday until midnight, so a marriage tonight would be considered legitimate, both in the eyes of the gods and the Council of Atlantis."

His mother struggled against Demyan's grasp. "Perhaps we should wait until my father awakens."

"If we wait," Demyan said, enunciating each word, "We may miss this opportunity to form a legal union. The next Solstice isn't for six months. Those unhappy soldiers might act in a...drastic manner." His mother's face paled.

The Chancellor leaned in to peer more closely into her face. "Are you feeling well, my dear? For truly, I'm sure there is no harm in waiting until winter as originally planned..."

"No!" roared Demyan. "We will be married TONIGHT." He paused to take a deep breath. "I will not put my soldiers at risk from further treachery by rogue Aequorean rebels, nor will I swim in circles while the Pacific clan mounts an attack on either the Atlantic or Southern Ocean. Perform the ceremony NOW."

"But...But Prince Demyan," spluttered the High Chancellor. "Marriage is a sacred rite, a public act, a ceremony of pomp which demands witnesses. Especially a wedding which will bind two clans together for hundreds of years." He shook his head. "I can not perform such a ceremony within the confines of a hallway. Tradition dictates such a wedding be held in a public place, before the people of both clans."

"Fine. Let us adjourn to the outer courtyards." Demyan tugged on the princess's hand. He turned to the merman ever present by his side. "Zan, would you be so kind as to dispatch the servants to spread the word? The princess and I will be married in the courtyard in one hour's time. While you are at it, you should take care of that other contingency we discussed earlier in my chamber."

Zan bowed at the waist. "As you wish, Sire." He swam down the hall and out of sight.

The High Chancellor's face lit with smiles. "Oh, yes. A courtyard wedding is a splendid idea! We can adjourn afterward to the surface to enjoy the spectacle of the drylander fireworks in the night sky. Their arcs of colored fire always makes me feel like a guppy once more."

The desperation on his mother's face tore at Shea. He clenched his fists and started forward, but Kae dragged him back. "The king said to watch and wait."

"Wait for what? That bully to win? I can't let him do this, Kae. It's not right!" He turned in time to see the High Chancellor swim in the direction of his chambers.

"I need to find my formal robes, and the wedding tablets to make it all official. I shall meet you in the large courtyard, where the parade took place at sunset."

Demyan nodded to the larger guard. "Stay with the old merman. Make sure he comes to the courtyard as fast as possible. You heard him, this wedding must take place tonight to be legitimate."

The Adluo guard bowed low from the waist. "Whatever you command of me, Sire."

Chapter Twenty Six

Shea followed Kae through the winding corridors of the castle to the entrance of the courtyard gardens. They'd left Lybio and Kira waiting with King Koios as he regained his strength, but Shea didn't want to take the chance that the marriage of his mother to the prince would be over before the king could get out of his bed. Not when he could stop it. Or at least delay it. He had no idea how, but he had to try.

They emerged through a doorway and saw a large crowd gathered in the courtyard. Elevated above the crowd, he saw his mother hovering next to Demyan under an arch of billowing white silk, held on either end by a dark-haired mermaid. As they watched, the merman Demyan referred to as the High Chancellor swam to join them, resplendent in flowing white robes.

They wove their way through the crowded courtyard, careful not to show their faces above the crowd, while Kae explained the old merman's importance. "The High Chancellor of Atlantis is head of the Supreme Council, and also head of the university. He's well over a thousand years old, and rumor has it he knows Poseidon on a first name basis. He doesn't usually leave Atlantis, but your grandfather invited him to witness the peace accords."

The High Chancellor began to pontificate to the gathered audience, on and on about the virtues of leading the Atlantic Ocean away from the ways of war, and binding the oceans' clans in peace. Kae stopped swimming and grabbed Shea's arm. "What exactly are we supposed to do to stop this ceremony?"

"I don't know yet," he said quietly. "We need to stall things until the king gets here. I think we'll be fine as long as the Chancellor guy keeps up the lecture and doesn't get to the ceremony part."

The Chancellor's long white beard flowed with the current, his high bushy eyebrows bouncing to emphasize his words. Finally his lecture wound down and he concluded by saying, "This marriage will form the perfect center to a new and lasting peace. I can see no reason to wait until the Winter Solstice to perform the ceremony to join your two clans."

A feeble cheer rose from the crowd. The deaths of King Theosisto and Prince Azul, as well as the uncertain fate of the Atlantic King, dampened the crowd's enthusiasm for a wedding, but not for the idea of peace.

"My father planned..." Princess Brynn said, but Demyan cut off her words by yanking her hard against him, knocking the breath out of her.

"My bride-to-be seems to forget her father lies unconscious." With his free hand he pushed a stray hair behind her ear. "And let's not forget, King Koios himself arranged this marriage between our clans."

"At the point of your sword," hissed Brynn. "Where my son is now." The crowd gasped collectively, and a low murmur started along the edges of the crowd.

Kae whispered, "I told you I heard rumors about your existence, Shea. It seems others have heard the tales."

Demyan raised his voice above the rumbling of the onlookers. "I think my poor darling princess is confused and distraught from the attempt on her father's life."

The High Chancellor nodded. "All the more reason to reassure the crowds, as you pointed out before."

"My soldiers will keep the peace." Demyan glanced at the Adluos in the crowded courtyard. "They'll do whatever I tell them. They all know the consequences for disobedience."

Brynn's eyes narrowed as she stared defiantly into his face. "I thought you said you couldn't control the ones who held my son?"

Oblivious to the tension crackling between the not-so-happy couple, the High Chancellor withdrew a thin marble tablet from deep within one of the many folds of his robes. He chuckled, waggling his bushy eyebrows. "I must have had a premonition to have brought the marriage tablet along on my journey. We need the proper words to mark this auspicious occasion."

Before Brynn could protest again, Demyan wrapped a muscled arm around her waist and squeezed. She gasped and bowed her head. "Yes, yes, that's all well and good. Let's get this over with."

"No, they can't get married," Shea yelled. "This is wrong!" His voice rang through the courtyard and other merfolk turned to stare at him. Demyan turned his head to see who protested, but couldn't pick him out of the crowd. Kae tried to hold Shea back but he wriggled out of her grasp and swam forward toward the dais. His movement caught Demyan's attention, and the prince quirked an eyebrow at him, a look of sheer annoyance on his face. His mother's head still bowed at Demyan's side, her face growing paler by the second.

Before Shea could get close to the platform, a commotion rose on the far side of the courtyard, cheers of greeting and cries of joy echoing from the castle walls. The High Chancellor lowered the tablet to peer over the gathered crowd. As King Koios emerged from the shadows at the opposite end of the courtyard, the cheers spread through the assembly like a tsunami. Everyone turned to stare. The garden's glowing lanterns illuminated the king's face from below, making him look stern and regal and larger than life.

"Father! Praise Neptune, he lives!" Brynn cried out in happy relief, trying to rush forward. Demyan pinned her to his side, tightening his grip.

"Perhaps not for long," Demyan hissed. "Hold your tongue and do as you're told, princess, or your son and his grandfather will suffer the same consequences as the Adluo royal family."

Brynn gasped, her head snapping to stare at the Prince. "You really killed them! My Aunt Jessamine and the Southern King! What of my cousin, Theo?"

"I told you before," he snarled, his mouth twisting into half a smile. "If I want someone dead, they die. Even if I have to do it myself as they plead for their useless lives." He glared at the trembling mermaids who held the ceremonial silk awning. "You two! Don't move. This ceremony will take place tonight!" He turned to the Chancellor. "Get on with it. Say the words!"

Brynn winced with pain as Demyan gripped her arm. Shea decided he couldn't wait any longer for the king to make it through the crowd. He swam over the heads of the onlookers closest to the platform. "Let go of my mother! You're hurting her!"

Demyan's eyes narrowed to dangerous slits. "You impudent mollusk! What do you think you're doing, you dryland bastard?"

"Putting an end to your cruelty. You can't bully your way through life and get away with it forever!"

"Murderer!" Brynn cried, finally twisting free of his grasp and swimming to her father's side. "Prince Demyan confessed to killing the Adluo royal family! And if he is behind Theo's death, he is guilty of poisoning you as well!"

Demyan's attention still centered on Shea, sneering at the boy. "You may have escaped my soldiers, but you won't escape from me. Who do you think you are, you squid-brained little eel?"

"He's my grandson," bellowed King Koios, moving so quickly he was a blur through the water. Shea's mouth dropped open as he marveled at the king's lightning speed. He certainly didn't look like someone who'd been in a coma just hours before. He came to an abrupt halt in front of the Adluo Prince, putting one hand on Shea's shoulder.

"Grandson?" Demyan sneered again. His hand gripped the jeweled hilt on his belt, but he didn't pull the sword from its holder. "You presume to claim your daughter's drylander whelp? To what purpose? He's a dryland-born bastard. A mongrel at best."

"He bears the Mark of Poseidon," the king proclaimed, ripping the torn vest from Shea's back, revealing the trident birthmark for all to see. The crowd gasped in unison and began to cheer even more loudly. Demyan's eyes narrowed to slits as he stared at the Mark.

"Three generations who all bear the Mark at the same time?" The High Chancellor waved his hands above his head. "But what can this mean? In all my years, this is unprecedented!"

"It means that my grandson is the heir to my throne. He will rule the Atlantic someday when I am gone." The king's booming voice carried throughout the courtyard, silencing the crowds. "And it means that my daughter, Princess Brynneliana – half Adluo by birth – shall take her rightful place on the throne in the Southern Ocean."

The soldiers grumbled loudly, and one shouted out above the din, "What of Prince Demyan?" All Adluo eyes were on the Atlantic King, as if awaiting the announcement of their own fates.

"Prince Demyan shall be tried for his crimes," the king announced. "Tried for the murders of King Anaxima, his wife, Queen Jessamine, and my nephew King Theosisto. And tried for poisoning Prince Azul, and attempting to poison me." A loud murmuring ran through the crowd. The king continued, raising his arms high, toward the surface. "If you will be steadfast and support your new queen, we can work together to make the Southern Ocean strong once again. Not with bloodshed, but through peace we shall restore prosperity to your waters."

The crowd erupted in wild cheers, but behind the king, Demyan shouted, "Never!" Shea turned toward the shout to see Demyan pull his weapon from its sheath and thrust it toward the king's back.

"Watch out!" Shea swam forward, fists extended to deflect the sword. His knuckles hit into the golden tip and pushed it away from King Koios, sending Demyan off balance. The mermaid servants holding the silk awning swam away screaming, letting go of the fabric which billowed away in the current. The dark prince snarled, and turned his weapon for a second thrust at Shea.

"Enough fighting!" The High Chancellor moved between them, arms extended to separate the combatants, just as Demyan's golden sword shot forward. It sliced through the thousand-year-old merman, thick red blood oozing as the stunned crowd watched in horror. Demyan pulled his sword free from the dead merman, genuine shock in his dark eyes.

King Koios pointed at Demyan. "Seize him! He is no prince, but a pretender who chooses war over peace!" Adluo soldiers were scattered throughout the gathered crowd of merfolk. They hesitated at the king's command, glancing from the solid presence of the Aequorean King to their own Prince Demyan, spattered with the Chancellor's blood. As one they let out a battle cry, and charged forward.

Toward the prince.

"No," cried Demyan, the fear in his voice obvious. "I am in command! You must obey! This is treason!" The soldiers paid no heed, chasing him with swords drawn. He fled beyond the glow of the courtyard lanterns into the darkness, thirty guards swimming in his wake.

Healers hurried forward to surround the High Chancellor, but his empty, staring eyes showed it was too late to save him, his blood slick upon the platform. Aequorean guards came forward to wrap the body in the abandoned silk awning, carrying it away from the courtyard before the scavengers arrived. A large crowd of mermaids followed the body into the castle, singing a sorrowful mourning song.

King Koios gathered the visiting dignitaries closer to make assurances as to his health as well as their own safety. Unlike the earlier confusion and panic after the deaths in the Great Hall, this time the crowds remained in the courtyard to hear the king's reassurances and explanations. Shea watched the way the merfolk listened to every word from his grandfather's mouth, the way his larger-than-life presence helped restore calm to the crowd. He wondered if he'd ever be nearly as self-assured and confident as the king, suddenly worried that he'd have awfully big shoes to fill someday. Or fins, rather. Hopefully, that day would be far, far in the distant future.

He was startled from his thoughts when Princess Brynn wrapped her arms around his neck, showering his cheeks with kisses. Useless tears filled her eyes. "You are safe, my son! And alive!"

He squirmed awkwardly in her embrace. "It's good to finally meet you, Mom."

The princess laughed, her eyes bright. "I'm so relieved to see you unharmed that I forgot!" She extended her right hand. "It's very nice to meet you, too, Mr. MacNamara. You've grown so much since I last saw you."

He started to put his hand out to shake hers, and then broke into laughter. "Who am I kidding?" He threw his arms around his mother's waist, his voice cracking. "I've missed you so much."

"You were safer with your father," Brynn said softly. When he didn't reply, she added, "I'll never leave you again."

"Ahem." The king's low voice interrupted, and Shea turned to see his grandfather hovering near them. "That may not be your promise to make, my dear."

Shea faced his mother. "I guess you're going to the Southern Ocean to be in charge. The king says I'll need to begin my studies right away if I'm to someday rule here in the Atlantic."

"But you can come south with me..." Princess Brynn started.

"There will be time to discuss and plan later," the king declared. "For now, let us enjoy the rest of the Solstice, and each other's company." He smiled at his daughter and added, "You have a remarkable boy here, Brynneliana. I am honored to call him my grandson, even if he's part human."

"Thank you, Father," she said quietly. Shea smiled.

The king raised his voice once again to address the gathered crowd. "Come now, let us all return to the feast! We have much to rejoice over. The Adluos and Aequoreans begin a new era of peace. Together. Starting today."

More cheers rippled through the throng of mermaids and mermen. King Koios led the way through the crowd, his daughter smiling at his side. Lybio and Kira followed after to attend them, with Kae and Shea bringing up the rear of the small procession.

Shea caught sight of Gregor at the edge of the crowd and waved him forward. "Gregor! We did it! We saved the king!"

Gregor bowed his head. "You did indeed, Sire."

"No, Gregor, *we* did it. That includes you, too. Kae and I would never have escaped without your help. Thank you. And please call me Shea."

Gregor stared at him, his eyebrows raised high on his forehead. "You're welcome, Shea." He smiled and started to fade into the crowd of guests.

Kae's hand shot out and encircled his wrist. "Oh no you don't! You must come join us for the feast!"

"Yes," Shea nodded. "I insist."

"But I'm an Adluo," Gregor reminded them. "Isn't it best if I sit with my own clan?"

Shea shook his head. "Didn't you hear my grandfather? We're all in this together, Adluo and Aequorean alike. Besides, I'm part Adluo, too."

Gregor chuckled. "I guess you are, Sire. I guess you are."

Chapter Twenty Seven

The breath caught in Zan's throat as he tried to make sense of the scene before him. Above the ocean, distant booms sounded from the drylander celebrations, showers of multi-colored sparks filled the night sky and rippled atop the waves below.

He'd been hovering near the surface along with the battle commanders, awaiting Prince Demyan's signal to advance with the rest of the Adluo troops. With King Koios still clinging to life, Demyan triggered his contingency plan to take control of the castle by force.

The scene in the castle's outer courtyard looked as if it were going according to plan, the white wedding awning raised above the platform and the crowd gathered to watch the marriage between the clans. From his vantage point, Zan saw some brief commotion before utter chaos erupted. Instead of the agreed upon signal, Zan watched Demyan flee into the darkness of the ocean, pursued by several dozen angry Adluo soldiers.

The battle commanders by Zan's side panicked, all speaking at once, demanding answers. As if Zan knew what in Poseidon's name had happened down below.

"Where is Prince Demyan going?"

"Did we miss the signal?"

"What do we tell the troops?"

"Should we still attack the Aequorean castle?"

"Shall we follow Prince Demyan with the rest of the soldiers?"

It took Zan several moments to sort his thoughts, his eyes trained on the confused scene in the courtyard. For a prince who liked to have contingencies for his contingency plans, Demyan hadn't mapped any schemes that included him swimming for his life from his own soldiers. Nor did Zan remember anything about planning to slay the High Chancellor in front of the gathered crowd, a crime worse than murdering royalty. The whole of Atlantis would turn against Prince Demyan now, so it was no wonder that his own soldiers pursued him to bring him to justice. Or even kill him.

Whatever came to pass during the wedding ceremony boded ill for Prince Demyan and his followers, whether they caught Demyan today or not. For now the best course of action would be to disperse the troops and swim far away from Nantucket Sound. He gave orders for the commanders to disband their units and swim home to the Southern Ocean to await further orders.

If Demyan lived, he would have a plan and regroup. If he should die...

For the briefest of moments, Zan caught a glimpse of a future without Demyan controlling him. With Demyan gone, he would have nothing to fear and no one to answer to. A future where his choices would be his own.

CHAPTER TWENTY EIGHT

Shea twisted the knob on Martha's front door, the house he now thought of as home. It felt like he'd been away for ages, when in reality he'd only been gone overnight. It was good to be home.

"Come on, Mom. Gramma will be thrilled to see you again." He held the door open for his mother to enter the hallway ahead of him. Voices drifted to them from the kitchen.

"Really, Leslie, there's nothing strange going on in the neighborhood. My grandson should be home soon and I'm sure Gregor is off visiting family. No one is actually *missing*, no matter what Ann McFadden told you."

"Well, Mrs. MacNamara, I'd like to believe you, truly I would…"

Shea entered the kitchen with a big grin, towing his mother behind him. "Hi, Gramma, I'm home! And look who came with me!"

"Shea!" Martha threw her arms around the boy's neck.

"I'm sorry if you were worried." He hugged her, burying his face in the familiar scent of bleach.

"It's my fault, Martha." Brynn put a hand on the older woman's shoulder. "He spent the night at my...house. We would've called...but the phones weren't working."

Martha released him and gave Brynn a hug as well. "I'm so happy to see you both. It's been too long, Brynneliana."

"I've missed you, too, Martha," she said, her voice cracking.

Martha let go and gestured to the policeman standing by the kitchen table, as if suddenly remembering he was there. "Leslie? You remember Tom's wife, Brynn, don't you?"

"A pleasure to see you again, ma'am," Officer Tandy said formally. "I heard you and Tom divorced?"

Brynn shook her head sharply, her smile gone. "No. We didn't."

Officer Tandy scuffed his polished black shoe along Martha's kitchen floor. "Sorry to hear about your husband's death."

"Thanks, Leslie. I appreciate it." She took Shea's hand in her own, as if unwilling to let him get too far from her side.

Officer Tandy pressed his lips together into a thin line before speaking again. "I thought you were gone. Knew you weren't in Oklahoma with Tom, but haven't see you...around."

The sparkle returned to Brynn's eyes. "Oh, my family is still around."

The doorbell rang. "Who could that be?" Martha hurried to the front door and opened it, Shea on her heels. He kind of hoped Kae followed him home, but was disappointed to see Hailey on the doorstep, holding Lucky's collar. The dog wagged his tail and barked a greeting to Martha.

"He was by the dock barking this morning," Hailey explained. "I saw him out the window, and thought I should bring him home. Why is there a police car out front?" Lucky ran into the house, tail wagging, poking his nose at Shea before running down the hall toward the kitchen. The dog stopped abruptly in the doorway and growled menacingly.

"Oh dear!" Martha hurried after him. Shea and Hailey exchanged a puzzled look and followed. When they reached the kitchen, Lucky stood on his hind legs with Officer Tandy pinned against the wall, one large paw on either side of his head.

"Would someone...please...call off...the dog...?" Officer Tandy's teeth were clenched so tight he could barely form the words. "I don't think...he likes me..."

"Lucky!" Martha stepped forward. The dog stopped growling and turned to her. He dropped to the floor, and went to sit at her feet, tail sweeping the floor as it wagged. "I'm sorry, Leslie, I don't know what could have gotten into him!"

"Maybe it's the 'no dogs on the beach' rule," Hailey said, smiling. She slid into an empty chair and turned to Officer Tandy. "So, did you figure out what happened to the crazy old man that went missing?"

"You mean Gregor Guenther? We're working on it, I can assure you," Officer Tandy said, trying to sound official as he wiped the copious amounts of dog drool from the front of his uniform shirt. "I'd better be going," Officer Tandy said, obviously uncomfortable. "There are missing persons to be found." He grabbed his mirrored glasses from the table, and slipped them up his pointy nose. "Ma'am," he said, nodding at Martha before heading out toward the front door.

There was silence in the kitchen as the screen door slammed shut. A minute later the police car's engine roared to life. Martha patted Brynn's arm. "Let's go sit in the living room for a minute to catch up, shall we?"

Shea turned to follow his mother, but Hailey grabbed him by the arm and punched his shoulder. "So what happened to you? I was worried."

He smiled. "Kae took me to find my mother."

Hailey released her grip. "So that's your mother, huh? She was here on Cape Cod the whole time? And so why couldn't I come along with you guys yesterday? I thought I was your friend."

"You are. It's just…"

Hailey leaned closer, cupping her hand against his ear. "I saw you and Kae in the river, Shea. You had a tail. You want to tell me something real?"

The challenging look on her face made Shea pause. He had no idea what to do about the situation. "Umm, is this going to be a problem?"

A slow grin spread across her face as she shook her head. "Are you kidding me? You know I've been obsessed with sea mythology since we moved to Cape Cod. And now I have an actual mythical creature for a friend? How cool is that! I can't believe you held out on me this long! Windmill Point is much weirder than New York City ever was."

Shea laughed. "It certainly can be. Come on, you've got to meet my mom." They followed the others to the living room. Shea wasn't sure how much information about his recent adventures or his new undersea life he was allowed to share with Hailey, for her own safety if nothing else. After all, Demyan was still out there somewhere. But in a way it was a relief to not have to hide who he was from his friend.

He was the son of a mermaid.

Hailey accepted that fact and still want him as a friend. He wondered if John would have the same positive reaction when he came to visit Cape Cod later in the summer. After all, John wasn't raised in a big city like New York and wasn't used to weirdness. Navigating this new life wasn't going to be easy. But watching his mother laugh at something Martha said, he knew he wouldn't trade his new reality for anything.

He introduced Hailey to Brynn. His mother smiled and shook her hand. "I've heard all about you. It's a pleasure to meet one of Shea's friends."

"He told you about me? Really?" Hailey's cheeks turned bright red. She turned to him. "I can't believe you told your mom about me!"

Shea laughed. "Of course I told her about you. You're like my best friend on Cape Cod."

"I'm like your only friend." Hailey punched his shoulder again. "I mean, who else do you even know? Kae? That creepy Mr. Guenther guy?"

"Which reminds me." Brynn handed two notes to Martha. "Gregor wanted you to give one of these to a woman named Ann?"

Martha nodded. "Ann McFadden. Is Gregor okay? Is he coming back to Windmill Point?"

"He's received a new assignment," Brynn explained, glancing at Hailey. "I've asked him to come work for me, down South, at least until I get things organized. My son seems to think Gregor is the best...man for the job."

Which reminded Shea of something Gregor said. "Gramma, Gregor said he made a promise to you? Does that mean you knew...why he was in Windmill Point?"

She shook her head. "Not when he first moved here, certainly. But I've had my suspicions over the years."

"But..." Shea paused, frowning. "You knew all about Mom and her...family stuff. Do lots of people...you know, *know* about...us?" He gestured at himself and his mother.

"Some do," Martha answered. "Some know and choose to ignore the truth. Others think the stories are fairy tales." She seemed to think that was a sufficient answer, and opened the note from Gregor and started to read.

"Kae says all tales have some truth to them," Shea mumbled. An image of her smiling face danced in his mind. He wondered when he would have a chance to see her again. They left so many things unspoken between them, things that needed to be said before they traveled to the Southern Court. If they were going to be living in the same castle, he didn't want it to be awkward. He still had no idea how she really felt about him, a thought that made his stomach churn uncomfortably.

"So Gregor is moving south," Martha said, as she refolded the note. "He didn't have time to come say his good-byes in person?"

Brynn shook her head. "I sent him on ahead with others he deemed trustworthy, to get things started along the right path. I'll be joining him in August."

Martha slapped her knee. "But you just got here! What happened last night?"

"You wouldn't believe it if we told you, Gramma. But Mom is now totally…in charge…down South, so we have to move there."

"Not *we*," Brynn said quietly, a sad smile on her face. She turned to Martha. "I must leave my son yet again, and was hoping he could stay here with you on Cape Cod a while longer? He's safer here than with me."

Shea jumped to his feet. "Wait a minute! I thought I could go with you."

"Remember what your grandfather said? Until the ones who caused the death of your father and so many others are brought to justice, you won't be safe. Not in my world."

"But I just met you..." Shea started. "And I just learned how to swim..."

"It won't be like before. You can visit for the Winter Solstice in December, and we can be in contact anytime you need me." She touched the *transmutare* at her neck, as if to remind him of its powers. "I don't intend to let you go ever again. Besides, soon enough it'll be time for you to head off to the university."

"University?" Hailey asked, interrupting. "But you're nowhere near eighteen yet."

"It's kind of like boarding school," Shea explained. "Like high school and college rolled into one. Kae was telling me all about it last night at the banquet..."

"Banquet?" Hailey asked, and her stomach rumbled. Martha and Shea both laughed. Hailey smiled. "Have I mentioned my mother can't cook? All of a sudden I'm hungry."

Martha rose from the couch. "It's no problem, Hailey. I'll whip up breakfast. Brynn, how long can you stay this morning?"

"As long as I want. I'll even help." She stood and followed Martha to the kitchen. "You'll be seeing a lot of me, if that's all right with you, at least through the end of July," she added, glancing toward Shea. "I need a chance to get to know my son."

Shea smiled at her, and then at Hailey.

"So that's your mom, huh?" Hailey asked, cocking her head to one side.

He nodded.

"She's certainly beautiful. And smart, if she's taking over the family business. But can she cook?"

He laughed out loud, and threw his arm around Hailey's shoulder. "I guess we'll find out!" They headed for the kitchen.

CHAPTER TWENTY NINE

Shea walked along the stretch of Windmill Point beach that he'd come to think of as his own, in more ways than one. The sun barely cracked the horizon, so he knew he had plenty of time before any lifeguards or sunbathers would arrive to spoil the peaceful morning. This was his time.

Lucky chased after a flock of seagulls, bounding straight through the waves in pursuit. So much had changed in Shea's life over the last two months. He didn't think he'd ever be able to see the ocean the same way now that he knew some of its secrets.

"Hey there, Garbage Boy."

He turned and saw Kae walking along the edge of where the sand and waves met. A rush of warmth flooded his body and a smile automatically pulled at his lips. Things between the two of them had been strained since the Solstice, but he couldn't help his body's reaction to her.

Technically, she worked for his mother. The king assigned her father as Shea's bodyguard. He felt like he was taking advantage if he even thought about kissing her, but he couldn't look at her without thinking about kissing her. Instead, he avoided her altogether. Which only made him think about her even more. And think about kissing her.

It was a vicious cycle.

He wanted to tell her so many things. He needed to find out what she was thinking and feeling about everything that happened to them... But he was afraid of what he might find out. Did she still feel that connection between them, or had she changed her mind?

The last few days without seeing her had been hard, like a vital part of him was missing. Even though he hadn't gone searching for her, he knew she wasn't near the beach in the mornings. Was she avoiding him? How could he even ask that?

He decided to play it cool. "Hey yourself. Where've you been?"

She bent to gather a particularly large conch shell. "Oh, your mother has been keeping me busy, packing her things for the move south." She turned and threw the shell far out over the waves, avoiding his eyes. "She wants me to go with her, to help her settle into the Adluo castle."

He felt his heart sink. "But I thought she wasn't leaving until the end of the summer. What's the rush?" He'd barely started to get to know his mother, and wasn't ready to say good-bye just yet. Especially if it meant saying good-bye to Kae, too.

"The king thinks there needs to be immediate action to settle any unrest that may arise in the Southern Ocean. Those poor Adluos have been through a rough time…" Her voice trailed off and she still wasn't meeting his eye.

"My grandfather is screwing up Mom's life again?" The thought left a bitter taste in his mouth. "This is so not fair. She didn't get to stay with my dad, she didn't get to raise me, and now she has to abandon me again? It's so wrong."

"We don't leave for another few weeks." Her fingers brushed his arm. "You should come visit the castle and see…her."

The hesitant touch surprised him. Almost as if Kae was afraid of him. Afraid of something. "Is everything okay?"

She nodded and looked away. "Come swimming with me?"

"I can't. My friend John is already on his way to visit. Gramma is taking me to the airport this afternoon to meet his plane. I'm not going to be able to come… swimming… until after he leaves." His eyes met hers, and he saw her pain.

"You aren't going to tell your friend about… anything?" Kae's question sounded more like an accusation.

It was his turn to look away. "He wouldn't understand. I've thought about it a bunch. What would I say? Hey, dude, my mom's a mermaid queen and I'm the son of a mermaid? Wanna see my tail?" He kicked at the sand.

"Did your other *friend* have trouble believing?"

"That's different. Hailey's a girl." Kae snorted and started to walk away, but he grabbed her hand. "Wait, don't go."

She turned and cocked her head to one side. "Why? You have your human friends to worry about. You don't need me. I'm only a servant, after all."

He took her other hand. "Kae, it's barely been a week and I'm already miserable without you. What am I going to do when you go south with my mom?"

She shrugged, staring into his eyes. He pulled her closer and wrapped his arms around her waist. She didn't resist, instead leaning against him, resting her cheek on his shoulder. Her hair smelled of sunshine and ocean breezes, and Shea thought his heart might break into little pieces if he had to say goodbye to her.

"Don't go," he whispered into her damp curls.

"I have to." Her voice was barely audible over the sound of the waves lapping the shore. He felt her warm breath against his neck. "Can't you come with us?"

"She won't let me. Not until they capture Demyan." Shea hugged her closer. "She says I have to stay with Martha, that I'm safer here this summer. She promised I could visit her for the Winter Solstice."

December had never seemed further away than it did at that very moment. How would he last that long without seeing Kae? Without holding her in his arms, or hearing her laughter? The tightness in his chest hurt so much he felt like he might explode right there on the beach.

"Wait a minute, did you say just for the summer? You have to stay with Martha for the summer? Does that mean...?"

One corner of Shea's mouth turned upward in a sad imitation of a smile. "She's still sending me to the University of Atlantis in the fall." Which wasn't any closer to where Kae would be, if she lived in the Southern Ocean and served in the castle. Maybe he should tell her now how he felt about her, so she would know how much she meant to him. Could he ask his mother to fire her as a servant, so there wouldn't be the weirdness between them? That would mean explaining things to his mother that he wasn't sure he understood... And he wasn't even sure how Kae felt.

The whole "heir to the throne" thing kind of threw their budding relationship into disarray. He knew his feelings for Kae only grew stronger because of what they went through together, but he didn't know if her feelings for him were strong enough to overcome all the class and clan issues that the merfolk obsessed over.

"University? Really?" Kae's face lit up, her smile radiant. "Me too, I mean, I'm still planning to attend university next semester. So we'll be there together!"

The tightness in Shea's chest started to loosen. "I didn't know... I thought you would have to stay and help Mom get settled into the new castle and all."

Kae shook her head. "Definitely headed to Atlantis in September."

"So this isn't good-bye. It's more of a 'see you later' thing." His heart soared as his whole perspective shifted gears. Yes, his life would be changing again when September rolled around, but he wouldn't be facing this next adventure alone.

Kae would be with him.

Suddenly, he remembered the burly Adluo guard who shook his finger in Shea's face that night in the hallway, outside the High Chancellor's quarters. His advice rang in Shea's ears even now, urging him to do the right thing.

"Kae," he started. "There's something we need to talk about, especially if we're going to be in Atlantis together."

Her brows scrunched together and she started to pull away from his embrace. "You don't have to say anything. It's because I'm a servant, I know. I promise not to embarrass you in front of the other royals."

He pulled her back before she could escape. "No! That's not what I meant at all." He shook his head, frustrated. "How can you even say that?"

"Say what? That I'm a servant? Because that's the truth," she said, the light in her eyes dimming. "I didn't know you were a royal when we first met, or I wouldn't have acted in such a familiar fashion. I promise to conduct myself with more decorum in the future." She tried to pull away again.

He held her tight, refusing to let go. "Listen, Kae. I realize we've only known each other a short time." He ignored the fact that she rolled her eyes and plunged on. "It feels like we've been through so much. Together. I mean, don't you know how I feel about you?"

"I guess I don't," Kae said, sounding cautious. Some of the darkness left her eyes, and Shea thought he saw a glimmer of hope there instead.

He gathered her even closer. "You mean everything to me." Which was true, he realized. She was his whole world, and he never wanted to live without her. And just as suddenly, he knew the words he wanted to say to her, to tell her right now before she swam out of his life without knowing the truth. "Kae, I... I think I love you."

She gasped, her eyes wide as if unable to comprehend his words. "But..."

He silenced her words with his lips, trying to convey with his kiss all the feelings he held in his heart. If she wasn't going to believe his words, maybe he could make her believe him this way. He closed his eyes, drinking in the salty taste of her lips, as if he were dying of thirst, and Kae returned his kiss with an intensity that matched his own. Everything suddenly felt so perfect and so right that he almost forgot to breathe.

He tore his lips away from her mouth and opened his eyes, to find tears escaping from the corners of Kae's eyes. "What's wrong with me? I think I'm leaking."

"They're tears," he whispered. "But mermaids don't cry, remember?" He tried to hug her even closer to comfort her, but that made the tears fall faster. "It'll be okay. It's not even two whole months, and then we'll be able to see each other every day."

Kae sniffed, and swiped at her eyes. "Every day sounds good."

"It does, doesn't it?" Shea smiled at her, his heart pounding in his chest at the thought of being with her every day. Sharing classes, sharing meals, sharing all the new experiences that Atlantis had to offer. Together.

"September isn't that far away." Kae rested her head against his shoulder and sighed. "With everything that needs to be accomplished between now and then, I'm sure the time will swim right by."

Shea wasn't as sure. "Every day without you will seem like an eternity," he said, feeling foolish despite the fact that he meant every word. Here he was making declarations of love, and she hadn't yet said the words to him. Could she have true feelings for him, despite the fact that he wasn't a full-blooded merman? His dad was only human, after all. Could a mermaid as beautiful as Kae fall in love with someone like him? The moment stretched on forever, his anxiety mounting with every breath.

Kae must have sensed his uncertainty, and answered his unspoken question. "I love you too, Shea MacNamara," she whispered into his chest. "It might be breaking the rules, but so be it."

Her words sent a jolt of excitement running through him and his breath caught in his throat again. *She loves me!* Nothing else mattered. "I've never been all that good at following rules," he said, planting a tender kiss in her golden hair. "I'm better at making them up as I go along."

"It's a good thing you'll be king someday. Then you can make as many rules as you like."

"I don't want to think about that right now. I want to get to know my grandfather, and learn all there is to know about your world."

"It's your world too," Kae reminded him.

"Our world," he said, smiling. "You can teach me about the Atlantic, and I can teach you about the world above the water."

"We'll see about that. I don't have a lot of time left here on Cape Cod."

"Then we'll have to make it all count." He cupped her cheek and traced his thumb across her lips. "Can I ask for something right now?"

"Anything."

"One more kiss?"

Kae's smile widened, her answer in her eyes.

Acknowledgements

My thanks go out to the many people who helped make this book possible. First to my husband, for giving me the chance to follow my dreams, and of course to my family for believing in me and listening to me babble about mermaids.

Big hugs to all my fellow authors I've connected with over this journey called publishing, especially those I met during our CMP years who helped me survive that leg of the journey. Nothing worth doing is ever easy. Hugs to all the other YA authors I've met along my journey, for your words of wisdom, advice and support. Special thanks to Shawna Romkey for being one of my first beta readers way back when, and to Katherine and Kate for being the best betas ever!

To Caitlin and Joanne at Where the Sidewalk Ends bookstore in Chatham, who hosted my mermaid release parties the first time around, and to the wonderful women at both Titcomb's Booksellers in Sandwich and Brewster Book Store in Brewster who sponsor fabulous events all year long. Indie booksellers rock!

I'm especially thankful to the lovely and talented Kate Conway for helping me realize my dream of re-launching my mermaid series into the world for a second chance, and for creating my beautiful new covers! Thank you from the bottom of my heart, Kate!

I also want to give a shout out to my readers, to everyone who has read these books and enjoyed them, to those who took the time to visit my website and Facebook pages to let me know how much you love Shea's story. Thank you for your notes, your emails and your reviews – especially the reviews. I'm thrilled when you take the time to let other people know you enjoyed what I wrote. And yes, I'm writing more. I promise.

Spending so much time on Cape Cod makes describing the beach and ocean easier, but other information needed to be gathered, such as the names and descriptions of different sea creatures and the geography of Oklahoma. Most of my research for this book was done online, but a special thanks goes out to Jane Sugden, who lives in the "real" windmill house and visits me at every book signing. It's a pleasure to be your neighbor, Jane.

I'm grateful that my mother lived to see me fulfill my dreams of becoming a published author. She instilled my love of books, and never stopped pushing me to try harder to achieve my goals. I miss her every day.

And a last heartfelt thanks goes to Nickey, my writing cohort and partner in both whine and wine. Everyone should be lucky enough to have a friend like you.

About the Author

Katie O'Sullivan lives with her family and big dogs on Cape Cod, drinking way too much coffee and inventing new excuses not to dust. Living next to the Atlantic influences everything she writes, including her young adult series about the mermaids who live near her beach. A recovering English major, she earned her degree at Colgate University and now writes romance and adventure for young adults, and something steamier for the young at heart.

Please visit her blog or find her on Facebook for the latest information on planned events, culinary disasters, news about mermaid sightings and upcoming novels.

Website: www.katie-osullivan.com

Blog: http://katieosullivan.blogspot.com

Facebook:

https://www.facebook.com/AuthorKatieOSullivan

Twitter: https://twitter.com/OkatieO

Coming December 2015

Turn the page to read a sample chapter from:

Defiance

Son of a Mermaid   Book Two

By Katie O'Sullivan

Defiance

Chapter One

Zan shivered as he felt his way along the uneven walls of stone, the cave as cold and black as a cloud of octopus ink. The message he'd received had been cryptic, but he was pretty sure he was in the right place.

"Right" being an extremely relative concept.

His eyes widened to their limits trying to see beyond the blackness of the murky Arctic cavern, but to no avail. *So much about this journey is wrong.* He flicked his tail and quickened his pace, thinking bitterly of the last year, doubting the path he'd chosen to swim. Or rather, the one he felt forced to choose. Choice was not a luxury afforded to one in his position.

In the span of a few short weeks, he'd gone from being the hunter to being hunted.

He exhaled heavily in the darkness as the tunnel led him downward, releasing the pressure building in his ears and feeling the bubbles stream from the gill slits underneath his now shaggy hair. He no longer looked the part of an Adluo soldier, but his altered appearance helped him blend as he passed through the small villages that dotted the floor of the Atlantic on his way north to this rendezvous point. Granted, the black hair billowing around his ears stood out, shining blue and green in the sunlight, but no one would connect him with the dark sorcerer of legends. In his years as Demyan's right hand merman, he'd kept his hair shorter than the dark stubble now sprouting from his jawline.

His eyes still straining against the darkness, Zan's mind wandered, thinking how close he and his comrades had been to accomplishing their mission and taking over the whole of the Atlantic.

After years of brutal and bloody battles, the Southern and Atlantic Oceans had finally come to an agreement. The end of war had been on the horizon, almost within reach, when he and the other Adluos made their way to Nantucket Sound for the final negotiations.

The oceans were now at peace with one another. But Zan was no longer a part of that peace.

He was an outlaw.

He'd been lucky to escape with his life, after being part of the plot to poison the Atlantic King at the Solstice Banquet. Assassination is not something ever taken lightly in the courts of Atlantis. Zan knew too well that the punishment for killing a member of the royal family is death. When he was young he'd made that mistake and had been paying the price ever since.

He'd left the Solstice celebration before Prince Demyan confessed to his own sins: poisoning the rightful Adluo heir as well as killing the boy's parents, the King and Queen of the Southern Ocean. Princess Brynneliana's drylander son miraculously appeared, bearing the Mark of Poseidon on his back and saving King Koios.

Zan had watched from afar, awaiting the signal to storm the castle with the rest of the soldiers. He saw the prince swim away, pursued by his own men after he killed the High Chancellor of Atlantis.

So why was Zan here now?

He shook his head in the darkness, trying to dispel the doubts. Why risk the potential for a quiet life in one of the small Atlantic villages, where he could raise crops and find a mate? Why was he now on the outer edge of the Arctic Ocean in these dark, subterranean tunnels? The answer was both simple and complex.

Zan owed Prince Demyan his life.

It was the prince who first noticed his innate magical abilities and saved him from a life in the dolphin stables – or worse. Demyan was the first to find Zan after the accident. Two young royals died that day, but instead of sending him to the High Court for judgment, Prince Demyan kept his secret. Demyan convinced the king to send Zan to the university to be trained as a sorcerer. Not only did Zan owe the prince his life for saving him that day, Zan's life would be forfeit still if the secret ever came out.

Now seventeen, Zan knew that while he was still a mere fry in the eyes of the elders, his magick was impressive, so strong that at times he still feared it might control him again rather than the other way around.

When the messenger arrived at the village where he'd been hiding, summoning him to this meeting, Zan had no choice but to obey. There was not a doubt in his mind. Which frightened him, and not only because Demyan knew exactly where to find him.

The message meant either the prince had gone completely insane with delusions of new powers, or succeeded in amassing a fresh army to continue his ongoing quest for underwater domination. Either way, it wouldn't have been prudent – or safe – to ignore the summons.

Up ahead in the blackness of the tunnel, Zan's eyes focused on a speck of glowing green. *A lantern! Finally!* His

327

heart began to pound, knowing each flick of his tail brought him closer to Demyan. Closer to either his own death, or his redemption. He would soon find out which.

Emerging from the darkness, he entered a high-ceilinged cavern carved from the white marble rock. Lanterns glowing with luminescent sea creatures studded the walls at regular intervals. He raised one hand to shield his eyes from the sudden brightness, searching for signs of life.

Slabs of white and off-white marble lined the floor in a checkerboard pattern, reflecting the green light and making the room almost unbearably bright after the prolonged darkness of the tunnels. At the center of the chamber stood a tall, rounded table, also made of white marble, with twelve empty chairs surrounding it.

"Hello?" Zan's voice echoed from the rocky walls. "Is anyone here?" He waited silently. No one answered.

Exhaling his frustration, he moved forward, eyes darting around the bright chamber. Two places had been set out on the table as if for a meal, one on either side of the large circle. Facing each other.

"Hello?" Zan called again. A small mermaid with dark blue skin and long flowing hair that matched the color of the marble table emerged from a doorway on the opposite side of the chamber. In her hands a gleaming silver tray with a single clear bowl in the center caught the light, reflecting it around the room in broken prisms. She placed the bowl in the middle of the table and a shudder ran down Zan's spine. The bowl was filled with small bluish-green berries, native only to the area around the Fiji Islands in the Pacific Ocean.

Eucheuma seeds.

"Zan! You got my message!" Prince Demyan's booming voice filled the entire cavern as the merman himself swam into the room. He stopped in front of Zan, folding his arms across his wide chest as the two mermen stared at each other. "You look like hell," he said with a wry smile. "What's with the long hair...and what's that growing on your chin? Is it black mold? Great Neptune's ghost, you even smell awful!"

Zan found his voice. "Thank you, Sire." He knew he looked frightful. He'd been on the run since the Solstice, not knowing where to go or who to trust.

Demyan, on the other hand, looked exactly the same as that Summer Solstice day when he'd almost accomplished his goal of taking over the Atlantic. How was such a thing possible? Zan opened his mouth to ask, then closed it again without saying a word. Such questions were not advisable, no matter how much the other merman smiled or joked. His was the smile of a sea snake, widening its mouth for the kill.

"But come, you must be famished." The prince gestured toward the waiting table. "Have a seat. Rest. Eat. There is much to be discussed as to my return."

"Your...return?" Zan said, his voice breaking roughly. "You're coming back to the Southern Ocean?"

Demyan laughed, his black eyes glittering coldly. "Hades help me, no. Brynn and her whelp are welcome to that barren wasteland." He took a handful of Eucheuma berries from the bowl and popped them into his mouth one by one as he continued. "No, the Southern Ocean isn't for me, Zan. It's so...limiting. I've developed a more global perspective, setting my sights on something bigger."

"Bigger? You mean like the whole Atlantic Ocean?"

"I mean all of it. The world." He pushed the bowl of seeds closer to Zan. "Have something to eat and I'll explain my vision for the future. Our future."

"Our future?" Zan repeated, feeling like an echo. "You...need my help?"

"Need is such a relative and transient term." The gleam returned to Demyan's black eyes. "I prefer to think of this as me offering you a position, but really more than that. I'm offering you a place in history! History that has yet to be written, but will be spoken of and remembered for centuries to come. Join me, Zan, and help me make my visions into reality, one ocean at a time."

"Are you offering me a choice?"

"No. Not really. I'm sorry if you don't feel up to the task of making history with me. You were always a good strategic thinker, a good second in command for someone so young, as well as a truly powerful sorcerer. But everyone can be replaced." Demyan inclined his head to one side, his eyes shifting to something behind Zan.

Afraid of what lay behind him, he leaned forward. "I accept your offer."

"Good choice, my old friend." The wide smile returned to Demyan's face.

Turning in his chair, Zan saw two Arctic mermen swimming away, their snow white hair flowing behind them. One hefted a long steel blade and the other dragged a canvas sack secured at the top with a long length of blackened rope. The sack itself writhed furiously.

Zan took in a long, slow breath, glad he hadn't met them, and gladder still he didn't know what was in the sack. He felt certain if he knew the contents, he would already be dead. "Who are they?"

"Do you know the Arctic mermen have developed some quite innovative methods of…persuasion?" Demyan's smile widened even further. "I used to think we Adluos were the best fighters in any ocean, but I think the Arctic mermen are better."

"Better? How so?"

"More subtle. More precise with their movements, so as not to waste time or energy. It's fascinating to watch them work, really." He grabbed another handful of the seeds. "Like artists, they are. The pity of the matter is they can also be quite overzealous. They keep going, and going, and going until really, you wish it would all just end."

Zan took in another long breath of the crisp Arctic water, grateful to know it was not to be his last. At least, not yet.